THE SHAPE OF YOUR HEART

DEBBIE HOWELLS

B

First published in Great Britain in 2023 by Boldwood Books Ltd.

Cover Design by Head Design Ltd

Cover Photography: Shutterstock

A CIP catalogue record for this book

Paperback ISBN 978-1-80415-026-9

Large Print ISBN 978-1-80415-027-6

Hardback ISBN 978-1-80415-025-2

Ebook ISBN 978-1-80415-028-3

Kindle ISBN 978-1-80415-029-0

Audio CD ISBN 978-1-80415-020-7

MP3 CD ISBN 978-1-80415-021-4

Digital audio download ISBN 978-1-80415-022-1

Boldwood Books Ltd
23 Bowerdean Street
London SW6 3TN
www.boldwoodbooks.com

For my family

When the world says 'give up', hope whispers, 'try it one more time'.

— UNKNOWN

Life can be all kinds of wonderful. It can also be all kinds of heartbreak – a subject in which my sisters are well versed. There's Alice, the eldest, who as a cardiologist fixes the physical manifestations of malfunctioning hearts. Then there's Sasha, a psychologist, an expert in the emotional rise and fall that comes with loving and losing someone. Rita, meanwhile, actually lectures at Bristol uni on the philosophy of love, from the ancient Greeks to the present day.

That leaves me, the youngest, by far the lowest achieving, though arguably the happiest of the four of us, because for all their expertise and knowledge of the workings of the heart, none of them have been in love – while for the last five years of my life, I've lived with Liam – and this weekend, we're getting married.

'You are sure about this, aren't you?' Sasha looked doubtful when I told her. 'You're both so young.'

'And un-sorted, is what you're trying to say.' I nudged her elbow in a little-sisterly way. 'But I'm not like you, Sash. And I am *so* sure about this. We're happy as we are – and one day, I'll get around to doing whatever it is I'm supposed to do with my life. Liam and I... you know how it is. It's like we're meant to be together.'

It was how it had felt, almost from the first day we met, a cold, crisp Friday in January, one on which, while my sisters were busy saving lives, I had a day off from the indie bookshop where I worked, up a narrow street in the heart of Truro. As far as I was concerned, it was a perfect day, a bracing wind blowing off the Atlantic, the spray whipped up, the waves rolling in, one after another, uncurling themselves on to the shore.

I'd always loved Cornwall's beaches, particularly this one isolated little cove. There was the exhilaration of the walk to get here, the climb down rocks on to velvety sand; the scouring of the high-water mark for shards of sea glass, tiny shells, pale driftwood, mermaids' purses, fragments of slate carved from the cliffs. Then alone on the pristine sand, I'd create pictures with what I'd found; impermanent pieces of art lasting the few hours until the incoming tide claimed them back.

But on this particular Friday, as I reached the rock where I usually sat, someone else had got there first. There on the sand was a perfect miniature of a tree, complete with a slate stem, sea glass leaves, strands of seaweed arranged into an elaborate root system.

I couldn't stop staring at it. It wasn't just that I'd never known anyone else to make collages the way I did, let alone in exactly the same place; this was the most beautiful thing I'd ever seen.

'I haven't quite finished.'

I turned in the direction of the voice, meeting eyes that were the same blue as the ocean in summer, a face that looked slightly wary. In a thick sweater and jeans, a scarf wound around his neck, he was dressed for the elements.

'It's very good.'

'I hope it will be.' Crouching down, he added some more pieces of sea glass.

'You can have these, if you like.' Opening my cupped hands, I held out the treasures I'd collected.

Turning to me, his eyes were quizzical.

'I was about to do the same – not a tree, though. Mine tend to be more abstract. The thing is...' I hesitated. 'I've never met anyone else who makes sea pictures.'

His smile was warm, reached the corners of his eyes. 'Because who would spend all this time, when in a few hours from now, every trace of them will be gone for ever.'

I was nodding. 'But I kind of like that. Human beings aren't exactly subtle, are they? I mean, we decimate the natural world at the drop of a hat. But these pictures... It's like leaving a sign that we were here for a while.' I shrugged. 'I'm quite glad we haven't learned to stop the rising tide – at least, not yet.' I liked to be reminded that nature was more powerful than any of us.

We sat on the beach together for hours that first day. Liam, as I found out his name was, had abandoned his career in the City in his quest for a simpler life.

A frown flickered across his face as he talked. 'It was great to start with. I worked hard and played hard. But it kind of lost its gloss. Everyone is always rushing everywhere. Almost no one takes time to be still for a moment – to notice something simple like a single bird – or to stand and look at the stars – and even if they did, the light pollution would ruin it. While here...'

But he didn't have to explain. As I already knew, Cornwall's dark skies were mesmerising.

Liam also had this dream, which he described to me in detail. 'It's a house – it doesn't have to be a big one. But it has sea views – and trees, so that you can hear the wind. It has a wrap-around veranda, so that you can sit outside even when the rain is lashing down. There's a garden – and a few chickens. Ideally, it would be off-grid, but that side of things could be a work in progress. But mostly, I'd like to live in a way that didn't impact on the environment. I mean, I used to love flying around the world, but it's amazing how many places you can get to by train.'

I wasn't a fan of flying. With only a few millimetres of metal keeping you in the air, I'd far rather stay firmly grounded.

He went on. 'Have you heard of the Camino de Santiago?'

I couldn't believe that out of all the places in the world, he'd mentioned this. The Camino is a network of routes across northern Spain, starting in the east and finishing in the west in Galicia, at the Cathedral of Santiago de Compostela. It was one of my dreams to complete that walk through the stunning countryside along the northern Spanish coast. 'I have, actually. I'd really like to walk it one day.'

'So would I. It's kind of weird, when you think that apart from the bit of France that sticks out...'

'Brest,' I added helpfully.

'Yeah, Brest. But other than that, between here and Northern Spain, there are just miles and miles of the Bay of Biscay.'

Which was all very well, but, 'What does that have to do with your house?' I asked.

His eyes were far away. 'I've always liked the idea that it could be a stopping-off point – for people walking the Cornish coast path. Nothing fancy, just somewhere to sit for a while, maybe get a cup of tea along the way... kind of like the way you can on a Camino.'

I liked the idea, too. It seemed a gentle way of interacting with transitory strangers.

Feeling the wind pick up, I pulled my jacket closely around me. 'Tide's coming in.'

'How about we watch my tree get submerged – then...' He paused. 'Can I buy you a drink?'

* * *

At their best, matters of the heart can be instinctive, and it didn't take long to realise I'd found someone special, who cared about the same things I did; whose vision of the future felt so aligned with my own.

But while my sisters had always been ambitious, I never had been. I liked a much simpler life: discovering secret places, or where nature had taken over. To me, there was as much beauty in a polished pebble or a single feather floating on the breeze as a priceless gemstone. It seemed incredible that Liam felt the same.

Over the five years since, Liam and I have made a hundred or more sea pictures, listening to the sound of waves breaking on the shores of dozens of coves; created magical gardens in many places, crafted the most dazzling, joyful memories together.

For the last three years, we've nurtured the neglected garden of our rented cottage back to life. We've even found his dream house – only it's become *our* dream house, with a garden, veranda and spectacular sea views. It's also a stone's throw from the coast path. Having had an offer accepted, we're waiting for the sale to go through.

But before we move in, tomorrow we're getting married. It's got rather out of hand – the small, intimate wedding Liam and I have always envisaged has become a large marquee in the grounds of my parents' sprawling farmhouse on the outskirts of Padstow.

As I am the first of her children to get married, my very organised, sensible mother wants it to be perfect.

'The roses are the wrong shade of pink.' Coming into the kitchen, she looks irritated. 'Honestly. After all the lengths we've gone to, you'd think they'd have got it right.'

'Mum, there is no such thing as the wrong shade.' Going over to her, I take one of her hands. 'Whatever it is, as long as Liam and I get married tomorrow, it will be perfect.' The honeymoon was going to be, too. To avoid flying, we've booked a ferry to Bilbao, then a train which will take us to Donostia–San Sebastián from where we'll start our long-awaited pilgrimage across northern Spain to Santiago de Compostela.

But she won't be placated. 'It's not good enough.'

I sigh. 'Shall I go and see?'

Going outside, I shield my eyes from the sun's glare as I walk across the garden. The lawn has been meticulously mown, fairy lights and bunting strung under the trees. By anyone's standards it's an amazing setting, but because it's my childhood home and I'm surrounded by memories, for me it's much more so.

The front of the marquee is open, and as I step inside, it's a breath-taking sight. The flower arrangements are wild, exactly as I'd envisaged them; the napkins various muted shades; the tables adorned with treasures Liam and I have mined from the beach – pebbles, sea glass, tiny shards of slate, with jam jars of mismatched flowers cut from my parents' garden – mint, rosemary, cornflowers, hydrangeas – maybe not quite what my mother had in mind, but representative of things that are significant to us.

I find the pink roses my mother was talking about. Maybe they're a little paler than we'd thought, but they're no less beautiful for it. Standing there, I imagine the space filled with our guests, my father making a speech, before my eyes wander to the small stage and the dance floor, where later on, we'll dance until dawn, because neither of us will want this day to come to an end.

I turn back to the house, and go to find my mother. In the kitchen, she's making canapes.

'There is literally nothing there to worry about. Everything is perfect.'

'It means they won't match the cake.'

'Mum. It doesn't matter.'

A frown wrinkles her brow as she sighs quietly. 'I suppose not.'

She wipes her hands on her apron. 'I really should go and feed the dogs.'

Leaving her in the company of her beloved Labradors, I go up the stairs to my old bedroom. Closing the door behind me, I think of Liam in our rented cottage where he's spending tonight with Max, his best man. Then tomorrow... I glance at my gorgeous dress hanging on the wardrobe, taking in its layers of soft tulle, the subtle beading on the bodice, and feel a thrill of excitement. The most beautiful dress I've ever worn, in which I'll walk down the aisle to marry the one and only man in the world for me.

* * *

The party starts when Rita's car pulls up outside the house. It's a beautiful evening, the sun shining through the huge old trees, casting shadows across the garden. When she comes in, Sasha's with her.

When they see me, their faces beam with excited smiles. 'Callie! You're getting married tomorrow!'

Both of them hug me tightly, until, unable to breathe, I push them away. 'Hey! You're squashing me!'

Rita hugs me more gently. 'I can't believe my baby sister's getting married.'

'I can't believe I have the three of you as bridesmaids! You need to come outside and see the marquee.'

As we make our way across the garden, the air is scented from the roses growing up the back of the house.

'Has Mum been bossy?' Rita asks.

'Superbly so.' I glance at my sisters. 'I've had to remind her whose wedding it is at least a dozen times. But it's been worth it, as you'll see.' Reaching the marquee, I stand back to let them in, watching the amazement on their faces.

'This is stunning.' Rita glances woefully at Sasha. 'Even I would get married for a party like this.'

Going over to one of the tables, Sasha picks up some of the sea glass. When she looks at me, her eyes are misty. 'It's gorgeous. You're gorgeous... I'm so happy you found Liam. I wasn't sure to start with – but you two really have something, don't you?'

I still remember what she said to me. *Don't you need to think about financial security? I mean, I know you love him, but you still need to think of the practical side of things.* Just because Liam didn't own a big house or earn a six-figure salary any more – neither of which were remotely important to me.

'We want the same things,' I say simply. Right from the start, it was how it always had been between us.

* * *

In the kitchen, as we're opening a bottle of champagne, Alice comes in. In jeans and a T-shirt, with her long hair tied back, she looks way too young to be a heart specialist.

'Nice of you to join us!' Sasha teases.

'I'm always the last, aren't I? Sorry.' Coming over, she kisses my cheek.

'You have a very important job.' I pour the champagne. 'Saving lives and that.'

'I actually did this afternoon.' Her face is sober as she takes the glass I pass her. 'But enough of that! I can't believe you're getting married tomorrow!'

'Is that my girls I hear?' My father pokes his head around the door. Since retiring from his law career, he's taken to a quiet life with a bumbling kind of ease. Slightly dishevelled, his eyes are full of love as he comes in.

'Hi, Dad!' One by one, my sisters hug him.

'Big day, tomorrow, hey?' He ruffles my hair affectionately. 'No idea where your mother is. Last I saw of her, she was muttering about something to do with changing the seating plan – yet again.' He looks perplexed as he takes the glass of champagne Rita holds out. As he raises it, his eyes are misty as he gazes at us. 'This really is rather lovely.' He clears his throat. 'I'd like to make a toast – to all of you.'

2

Waking up on the morning of my wedding day, I lie there for a moment. The birds are singing, the distant sound of the sea reaching me, a smile spreading itself across my face, my heart bursting with love as I think of Liam. I feel a pang of anxiety – I know he'll be nervous. Liam's never enjoyed being the centre of attention. When he first met my family, he found them a little intimidating – though he loves them now. But I know he's looking forward to today as much as I am.

Going over the window, I pull the curtains back. It's the perfect day I wished for, the sky blue, the low sun sending rays of hazy light through the trees. Gazing out, I think how lucky I am that my parents can host our wedding. The lengths they've gone to so that everything has been thought of – they've even organised a car for Liam's mum.

I glance at my phone. It's only 8 a.m., giving us about an hour before the hairdresser arrives. After going downstairs to put the kettle on, by the time I've made a pot of tea, my sisters emerge from upstairs – Alice in flowery pyjamas, Sasha in a shapeless T-shirt dress. Only Rita looks wide awake – in her sports gear, she's obviously been for a run.

As they come in, a sudden pang of nostalgia hits me for everything that's happened in this house. Our growing-up years; the Christmases we've shared; the sisterly squabbles that all siblings have, that have turned into this wonderful, unconditional love we share.

I pass them all a mug of tea. 'I just want to say...' I break off, hesitant all of a sudden. 'You three, you're the best. I'm so lucky to have you. I really am.' I swallow the lump in my throat. 'And now I'm going to cry!'

'Don't you dare, because you'll set us all off.' Rita's voice is husky.

'We are lucky,' Alice says quietly. 'I should remind myself more often, because it's only in moments like this that you stop and take the time to actually think about it.'

* * *

After the hair stylist arrives, she curls Alice's hair into soft waves. As she starts on Rita, Sasha comes in with a bottle of champagne and four glasses.

'Just the one,' she says firmly, opening the bottle and filling the glasses with pink fizz. 'We can't have you piddled before you walk up the aisle.'

Sitting on the bed, Alice paints my fingernails and Sasha my toes, while Rita's thick hair is persuaded into a lesser state of unruliness. Then after Sasha is done, it's my turn.

'You all, out of here,' I tell my sisters. 'I want to see the full impact of my transformation on you.'

Rita shakes her head. 'We're staying, I'm afraid.'

I give her a mock-stern look. 'You may be older than me, but you are not pulling rank on my wedding day. Come on! Vamoose, the lot of you.'

Waiting until they close the door behind them, I sit at my dressing table, watching the hair stylist curl my hair before pinning some of it loosely. It seems incredible that after all the planning, the anticipation, this day is here; that a couple of hours from now, I'll be arriving at the church.

As the hair stylist finishes, there's soft knock on my door. 'Callie?'

'Come in, Mum.' I turn to face her. 'What do you think?'

For a moment she doesn't speak. 'You look beautiful.' Usually unemotional, she blinks away a tear as she holds out something. 'I don't know if you have a something borrowed, but I wore these on my wedding day. I'd love you to wear them.'

Opening the little box, I gasp as my mum's diamond earrings sparkle back at me.

'Try them on,' she says quietly.

Going over to my mirror, I carefully put them on. Like everything else about this day, they're perfect, understated even as they sparkle in the light. I turn back to my mother. 'I love them.'

'Good. They look lovely on you.' Glancing at her watch, she clears her throat before reverting back to her typical self. 'Good heavens. I can't believe the time. I haven't even done my nails – and the cars will be here soon.'

Feeling my excitement build, I smile at her. 'I need to get dressed, don't I?'

* * *

In my dress, I take a moment to gaze at my reflection. My eyes shine back at me, my tan setting off the dusky colour of my dress, while my hair is just as I wanted it. Adding a last slick of lip colour, as I glance around the familiar walls of my bedroom one last time, a feeling of gratitude fills me, for the past, for everything that's brought me to this moment.

Closing the door behind me, I make a grand entrance down the stairs of the house I grew up in. At the bottom, my sisters are waiting in the bridesmaids' dresses they chose themselves. Their faces light up with love, another moment I commit to memory.

After Mum and my sisters go ahead in the first car, I have a moment with Dad. Typically seen pottering around in jeans and an ancient sweater, in a dark suit, apart from his slightly unkempt hair, he's unfamiliarly smart.

'I know I gave you a bit of a hard time when you and Liam were first together.' His face is solemn. 'I wanted you to always have the best of everything.'

'I know. And I do – the important things aren't about money, Dad.'

'You're right. I'll even go so far as to say you've taught me that. Liam is a good man – and he loves you. I do too,' he adds.

My heart is full to bursting as I reach to kiss his cheek. 'I love you, Dad. Thank you, for today – for this incredible wedding.'

'Your mother's loved every second,' he says wryly. 'I'm not sure what she's going to do with herself once it's all over. Anyway... the car's outside.' He glances at his watch, before offering his arm. 'I think it's time. Shall we?'

* * *

As we drive to the church, I take in the familiar Cornish countryside I've always loved, the green of summer broken by grass verges peppered with wild flowers, the swallows soaring in a cloudless sky. On my lap, I'm holding my bouquet. More of a small, wispy posy, it looks as though it's been just picked from the hedgerows.

As we reach the church, the car slows down.

'Ready?' My dad winks at me.

My heart flutters with excitement. 'Never more so.'

But when we stop outside the church, Rita hurries towards us. As my dad lowers the window, her face is anxious. 'Liam isn't here yet. Can you go around the block again?'

An uneasy feeling grips me. 'Have you called him?'

Rita's worried too. 'Several times.'

My stomach lurches as I meet her eyes. 'He wouldn't stand me up like this.' It hasn't so much as crossed my mind. But suddenly I'm worrying. Has he had second thoughts? Was the big country wedding too much for him?

'We'll do another lap,' my father says firmly. 'Most likely he's had a problem with his car and he'll be here any minute.' He leans forward to the driver. 'Can you drive on?'

'Something's wrong,' I say as the car drives away. I can feel it, deep in my bones. 'No way would Liam do this. He was planning to get to the church ages early – so that he could talk to people as they arrived.' With each passing second, my fear is growing. As a helicopter flies overhead, I start to panic. 'That's the police helicopter. What if Liam's been in an accident?'

My father stays calm. 'I'm sure he'll be waiting for you at the church. Shall we go back now?'

In spite of his attempt to reassure me, I have a feeling of foreboding I can't shake. I try to tell myself I'm jumping to the wildest of conclusions; that nothing has happened, that Liam's car had a flat tyre. But when we reach the church, seeing my mum and my sisters walk towards the car, taking in their tear-stained faces, I feel my heart twist, before it stops for one heart-breaking moment. As it restarts, I realise that Liam isn't coming today or any other day; just like that, everything's changed.

* * *

I don't remember anyone helping me out of my dress and into my pyjamas. Lying in my bedroom, the shock is too great for me to think about anything other than one fact: *I found my once-in-a-lifetime love, but now I've lost him.*

As I replay my mother's words, it feels like I've been savagely uprooted from the life I loved and plunged into a hideous nightmare. *There was an accident... A witness said a car came out of nowhere. Max didn't have time to react...*

At some point I'm dimly aware of Sasha coming in. Lying next to me, she strokes my hair then rests an arm over me. A little while later, Alice comes in. Crouching on the floor beside me, she takes one of my hands.

As Sasha's arm around me tightens, I conjure Liam's dear face, the eyes that were filled with kindness, and remember the feel of his thick dark hair, his body against mine – the body I'll never touch again. My mind fills with horrific images as I imagine the crash, the impact that took Liam's life away; a life we were meant to share.

It feels as though the world has closed in around me, as a torrent of thoughts fills my head. I don't have any idea how I will get through this. If it was going to end like this, what was the point of Liam and me meeting? But having known him and loved him, without him in my life, I can no longer see the point in anything.

3

Time heals, people have been all too keen to tell me. Leaving out the *sometimes*. And a year later, I cry less, I can say Liam's name out loud, but I am no closer to moving on.

Unable to afford the house we were going to buy, I'm still living in the cottage we rented together, huddling within walls that are comfortably familiar, where every corner echoes with memories of us. Meanwhile, the garden has become my haven – I know every pebble, every plant, the walled corner where tiny ferns have taken root, their fronds softening the grey of the Cornish stone.

After weeks off work, I went back part-time, but it's as if I'm going through the motions. Every few days, my dad comes over. He doesn't say much, just drinks the tea I make him, pats my shoulder when I cry, then asks me to show him around the garden.

'This was the first thing Liam bought me.' I point to the jasmine that clambers up a sheltered wall. It came from a garden in the grounds of an old house that was being done up into modern apartments, the kind I detest. I must have told him the story a dozen times or more, but my dad lets me talk, nodding silently.

When Mum comes over, she talks about anything but me and

Liam: like someone she's met at bridge club or the gardener letting her down. The nearest she gets to anything of meaning is when she says, 'You are OK, aren't you?'

'Of course I am.' I blink away tears, knowing she doesn't want to hear the truth, that my cracked open heart will never get over this.

In all this, my sisters endeavour to rearrange their lives around me, taking turns to spend their weekends with me.

'You don't have to do this,' I protest – albeit half-heartedly, when Rita and Sasha turn up together.

'You really should stop saying that,' Sasha says gently. 'We're here because we want to be, Cal. This is what sisters do for each other.'

* * *

In this weird, disjointed life I find myself in, some days I make it to the beach, where I spell Liam's name a hundred ways: scored into the sand with one of my fingers, delicately painted with coloured sea glass; moulded out of pieces of slate, or in thick ribbons of seaweed draped to form the letters; when I run out of ideas, whispering it into the wind.

Now and then, I visit the site where Liam died, torturing myself as I imagine the accident; leaving a posy of flowers picked from the garden. Other days I go to the church, where instead of being married, days later his coffin was buried. Sitting on the grass, I hold silent conversations with him, trying to curb my frustration when he doesn't reply, instead crying tears of grief into the grass growing up over his grave.

The truth is, I don't understand. When love is supposed to connect people across universes, between this world and the next, given how powerful ours was, surely I should be able to hear him.

But after a year of hoping, of hearing nothing, there's only one conclusion I can come to. No matter the belief I've held on to that there's something else beyond this life, I see it as proof that there is a finality in death. It's the end. The closing of a door. There is no afterlife, no ethereal connection between us.

It's a realisation that's devastating, leaving me at my lowest ebb, forcing me to face the reality I've lost Liam for ever. Holed up at home, I cry for days on end, before pain-racked, exhausted, I think about ending it.

Going to the bathroom, I stare at my face in the mirror for a moment. It's like looking at the ghost of who I used to be, at someone for whom life is over.

Right on cue, my mobile buzzes. Picking it up, I feel a jolt as I gaze at Alice's face, before thinking of all my sisters, then my parents. However broken I feel, however wretched life seems, since Liam died, they've been unceasingly there for me. Warmth creeps into my frozen heart, and with it comes a realisation. Things may feel a lifetime away from how I imagined they would be, but life isn't perfect. It can be messy and heart-breaking. But in spite of the pain, I still have so much to be grateful for.

* * *

The days are still too long, the nights longer. In the emptiness of my world, nothing's changed. The passing of time has slowed, one in which I've learned to study a rose for hours – taking in the delicacy of the petals, the intoxicating scent. I can describe each inch of this garden – the tiny violets that have colonised between the bricks outside the door, the succulents that thrive in the sun. The rosemary, sage and thyme that have flourished against the back of the house, the apple mint that's spread into the lawn so that when I mow the grass the air is perfumed with its sweetness.

Typically one of my sisters calls me every day, but one evening it turns into a video call with all of them.

'We're coming to see you at the weekend.'

'No.' Gazing at their smiling faces, I feel myself panic. One I can cope with; at a pinch, two. But all of them... Shaking my head, I know why they're doing this. On Sunday, it's exactly a year to the day Liam died. 'I think this weekend I'm better off alone.'

'You're outvoted,' Alice says quietly. 'You may as well give in gracefully.'

'I don't have anywhere for you all to sleep.' It's the first thing that comes into my head.

'You have two double beds,' Rita reminds me. 'We can share.'

'But that means I have to go shopping. I don't have time.'

'I've already done an online shop,' Alice says calmly. 'It's being delivered on Friday.'

Fast running out of objections, I play my trump card. 'I may not be here.'

Sasha looks outraged. 'Where else are you going to be?'

I sleep fitfully that night, as I can't help thinking back to this time last year. It isn't a day I want to mark, but it doesn't matter what day it is, really. Memories of Liam are omnipresent. Picking up the photo I keep beside the bed, I gaze at the familiar eyes. Liam knew me better than I did. But I know what he would say. *They're your sisters, babe. They love you. They should be here.*

4

NATHAN

Having always gone for high spec, high tech, when I first see this house, I'm not sure about it, yet I have this feeling in my bones that it's the one. It feels a little like falling in love – albeit slowly; and with old, irregularly shaped bricks and ancient timbers instead of a gorgeous woman, but it passed the tried and tested heartbeat test.

'It's not at all my style,' I say to Rena, the estate agent, aware of my heart beating faster.

'I've shown you three you said were exactly your style, but you didn't like any of them,' she reminds me.

'I know.' They'd been the kind of properties I'd lived in before – with clean lines, polished concrete, light white spaces, an area of decking instead of a garden. When this place is the antithesis of all that, I don't understand, either.

Curious, as I go inside, I notice the slate floors and a big old wood burner, but the kitchen is up to the minute, the walls painted in gentle colours. Upstairs are two bedrooms with floors that can only be described as undulating, while the bathroom is brand new with a huge shower and a floor-to-ceiling heated towel rail. But it's the far-reaching views I can't stop looking at.

I find myself liking this house more and more. Going outside, I take in a different view, this time of the sea. There's a long garden, that I'd probably end up concreting over; but it's the terrace that clinches it. It runs along one side of the house, with an overhanging roof that will give shade in summer and shelter in winter.

'You can't buy it just because you like the terrace.' Robin sounds bewildered when I tell her about the house. But my sister is nothing if not methodical and organised. Her head wins over her heart every time.

'When you haven't even seen it, you're not entitled to an opinion,' I tell her. 'Come with me tomorrow and check it out.'

Robin's blue eyes are wistful as she gazes at me. 'Have you thought that maybe I don't want you to move?'

For the last year, I've been living at Robin's. She's been my port in a storm, but things are changing. It's time I stepped out into the world again. I shake my head. 'You can't wait to get me out of here – and you have Max now.' Max is the latest man in her life – a really nice guy. 'I've loved being here. But I've been cramping your style, Rob. You know and I know…'

She sighs. 'How far away is it?'

'Not far. About twenty minutes,' I say firmly. 'You can come for dinner. It'll be like old times.'

* * *

When we get there the following day, as soon as she sees the house, a cloud crosses Robin's face. 'It's too remote, Nathan. You don't even have any neighbours. What if…'

I stop her. 'I'm going to be fine here. You have to stop worrying about me.'

Her eyes are anxious. 'Why don't you stay with me a little longer?'

'Sshhh.' I hold a finger to her lips. 'Can you hear that?'

As we stand there, she looks puzzled. 'I can't hear anything.'

'Exactly.' I nod. 'That's what I want – just the birds, the insects, even the wind.' I've been craving this kind of peace in a way I never have before; viscerally.

Robin frowns. 'This is so unlike you, Nathan. I mean, you like modern. And towns. Bars and life.'

I hesitate. She's right, but for whatever reason, they don't hold the same appeal any more. 'Change can be what we need sometimes. Come on. I want to show you the terrace.'

Taking the path that leads up to the front of the house, I show her around the side. 'I'm thinking a table and chairs at one end, maybe an outdoor sofa at the other.' I gesture towards the garden. 'Tell me you don't love this.'

Blinking her eyes, Robin gazes out across the garden. 'This all belongs to the house?'

'All one and a half acres,' I say proudly. 'But there's too much work here – you know me. I don't have a clue about gardens. I'll probably get a contractor in to do some hard landscaping.'

'It might be easier to manage. Seems a shame, though. At some point, someone must have gone to a lot of trouble with it.'

A thought comes to me. 'Or I could develop it and eventually sell it.' It's what I've been doing for years, after all.

'I wouldn't build on it.' Robin's still gazing across the garden. 'I would make it beautiful again.'

'I'll think about it.' Only just realising the amount of work I'd be taking on, I'm not in a hurry to make a decision – nor do I relish the thought of living on a building site. 'I just have this feeling I can't explain: it's what I need,' I say quietly.

* * *

What I also like about this house is that in spite of the sea views appearing distant, once I've bought it I discover it's only a ten-minute drive to the nearest beach. But before I go exploring, I have my stuff to move in – not a huge amount for a thirty-something man. I've been at Robin's far too long, and I'm looking forward to putting my stamp on this place.

Having perused local furniture shops, in the end I decide to keep it simple – my main purchase being a huge, comfy sofa that I buy second-hand for next to nothing. Then after trawling upcycling sites, I find a retro kitchen table and matching chairs. What I do splash out on is the bed, my theory being that when you spend a large part of your life horizontal in one, you might as well do it in comfort.

Of course, the walls are still bare. I also need some bookshelves, as well as a desk. Catching myself, I frown. In the past, the idea of books on shelves would have felt like unnecessary clutter. But in a house like this, everything is different somehow.

I'll start scouring second-hand shops, and seeing what else I can find. But all in all, it isn't looking bad this first evening, confirmed when Robin and Max make an impromptu visit.

'We have fish and chips – and beer.' Max drops the bags on the kitchen table.

'Smells amazing.' Suddenly I realise how hungry I am.

'I've brought you a couple of throws – I haven't used them in ages so I figured you may as well have them.' Robin passes them to me.

'Thanks.' Homely touches are really not my forte – apart from the surfboard leaned up against the wall in an empty corner, if you could consider that as such.

'This is really nice.' Glancing around, Robin looks slightly puzzled. 'And kind of surprising, if I'm honest. What happened to minimalism? I mean, you have stuff.'

'Only a very little.' Opening three of the beers, I pass them one each. 'Would you like a tour?' I lead them through to the sitting room.

'What a fireplace!' Max sounds envious as he follows me in.

'Good, isn't it? I'm going to stack logs either side of the wood burner. This...' I open the door into a large cupboard, 'is my study – or will be.' Going upstairs, I show them into my bedroom, where I've already made up the bed in faded green linen, before showing them the second bedroom, then the bathroom.

'This is a cool place, mate. I really like it.' Max looks impressed.

I nod. 'Me, too. It's weird, though.' I frown slightly. 'I haven't even been here an entire day yet, but already it feels like home.'

It's been a long day and back downstairs, I'm ready for fish and chips. Opening more beers and taking it all outside, I proudly show off the garden table and chairs that were delivered this afternoon.

'Would you like some cushions?' Robin sits down. 'I have some I don't need. I'll drop them in to you.'

'All donations welcome.' I raise my beer bottle. 'Cheers. And thanks, little sister – for putting up with me for so long.'

'You're always welcome.' Robin picks up a fork. 'It is funny, though. I honestly saw you buying one of those modern apartments in Padstow. But now you're here... It kind of suits you.'

'It feels right.' And it does, in a way I can't explain. 'I definitely want to change the garden, though.'

'I'd help you if I could.' Max sounds apologetic.

'Hey, no worries. I know you would.' He's still healing from an accident, which has left him scarred in more ways than one. 'But gardening or not, you're welcome here, any time. Both of you.'

* * *

With everything slowly getting sorted, I take a break from unpacking the remaining boxes and drive down the lane to the beach.

One of Cornwall's lesser-known beaches, it's inaccessible by car and disappears underwater as the tide comes in. Stopping in the small parking area, I get out, standing there for a moment, taking in a view that seems to stretch for ever.

By chance, I've timed it right and the sea is some way out. Climbing down the rocks, I feel my feet hit the sand. It's a while since I last went to a beach – too much life, stuff has got in the way. But as I breathe in the saltiness of air filled with the sound of the waves breaking, I promise myself that's going to change.

There's something about the sea – the constant motion of the water, the way no two days are ever the same. Today it's a vivid green-blue that contrasts with the clouds that are gathering. Glancing down, my eyes settle on some small shells, then newly washed pebbles as I find myself bending down to gather them.

Studying the shells more closely, I make out the flecks of colour in them, the intricate patterns, the way they glisten where the sun catches them, aware that I've never really taken the time to notice them before.

I glance towards the sea. It's surging with energy, the water white where the waves are breaking on to the shore, the pale sand contrasting against slate cliffs. It seems unbelievable that in the height of summer, apart from me, there's only one other person here.

Standing there a moment, I watch as she stops now and then, bending down, picking up shells, just like I have. I glance around to see if anyone is with her, but as far as I can tell, she's alone – a solitary figure in jeans and a white T-shirt, with honey-coloured skin and the wind in her hair.

5

CALLIE

I tell no one how close I came to giving up and in the days that follow, change is still painfully slow. But it's as though I had to reach my lowest point to begin to claw my way out of this.

The morning before my sisters arrive, I head for one of the beaches Liam and I used to love. As I collect tiny shells, my heart leaps almost instinctively as I see a man doing the same. Shocked, I stand there for a moment, watching him. In height and build, he reminds me of Liam – though, as he comes closer, apart from the fact that he's wearing jeans and a T-shirt, he doesn't look anything like him.

He appears oblivious to me as he carries on along the high-water mark, now and then bending down, scrutinising his bounty, before eventually he walks up the beach towards the car park.

The wind picks up and I shiver slightly. Finding an empty stretch of sand, I arrange my shells into a heart shape. But the weather doesn't hold, and feeling the first raindrops start to fall, I give up and make my way home.

I arrive back just before the heavens open. Opening a window, I gaze out at the garden, breathing in the scent of rain on dry earth.

After long, hot weeks, the downpour is welcome, as is the respite from the heat, revitalising the parched ground.

If only it could do the same to my heart. I think of the year that's passed since Liam died; how I watched the bleached colours of late summer turn to autumn's glorious shades, before the leaves fell and the stillness of winter set in. It was a winter to hermit away and wait for spring to breathe new hope into my life. But I'm still waiting.

* * *

In honour of my sisters' arrival, for the first time in weeks, I properly clean the house. When the rain stops, I even go outside and pick an armful of flowers and foliage to arrange in a couple of jugs. But as I stare at them, all I can think of is our wedding flowers, Liam's funeral flowers.

By mid-afternoon, the shopping arrives – a veritable mountain of food and wine that leaves me wondering how long my sisters are planning on staying. I cram it all into my not very big kitchen, only just finishing when they arrive in the little Alfa Romeo that's Rita's pride and joy.

Standing in the doorway, as I watch them climb out, I can't help envying them their energy, the brightness of their smiles, while in my cut-off denim shorts and halter neck vest, I feel dull and faded.

Coming over, Rita flings her arms around me, before Alice and Sasha do the same.

'I can't believe we're all here together! I've just remembered something...' Running back to the car, Rita retrieves a plant from the back. Coming over, she passes it to me. 'For you – from all of us.'

'Thank you, it's beautiful.' A white rose. The symbolism isn't lost on me. 'New beginnings, huh?'

Alice looks as though she's been caught out. 'We thought you'd probably find a corner in your garden for it.'

'I will. Come on in. I hope you're hungry – there is enough food in here for about twenty people.'

With my sisters in the cottage, it seems smaller somehow. Going through the double doors that are open at the back, I leave the rose on the low wall that demarcates the terrace from the lawn.

'Oh, wow.' Sasha comes and stands beside me. 'Callie, I'd forgotten how awesome this is.'

As the others come out, they stand there in silence.

I turn to look at them. 'What is it?'

'It's your garden...' Alice is speechless.

'You lot are never short of anything to say.' I'm starting to feel anxious. 'What's the matter with you?'

Alice steps on to the lawn. 'It's a work of art, Callie. A little paradise... Everything about it – the colours, the textures, the scent...'

They're starting to weird me out. 'OK,' I say cautiously. 'But you've seen it all before, and this is what I do – or have been doing. Liam and I started it together. I just kept going.'

'Everywhere you look, it's a scene of its own. Like that bit.' Rita points to a section where driftwood and slate set off the muted blue of sea holly and clumps of grasses.

She's right. The driftwood is from the beach where Liam and I met, the sea holly a reminder of the first bouquet of flowers he bought me. The grasses because we both loved the sound of the wind rustling through them, the slate picked up from the beaches together, while each pebble marks a day in the life that for a while belonged to both of us.

'Your wedding is here.' Alice says softly. 'So is our childhood home, the beach, the woods, even...'

'It has your memories in it.' Sasha says quietly. 'Of you and Liam.'

I shrug. 'Aren't all gardens a bit like that?'

'Not like this.' She's silent for a moment.

'Your rose could go there.' Rita points to the only empty space.

'That's Santiago de Compostela.' I stare at the bare soil that Liam and I had planned to plant after the honeymoon we were going to spend walking the northern Spanish coast, except that now it's come to represent the aching void in my life. I change the subject. 'Would you like tea?'

'There should be some gorgeous rosé in the shopping that was delivered,' Alice takes over. 'There's some Pinot Gris, too.'

'All chilling in the fridge,' I say before she asks.

* * *

That night, Sasha cooks pasta and a rich tomato sauce, insisting I sit on the sofa, where, sandwiched between Alice and Rita, I watch her cook.

When she's finished, we eat outside in the dwindling daylight. As it fades to darkness and myriad stars come into view, the small flowers of night-scented stock unfurl, releasing their fragrance. Breathing it in, the familiar ache in my heart is back. Feeling a single tear snake its way down my cheek, I wipe it away.

'You OK?' As Sasha speaks, all my sisters turn to me.

'I'm fine.' My voice wavers. 'It just goes like this sometimes.' In the silence that falls, I guess what's coming.

'I wish you'd move in with me,' Sasha says quietly. 'It would do you good to have a change of scenery – and company. You'd get another job easily enough – and there's loads going on in Bristol. I know you'd love it there.'

Her spare room is lovely – airy and light, with a view across a park. 'I can't.' I shake my head, looking around at the garden that's helped me survive the last year. 'Without this, I wouldn't know who I am.'

'Wouldn't it do you good to get out of the house?' Alice says gently.

'I go to the beach – and one or two other places.' I shrug. 'It's enough.'

'Are you OK for money?' Rita says. 'I – we were talking about it on the way here. We can all afford to help.'

'You're all so kind...' I look at their faces. 'But I don't need money. Liam had life insurance. What I need...' My voice breaks. 'Is to start to feel better. *But I feel so stuck.*'

'It takes time,' Alice says.

'Yes – but it's been a year. How much more time?' There's desperation in my voice.

'It takes as long as it takes.' Reaching across the table, Alice holds my hand. 'It's different for everybody.' She pauses. 'It will get better, Cal – maybe not yet, but one day.'

A sob sticks in my throat, because there's something I can't get my head around – because part of me can't, doesn't want to, feel better. Shaking my head, I stare at the table. '*When Liam's dead, it doesn't feel right that I should be happy again.*'

'Oh, Callie...' Beside me, Rita puts her arm around me.

'I get it,' Sasha says softly. 'And it's never going to be the same. It never can be. And I understand how, right now, the idea of feeling good again racks you with guilt. But there are a hundred paths to happiness, Cal. At the moment, there's a roadblock in front of you, and you feel stuck where you are. Maybe, for now, you even need that roadblock. But once you've found your way around it or even over the top, life will start to open up again.' She pauses. 'But that will only happen when the time is right.' She pats my hand. 'This is still the shit bit. And it must feel like the most horrible dilemma to want a future that won't have Liam in it... But whatever happens going forwards, whoever you meet, nothing's going to take anything away from the fact that you loved him.'

Even the thought of meeting someone else is somewhere I can't go. But I can't help thinking she's right. Maybe, now, I do need this roadblock. I'm still reeling, grieving, missing Liam. I'm not ready for anything else.

Rita tops up my glass. 'Drink this. I'm going to put some music on.'

I look at her, startled. 'I haven't played any music – since...'

Sasha rolls her eyes at me. 'Then it's high time you did. I have a speaker with me somewhere.' Going inside, she roots around in her bag before coming back out and scrolling down her phone to select some tracks. 'This will do.'

In my slightly drunk state, listening to loud music and watching my sisters dance in the darkness, from somewhere the glimmer of a thought comes to me, slowly taking shape in my head.

There is nothing wrong with this.

It's followed by another.

I know it doesn't feel like it right now; that you can't imagine anything changing, but it will. And you'll be OK. You've got this.

* * *

Over the last year, I've got used to my sisters dragging me out of the house, and on Saturday morning, when they suggest we go surfing together, I know better than to try to talk them out of it. Climbing into my car, they chatter noisily as we head for our parents' house. Gathered around the kitchen table, it's like old times as we drink coffee and eat the poached eggs on toast cooked by our mother, before gathering up our surfing gear and heading for the beach at Polzeath.

Polzeath is the beach of my childhood days, when I used to be in awe of my older sisters paddling out and catching waves, though it wasn't long before I plucked up my courage and went to join them. Today when we arrive, the sun is warm in a cloudless sky, the offshore wind meaning the waves are clean and glassy. After parking on the beach, we pull on our wetsuits before untying the boards from the roof of my car.

I haven't surfed in over a year. It's felt inappropriate, too joyful, when my aching heart has been raw with sadness. But today, when I hang back, my sisters aren't having any of it.

'You all ready?' Alice's wetsuit shows off her lithe figure. 'Let's go!'

Reaching the water, I push my board out past the breaking waves. As I slide on to it, it's like being reunited with an old and trusted friend. Paddling out, it takes a while for my sisters to catch me up. By the time they do, I've caught a wave.

As the familiar exhilaration courses through me, I feel euphoric for a split second before guilt crashes over me. I ride the wave to the shore and wade through the shallows on to the beach, where sitting on the sand, I watch my sisters. Sasha wobbles before she bails; Rita spectacularly nose-dives. Only Alice makes it gracefully to her feet and stays there.

Reaching the shore, splashing towards me, she calls out. 'Come on, Callie. You have to join us.'

Getting to my feet, I'm about to tell her I don't feel like it, when something different fires up inside me. Instead of wallowing, I'm angry all of a sudden – with Liam for dying, at myself for being alive, for feeling so stuck.

There's a melting pot of emotions churning inside me as I push my board out again, the sun dazzling my eyes as I catch Alice up.

'You were very good,' I tell her. 'The others, really not so!'

'I'd forgotten how much I love this.' Alice's face is radiant. Reaching the others, she calls out. 'What happened to you two?'

'Rookie mistake. Next one, I'm on it.' Rita tries to sound confident.

Beyond the waves, I sit on my board, watching as this time all three of them get to their feet and make it to the shore. I start paddling after them, the surging energy of the water suddenly contagious. Getting to my feet, I catch the wave; in the moment it feels a little like chasing happiness.

* * *

Surfing is restorative and that evening as we cook, we sing and laugh and drink more wine.

'I have a question for you,' I say during an interlude.

Sasha looks surprised. 'For who?'

'All of you.' Buoyed up by the wine, I eye their faces. 'How come all of you are single?' Before they can interrupt, I hold a hand up. 'Not that there's anything wrong with single – because it probably has a lot going for it. But are there literally no boyfriends – or girl-friends – between the three of you?' I say pointedly.

Rita's cheeks are pink. 'Shall I go first?'

'Someone has to.' I fix her with a stern gaze.

'OK. He's a student, far too young, classic uni lecturer dilemma... Bit like a doctor shagging a patient.' She glances at Alice. 'Oops. Sorry, Al. I didn't mean you.' She turns back to me. 'He's gorgeous and the sex is good – but that's kind of the extent of it.'

'So it's still going on?'

Rita shrugs. 'It's an on-and-off thing. I should probably end it.'

'If you're not sure about him, maybe you should. Next?' I glance at Sasha.

She sighs. 'There was someone for a while – quite a while, as it turns out. And before you say anything, he wasn't a client. I met him at a party. He was there alone – he told me he was married – unhap-pily, he said. Don't ever believe a man who says that to you, because it's incredible how easily they lie. He said he was waiting for the right moment to tell his wife it was over between them, but of course, when all this time passed...' She shrugged. 'I realised it was all talk and he had no intention of leaving her. A bit like Rita said – another classic – a selfish, egotistical man who thought he could get away with shagging two women. And for a while, he did.'

'Bastard. You're better off without him.' I turn to Alice. 'You're being very quiet.' Seeing the small smile that plays on Alice's lips, the strangest feeling comes over me. 'There is someone, isn't there?'

She hesitates. 'I wasn't going to say.'

'Why not?' Sasha and Rita say in unison.

Alice turns to me. 'After what you've been through, it would be pretty insensitive of me, wouldn't it?'

'No,' I mumble. 'It wouldn't. It would be great. You deserve someone lovely. *You deserve to be happy.*' She does, but it makes me miss Liam even more. I wipe away the tear that rolls down my cheek. 'Honestly, take no notice of me... Who is he?'

'Well, he's a junior doctor who wants to be a surgeon. So yes, he's a little younger than me. His name is Adam – we've been seeing each other for six months – and so far, it's really good.' She looks around at us. 'Why are you looking at me like that?'

'Because you didn't tell us?' Sasha sounds put out.

'I thought if it crashed and burned, it was easier not to. But now that we haven't, I have told you.' She smiles. 'Eventually!'

'So it's serious.' Rita is stunned. 'I can't believe we didn't know this. We need to meet him, don't we? Any other secrets, while we're on the subject?' When no one says anything, she goes on. 'Right. I'm starving. Let's eat.'

* * *

The rain holds off and Sunday is a chilled day, spent lazing in the garden. But on the day that should have been my first wedding anniversary, it's impossible to staunch the flow of memories – of getting ready, of how happy and carefree life had felt; of driving to the church with my father, only to find out Liam wasn't coming.

'I know it's a tough day, Callie.' Coming over, Alice hugs me.

Tears fill my eyes. 'Yes.'

All morning, I'm conscious of their thoughtful glances, their love. But even with my sisters here, I'm restless, unable to settle, the day passing slowly until late afternoon, it's time for them to leave.

'I wish you were coming with us.' Sasha hugs me tightly.

'I'll be fine here.' As Alice and Rita come over, I hug them all back, until I extricate myself from their arms. 'I know I tried to put you off, but thank you so much for being here. It's been fun.'

Rita pretends to wince. 'Did I hear you say *fun*?'

But it has, I'm realising, in more ways than one. My sisters, the sea, surfing, all of them have worked a kind of magic. Standing there, I watch them cram themselves into Rita's car before waving them off, feeling oddly bereft as they drive away.

* * *

After they've gone, I drive to the beach. The tide is low, the cove quiet and reaching the sand, I slip my shoes off. As I walk, I search for treasures, collecting the tiniest pieces I can find – broken shells, fragments of slate, tiny stones.

Heading back up the beach, reaching a place where the sand is drier, I sit down and start designing. I start with an elaborately curled A, for Alice, followed by S and R, so deeply engrossed in my work I don't notice someone watching me.

'That's cool.'

The voice startles me. Looking up into a pair of clear brown eyes, I realise it's the guy I saw last time.

'Thanks. It's a thing I do.'

'D'you want these?' He holds out a handful of tiny shells.

'Thanks, but I think I'm done.' Adding the last shell fragments to my R, I get up. 'You should have a go.'

He looks uncertain. 'Care to help me?'

I hesitate again, and make my excuses.

Turning, I start walking back to my car. Halfway back, I pause, thinking of the guy and his shells and I consider changing my mind. But today, of all days, isn't the time.

6

NATHAN

There are a few people on the beach when I get there, but I recognise her instantly – the girl with the wind in her hair, sitting on the sand totally absorbed in what she's doing. Seeing the intricate letters, I find myself intrigued by her.

But she seems anxious to get away and as she walks up the beach, my desire to go after her doesn't make sense. I mean, she's made it pretty clear she'd rather be somewhere else.

Nevertheless, there's something about her that seems familiar. I gaze down at the sand, at the letters she's formed out of the tiniest pieces – A, S, R – wondering what they stand for.

Then sitting down, I pile the shells I've gathered on the sand, thinking for a moment, before starting to form a question mark.

* * *

On Monday morning, I wake up early. Lying in bed, I listen to the birds. I can't get my head around how such tiny creatures produce such a brilliant, vibrant song. Nor can I understand why I haven't thought about it before. But I can't afford to just lie here. Work is calling and I still have a desk to buy.

After showering and dressing, I skip my usual coffee, deciding I'll get one in town. As I walk out to my car, I turn around for a moment. Looking at the house, a funny feeling comes over me. I already love its quirkiness – the old brickwork and the battered weather-boarded extension. But there's a heart to it, too. It feels like a good place to call home.

I've never felt this way about a house. But I know it's about more than just the building. It's the surroundings, the absence of background noise from traffic; the sense of timelessness that comes from being surrounded by nature. So very different from where I used to live, yet somehow the perfect setting to begin a new chapter of my life.

Whistling tunelessly, I head out to my car. Cornwall is always busy in the summer months, the payoff being that in winter, it isn't. But this is late summer, the tourists and second home owners here in droves and the nearer I get to Truro, the more crowded the roads become.

By the time I've found somewhere to park, it's already warm. Dodging families and children wielding ice creams, I head for the centre. As luck would have it, there's a market going on. Perusing the various stalls, I stop at one selling an array of what I guess to be gardening tools. But as I try to identify what I need, I'm rapidly realising that enthusiasm is only going to take me so far.

'You look baffled.' The voice comes from behind me.

Turning around, I find beach girl watching me, amusement in her eyes.

'Hi.' I try to hide the surprise I'm feeling. I mean, when I saw her on the beach, she hadn't been able to get away quickly enough. 'I've just bought a house – with a garden that needs a lot of work. I'm realising I don't really know where to start.'

'With this.' She points to an earth-encrusted fork that has clearly seen better days, then to a spade. 'Maybe this, too. They're good quality – and a good price.'

'OK.' I find myself mesmerised by the blue of her eyes, her dark lashes, the long hair that's darker than I'd realised, strands of it lightened where the sun has caught it. 'You're looking at a complete beginner. I know nothing about gardening.'

'I know a bit.' Her face clouds over slightly. 'If you don't have any tools, you'll probably need a wheelbarrow – and a rake. It depends what you're doing, really, but once you start planting...' She rattles off a list of implements I've never heard of before.

'I think I'll start with these.' I look at the stall holder. 'Do you have a wheelbarrow and rake?'

After he'd produces them from his van, I frown. 'Actually, I also need a saw and some heavy-duty cutters.'

'Secateurs, you mean,' beach girl says. 'It sounds like you have quite a project on your hands.'

'You could say.' I can't take my eyes off her. 'To be honest, it's too much for me. I'll probably end up getting someone in to clear it.' I hand over the money. Piling the tools into the wheelbarrow, I turn to beach girl again. 'Thanks. You've been really helpful.'

'You're welcome.' She pauses. 'I'd think about it before you start cutting down your garden. Plants take a long time to grow – and they become home to so many wild creatures.' She stops herself. 'Sorry. It's really none of my business.' She glances at her watch. 'Happy gardening! I have to go.'

I want to ask her to come for a coffee, anything to keep her here just a little longer, but she's already walking away, her golden hair swinging behind her. As I start to push the wheelbarrow, the tools slide out and clatter noisily to the ground, turning several heads as I feel my face turn red. Picking them up as casually as I can, I head for my car.

I abandon my pursuit of a desk. With the wheelbarrow inside it, there isn't room in my car, for one thing. Maybe I'll do another Facebook Marketplace search and find one nearby. Except that's the downside of living out in the sticks – the only one as far as I'm concerned – the concept of 'nearby' simply doesn't exist.

Back at home, I unload my car and arrange my purchases on the terrace. It's a satisfying feeling to think that I can now make a start, the only problem being I didn't have a clue how to.

Walking through the garden, I take my first up-close look at what's been planted there. I can see there's a whole range of plants, but I'm utterly flummoxed as I try to distinguish between flowers and weeds. Research is required – or maybe a book would help. I fantasise about running into beach girl again, maybe asking her advice.

Not sure where to start, I make myself a cup of coffee and take it outside. Sitting on the terrace, I get out my phone and started scrolling down Marketplace ads to hunt for a desk, but as I fail to find one, a bookcase catches my eye. Finishing my coffee, I go inside again to check the measurements of my study. It would fit perfectly.

I message the seller, someone who goes by the name *dog rose days*.

Is this item still for sale?

They get back to me a few minutes later.

Yes.

Can I come over and take a look?

Having taken down the address, I go back out to my car again. As luck would have it, it's only about twenty minutes away. The drive takes me along winding country lanes, the steep sides of which are edged with the stone walls that are everywhere in Cornwall; overgrown with long grasses and wild flowers.

I turn up a particularly narrow lane, before coming to a small cottage that stands alone. White-painted, it has small windows and a maroon front door. Parking behind another car in the layby opposite, I get out and knock, waiting only seconds before it's opened by someone. As I see her face, a feeling of astonishment comes over me.

It's beach girl.

7

CALLIE

'It's you.' Slightly shocked, I gaze at the guy. It's the weirdest of coincidences that having seen him in Truro earlier today, here he is now, standing on my doorstep.

He looks equally surprised. 'Hello.'

I pull myself together. 'You've come for the bookcase?'

'Yeah.' He pauses. 'It sounds exactly what I need – I think I told you, I've just moved. I have this tiny office space – which your book-case should fit perfectly.'

I have the strangest feeling as I stand back to let him in. 'You'd better come and see.' As he steps inside, I close the door behind him. 'It's over here.' I lead him through the kitchen part of the open-plan living space. 'This is it.' But instead of looking at the bookcase, his eyes seem fixed on my garden.

'Sorry.' He turns back towards me, then properly looks at the bookcase. 'It's great. I'll take it. Sorry,' he says again. 'It's just that your garden is really something.'

'Thanks.' I fold my arms. I can't quite put my finger on it, but there's something about this guy that makes me uncomfortable.

'I'm Nathan, by the way.'

I already know from his Marketplace profile, while mine, *dog rose days* is nicely anonymous. 'I'm Callie.'

Slightly awkwardly, he says, 'I hope you don't mind me asking, but would you mind if I had a look out there?'

Remembering what he'd said in Truro about having taken on an overgrown garden, I shrug. 'Be my guest.'

I watch him go outside, stopping to notice details, slowly working his way around the old wall, the borders, the brick shed at the end that's covered in honeysuckle, before he comes back.

He looks slightly dazed. 'It's the most beautiful garden I've ever seen.'

I feel a flicker of warmth. 'Thanks.'

'Did it take long? To get it looking like that?'

'About three years.' Years of love, blood and sweat – followed by a year of tears. 'You kind of learn as you go along,' I say to encourage him. 'When things start growing, it's the best feeling.'

'I feel inspired,' he says humbly. 'Honestly. I'm so glad I came to get your bookcase.' He fumbles in his pocket and gets out some money. 'You said fifty?'

I nod. 'I decided it was time for a bit of a clear out. It's why I was in Truro this morning – I was dropping some books at a charity shop. Not my books...' I've no idea why I'm telling him this. 'They were my fiancé's. He died,' I add, by way of explanation, feeling myself frown. My voice hasn't even wavered.

There's shock on his face. 'I'm so sorry. That must have been awful for you.'

'It was. Still is, if I'm honest.' This time, my voice trembles slightly. 'Anyway, I'm glad his bookcase is going to a good home. Shall I help you load it up?'

'Yes. Thanks. Great.' He sounds slightly flustered, but then I have just told him the saddest story ever.

The bookcase isn't heavy and we manoeuvre it through the door and into his car.

He pushes the door closed. 'Thanks again.' As he stands there, he looks as though he wants to say something. But he clearly thinks better of it.

'You're welcome. Enjoy the bookcase.' Folding my arms, I watch as he turns the car around before driving away.

Going back inside, I'm unsettled. The guy is nice – Nathan – I read his name on his Facebook message. I almost asked him if he'd like a cup of tea, but I stopped myself. Still caught between the past and present, I have no idea how I'm supposed to do that kind of thing, nor if I'm ready for tea with someone new.

Glancing around my living space, I take in the piles of books I still have, stacked higgledy-piggledy on the built-in shelves. I've come to think of them as old friends and I have hundreds of them, collected over the years, belonging to various stages of my life. But as I take in the several titles on grief that are recent additions, it occurs to me that what I need to find now is a book for the next part: beginning to live again.

Having started my clear-out, I need to keep the momentum going. Going upstairs, I swallow the lump in my throat. Since Liam's accident, I've kept this cottage exactly as it's always been. But I've a feeling it isn't helping me; my inability to change anything is keeping me stuck exactly where I am.

Carefully, I fold each item of Liam's clothing. Every one of them holds a memory: the grey sweater he was wearing the day we met; the woollen socks he used to wear with his walking boots when we went for a hike. Things I've bought him, lovingly chosen. Each shirt – a couple from his city days; the white linen one he wore on the hottest days; the patterned one he was wearing the day he asked me to marry him.

But without Liam in them, they are just clothes, I tell myself, adding them to another bag until every last one of them has gone.

As I take the bags downstairs, I'm fighting the urge to put them back in the cupboard. Before I can change my mind, I carry them out to my car. Locking the house, I drive to the nearest charity shop.

After dropping the bags off, I don't go home. Instead, I drive to the coast path that starts from the beach in New Polzeath, a place where Liam and I used to walk. It's the best of late summer days and the beach is crowded, though less so than the main Polzeath beach around the headland.

As I walk, around me the long grasses are sun-bleached, the sky an intense blue. There are sheep dotted across the scrubby hills that slope steeply down towards the sea. Passing only one or two other walkers, the further I walk the quieter it becomes.

I imagine Liam walking beside me, the way he'd point out a buzzard or a swallow, or stop to listen to the sound of the wind, bending down to look at a wild flower we hadn't seen before. Liam got that about details – how it wasn't about the obvious, it was about the tiniest, simplest of things.

I walk until the sun sinks lower, sending long shadows across the path, lighting the sky in shades of peach. But as I turn to head back towards my car, I question myself. What do I really want? If I can start to imagine a life going on from here, where do I want to live? I have a whole lot of life left – *hopefully*. Is it wrong to imagine being happy again?

* * *

It's dark by the time I get home. I open the double doors on to the garden, standing there for a moment, assailed by the array of scents that seem magnified in the darkness. Rose, mint, lavender, geranium, honeysuckle, each one of them identifiable in its own right, yet blended, forming the most perfect of fragrances.

Turning around, I survey the room. Like everything else in this house in the last year, nothing has changed, yet suddenly I need it to. I start shifting the sofa so that it's closer to the garden, before moving the dining table and chairs so that they're closer to the kitchen. Then I start taking down one or two pictures that have been there so long, I don't even notice them any more.

Leaning them against the wall, I study the room, my eyes turning to the framed photo of Liam and me on the fireplace, noticing the flowers in the vase next to it have wilted. Throwing them away, I go outside, cutting a single rose to replace them.

I reposition the vase next to the photo, standing there for a moment as a trace of its scent reaches me, watching as one or two of the petals drop gracefully, until I'm distracted by a knock on the door. Wondering who it is, I go to answer it.

'Hey!' When I open the door, Max leans down and kisses my cheek. 'Thought I'd pop by – it's been a while.'

It has been, but Max and I will always remind each other of the saddest day in both our lives.

'It's good to see you! Come in.' I stand back to let him in. 'How are you?'

'Pretty good.' It's the best he can manage, but like me, Max battles with survivor guilt. He closes the door behind him.

'Would you like a beer?'

'A beer would be great.'

Going to the fridge I take out two bottles. Passing one of them to him, I watch his eyes dart around the living area, taking in the changes I've made.

'You've been busy, Cal.'

'I've done a bit of clearing out.' My eyes don't quite meet Max's. 'Books, clothes, stuff like that... I thought it was time.'

He nods soberly. 'It's probably a good thing. I don't suppose it was easy, though.'

'Not really.' I try to force a smile. 'Shall we take these outside?'

The garden table is lit by the outside light and as we sit down, I'm reminded of the many evenings we spent here, the three of us; how there should have been many more. But as I know too well, thinking like this isn't going to change anything.

'So, where've you been, stranger?'

'Well...' He hesitates. 'A lot's been happening, actually. I've met this girl.'

'Wow.' I stare at him. 'Who is she? How?'

'I met her at a party a couple of months ago. She's very cool – and she's feisty. She has a great laugh – she's also gorgeous...'

I'm incredulous as I listen to him. 'So how don't I know?'

He sighs. 'To be truthful?'

'Generally the best way.' Leaning my elbows on the table, I rest my chin in my hands.

'I feel bad.' He shrugs. 'That I survived the crash and Liam didn't. And I feel guilty that I've found someone I'm happy with, when you...' He sounds choked.

It's almost exactly what Alice said.

'When I've lost him?' I swallow the lump in my throat.

He nods, his eyes bright with tears. 'I think about him every day, Cal.'

As well as the sense of loss we share, Max wears the visible scars from the accident. Reaching across the table, I take his hand. 'I know. I do, too. But we both know the accident wasn't your fault, Max. It's one of those shitty things that there will never be any explanation for.' It's one of the things I battle with, the pointless-ness of it. My voice trembles. 'I'm really glad you've met someone. What's her name?'

His face brightens. 'She's called Robin. I think you'll really like her. You should come over to dinner with us.'

'You're living together?' For the second time, my mouth falls open.

'I just moved in with her.' His cheeks flush slightly pink.

'It's serious.' I'm dumbfounded. 'It isn't too quick, is it?'

He shakes his head. 'That's the strangest thing. It doesn't feel as if it is.'

I try to sound enthusiastic. Max has been through so much. He deserves to be happy. 'This is wonderful, Max. After everything that's happened... I'm really happy for you.'

'You're sure? I keep thinking how insensitive it seems to feel so happy...' His voice drops.

It's only as Max voices my own thought, I realise it isn't right. 'I know exactly what you mean. I've been feeling the same. But hearing you say it... it really isn't insensitive. Life goes on – and Liam wouldn't want us to be unhappy.' And I mean it. But despite my words, I'm just not there yet.

A look of gratitude fleetingly crosses his face. 'I know. But thanks for saying it, Cal.'

'Not easy, is it?' I say gently. 'Finding your way when you've lost someone?'

'Changes everything, doesn't it?'

Both of us are silent for a moment before he changes the subject. 'Why don't I speak to Robin and fix a date?' He looks at me hopefully.

I hesitate. 'At some point. But right now, I'm still taking baby steps, Max. Meeting new people still feels too big.' I shrug. 'Maybe in a month or two.'

'I understand.' He pauses. 'Are you OK, though?'

'OK enough.' I meet his eyes, knowing it's true. 'Liam would be so happy for you.'

* * *

After a year of nothing changing, just like that, it's as though one small yet momentous step has shifted me from one stage of grief into the next. It's one where the house still rattles with emptiness; where each day I think of a million things I want to say to Liam. But I can mention his name, gaze at his photo, while instead of my heart cracking open, it bursts with a sad, aching kind of love for him. There's a kind of comfort in realising that maybe grief doesn't go, but that the memory of someone you've loved and lost doesn't disappear, and instead slowly becomes an integral part of you.

I take this new realisation to the beach, feeling the wind whip my hair back as I slip off my shoes and run towards the sea. Standing there, I watch the sun setting, looming larger as it sinks towards the ocean, casting the beach in its golden light. Bending down, I pick up little pebbles and stones, nuggets of gold in the sun's glow, pressing them into a heart-shaped collage on the sand.

On my way back to my car, I catch sight of something in the sand. Wandering over to it I see a flower, albeit a slightly crooked one with a seaweed stem, the petals formed from empty mussel shells.

I pause for a moment, gazing at it. Apart from Liam, I don't know anyone else who makes sea pictures – unless... Remembering Nathan's handful of shells, I can't help wondering if maybe it's his.

8

NATHAN

The bookcase turns out to be the perfect size for my office space. It's a little weird, though, knowing it belonged to Callie's fiancé before he died. I can't help thinking how tough that must have been for her.

I wonder how long ago it happened. I'm guessing not that long – it would explain her reticence, the way she seems to hold back. She's probably still navigating her way through her grief.

As I know too well, life sucks sometimes. I've had my own run-in with the grim reaper – a close call, until the Universe intervened with another chance. It's why it's become important to make changes to the way I live, the biggest of which has been buying this house.

The thing is, as I've learned, you can't count on tomorrow. The only bit that's certain is now, meaning you should make the most of each day. So why wasn't I taking my own advice – calling Callie instead of procrastinating? But I know why. She's grieving and grief takes its own sweet time. For her, right now is way too soon. But that she is clearing stuff out has to be a good sign.

* * *

As I get into more of a routine, I spend most of the day on the property development project I'm managing, then in the evenings, dig up the brambles at the end of my garden that are about the only thing I can positively identify as a weed. It's arduous, back-breaking work, but it's exercise at least, as well as one less thing I'll have to pay someone else to do. And there's the upside that already I'm noticing a difference.

A few days have passed since I last went to the beach. Saturday lunchtime, needing a change of scene, I head down there with a sandwich. There's an offshore breeze blowing, the sun high in a blue sky dotted with small clouds. Sheltered from the wind, I watch surfers gracefully riding the waves.

Once, I would have been one of them, taking every opportunity to be out there no matter the weather. And today is pretty much perfect. Closing my eyes, I let my mind wander, wondering how it would feel to be sharing this with someone, liking the idea that there might be someone – one day. *Maybe someone like Callie, sitting here on the sand beside me, the wind catching her long hair, her eyes bright with happiness again...*

But sometimes these things aren't to be. And while I, too, am in the midst of a process of change, it probably isn't the best time to meet someone.

Getting up, I start searching for shells and sea glass, now and then glancing up to watch the surfers again, contemplating that maybe it won't be too long before I can get myself back in the water.

'Beachcombing again?' The voice comes from behind me.

Recognising Callie's voice, I'm already smiling as I stand up. 'Hi! Guilty as charged!'

'So am I!' She holds out a cupped hand filled with sea glass.

'Selective, aren't you?' I raise an eyebrow at her. 'I've just had lunch down here. I hadn't been out for a few days.'

'Nice.' She peers at my collection of shells. 'So what are you going to make?'

I say the first thing that comes into my head. 'A surfboard.'

Her eyes lit up. 'Do you surf?'

'I used to. I was addicted to it, to be honest. Everywhere I went on holiday, there had to be waves. I haven't surfed for a while, now. But I happen to think a surfboard is like a beautiful piece of art. I have one in my sitting room, as a matter of fact.'

She looks interested. 'I agree. I love my board. I hadn't surfed for ages – but I went the weekend before last, with my sisters.' Her eyes are bright as she remembers. 'It was pretty awesome, actually.'

'There is something about it, for sure.' The might of the ocean and sense of exhilaration; the unpredictability of the waves that gives you a feeling of always challenging yourself. 'Shall we make a start?' For some reason I don't consider that she isn't going to do this with me.

'Sure.' She walks beside me further up the beach to where I sat to eat my sandwich. 'So why did you stop surfing?' She looks curious.

I hedge. 'I suppose I've been quite busy, one way or another. I wasn't well for a while – but that's behind me now. Then I moved... and since then, I've been trying to get my business back in shape.'

'And now you have a garden, too.' Sitting down, she looks at me. 'OK, it's your surfboard. You start.'

'OK.' Aware of her eyes scrutinising me, I start marking out the edge, before she joins in. As she lays out the pieces of glass in a geometric pattern, now and then, I feel a jolt of electricity as her hand brushes against mine, before she lightly touches my arm.

'You've cut yourself.' She's inspecting the scratches.

'Savage wounds inflicted by brambles,' I say wryly, trying to ignore how her touch feels.

'You need gloves. Brambles can be brutal.' Sitting back, she looks at our combined effort and her eyes light up. 'That is one cool surfboard.'

'It certainly is. It seems a shame that in a few hours it will be gone for ever.' I notice Callie glance towards the waves. 'Is it making you wish you were out there again?'

Her cheeks flush slightly. 'Kind of.' She pauses. 'I used to surf with Liam. Going on my own isn't really my thing,'

'So what is your thing?' I ask softly.

She's silent for a moment. 'I guess I'm kind of rediscovering that. Everything's different since my fiancé died. I'm readjusting – but... My thing?' Her eyes gaze into mine. 'It's my garden; but I suppose, more generally, it's noticing the small things. Like the million shades of blue that make up the sky.' She glances upwards, before going on. 'Or the way clouds change shape, or how colours intensify when it rains.' She hesitates. 'I love all the scents around us – not just from flowers, but the earth, the sea, the rain.' Pausing, she looks at me. 'Isn't it miraculous how tiny birds sing so loudly? Or the way we couldn't survive without bees? Then there are butterflies – how does a caterpillar metamorphose into something so delicate, with such beautifully patterned wings?'

I gaze at her, entranced. I don't have the answers, but from her air of calmness, I get the feeling she isn't looking for any.

'It's moments like this, too.' She hesitates, her cheeks flushing slightly pink again. 'They're unexpected. I really liked your sand-flower,' she says shyly.

'Thanks.' As we look at each other, I try to think of something profound to say. But instead, I come out with, 'I don't suppose there's any chance you could come and see my garden?' Then, conscious that 'garden' sounds horribly like a euphemism for 'etchings', I quickly go on, 'I have no idea what to do with it. The easy solution is to get someone in – I was thinking concreting over the grass, minimal planting...'

'It would be a shame to do that,' she says quietly. 'Your garden is its own little ecosystem. It's probably home to tens of thousands of insects. If you concrete over it...' She tails off.

'I know to someone like you it probably sounds terrible. But there are too many plants – and I don't have a clue which of them are weeds. As you've already seen, I've identified the brambles.' I hold up my scratched arms. 'If you do decide to come, I won't take up much of your time. And I understand you're probably really busy.'

She's silent for a moment. 'OK,' she says quietly.

'Really?' A feeling of relief floods through me. 'That's great! I mean, thank you!'

'How about tomorrow?'

'Um, yes. Tomorrow is great.' Taken by surprise, I'm floundering again. 'I need to tell you where I live, don't I?'

She hesitates for a moment. 'Send me a pin.'

* * *

The next morning, I feel a ridiculous sense of excitement that Callie's coming here, the only problem being I'm not sure entirely what she sees this as – a chat about gardens, or whether she's expecting more than that. But if it turns into lunch, I can always take her to a pub.

Tidying the house, I've lost track of time when I hear a car pull up outside. Imagining her taking a good look at the garden and seeing how neglected it is before changing her mind and driving away, I go to the door just as she knocks.

'Hi! I was just looking at the view out here. It's incredible.' She's wearing a loose-fitting cotton dress in shades of green.

'It's quite something, isn't it? Come in.' As I stand back to let her in, I catch the faintest trace of scent.

She glances around. 'This is really nice. How long have you lived here?'

'A couple of weeks – though it feels like longer.'

Her eyes scan the room. 'I see what you meant about your surfboard. Looks cool over there, doesn't it?'

'I think so. Would you like some tea? Or coffee? Or there may be some Coke in the fridge...'

She's smiling. 'Tea?'

Filling the kettle, I switch it on. 'Shall I show you outside?' Forgetting about the tea, I lead the way through the back door on to the terrace.

As she steps outside, instead of enthusing as I'd hoped she would, she looks thrown. 'This is really weird,' she says at last.

I watch her frown. 'What is?'

'This terrace... the garden...' She stands there for a moment, before turning to me. 'I'm sorry. It's just so like the house that we were going to buy. It's a shock, that's all.' She seems to rally herself. 'I can see what you mean about the garden, though. It's huge. Shall we walk through it and I'll try to tell you what everything is?'

'That would be really helpful.'

Going down the steps on to what would hopefully, one day, become a lawn, she touches the tree. 'This is a magnolia. They're glorious – wait till next spring. This one...' Her fingers brush through the leaves of a shrub with oval leaves and tiny red berries. 'This is an amelanchier. They're really subtle – and different every month of the year.' She surveys the tangle of plants around her. 'I see what you mean about the weeds. You probably need to try to dig up the buttercups and nettles...' She points at what looks like a veritable ocean of them. 'It's easier after it's rained – the soil is softer. Here...' As we reach another section of the garden, she sounds excited. 'This is a proper herb garden – there are tons of things.' She starts pulling out some tiny strands that cover the soil. 'These are all weeds, but you have sage, rosemary, thyme, mint, chives...' I take in the names as she indicates each of them. 'You can't concrete over this. It's a beautiful garden. All it needs is a bit of love.'

I'm not sure what to say. 'I'm afraid I'm not the person to give it to it. I know nothing about plants.'

She's still looking around. 'You could always learn.'

We carry on walking, reaching the patch that I've started clearing of brambles. 'I'm thinking of growing veg – easy ones, if such things exist.' Despite the cavernous gap in my knowledge, I've decided it can't be too hard to grow potatoes and tomatoes, maybe runner beans. 'This is an awful lot to ask, especially considering you barely know me, but I don't suppose there's any chance you could help? I'll happily pay you.' But even as I speak I realise it's probably too big an ask.

She's silent for a moment. 'If I did, there would be a condition.'

My heart lifts. At least she hasn't dismissed it out of hand. 'What's that?'

Her clear eyes fix on mine. 'No concrete,' she says simply. 'I couldn't be a part of destroying this place.'

I think for a moment. 'And if I agree?'

'I don't want you to pay me,' she says quietly. 'Can I think about it? It might be a good thing – for me, as well as your garden... but I don't want to make any hasty decisions. Is that OK?'

'Sure.' After what she's been through, I can understand why. 'But if you do decide to help me, I must at least pay your expenses. In the meantime, how about that cup of tea?' I half expect her to say she has to be somewhere else. But to my surprise, she smiles.

'OK.'

As we walk back to the house, I try to remember the last time I felt so at home with someone. I barely know her; it doesn't make sense. Whether we'll become friends in the future, or more than that, is neither here nor there. But the timing seems right. There's no question I need her help, and she, meanwhile, is finding her way forward. In a sense, both of us in some way have needed to find each other.

9
_____

CALLIE

When Nathan asks me to help him in his garden, my gut feeling is to say yes. But grief does odd things to gut feelings; as does guilt. When my emotions can swing all over the place, I'm no longer sure whether to trust myself – on top of which after a year of living in isolation, this feels huge.

Worried it's the roadblock again, in the end, I call Sasha.

'Weird things are happening,' I tell her. 'I keep running into this guy. He's really nice – and there's nothing going on – but he's just bought this house and he wants some help with the garden.'

'Yeah, right,' she says uncertainly.

I frown. It's unlike Sasha to be cynical. 'He's not like that. He genuinely doesn't know the first thing about plants. He was going to concrete over the whole lot. But I told him what a bad idea that was, and now he says he wants to learn – and he wants to pay me.'

'It sounds like your kind of thing, doesn't it?' she says more gently. 'So what's the problem?'

'I'm not sure,' I say carefully. 'It's like I can't decide whether to do it or not.'

'Well, what are the pluses?' Sasha says practically. 'There's the money, for one thing.'

'I don't want to be paid.' If I do it for free, it will feel more on my terms, while money would mean I'd feel obligated.

'Sounds bonkers to me – but at least it's a decision. You'd enjoy it, though, wouldn't you?'

'I think so.' I wait for her to say that it would get me out of the house, but she doesn't.

'So what's the problem?' She sounds slightly exasperated.

'I don't know.' I'm quiet for a moment. 'Thanks, Sash.'

'Is that it?' Sasha says.

'I'm going to sleep on it.' But as my thoughts untangle themselves, it's suddenly clear. I'm not sure because I like him. And last time, like turned into love, which turned into heartbreak and the worst kind of pain. I can't ever risk doing that to myself again.

Going outside, I gaze up at the sky. It's hard to explain, but going to Nathan's garden today held significance of mammoth proportions. And I know why: it's a step away from the familiarity of the grief that's held me in its grip; grief that I'm scared to let go of.

I watch a family of swallows dip and soar, and tears prick my eyes. I've always been in awe of the journeys these tiny birds embark on, but as I look at them, I'm thinking how for me, too, it feels immense that I'm stepping out into the world again.

* * *

The next morning, I have it all worked out. I may like Nathan, but that's all it's ever going to be. There will be no dates, no long coffee breaks, just hopefully the beginning of a healthy and limited friendship – based on gardens.

Liking how that sounds, I text him.

Yes. Can I start this morning?

Seeing as I'm up early, I decide there's no time like the present. In any case, I can't imagine him saying no. Sure enough, as I'm gathering my sunscreen and gardening gloves, my phone buzzes with a text.

Come over whenever you like.

I collect a few more things together and drive over to Nathan's. It's a gorgeous morning, the roads quiet, the sun still low, bathing the landscape in golden light, and as I drive along unfamiliar lanes, I take in the breath-taking views around me.

When I reach his house, the curtains are still closed. Noticing the wheelbarrow and gardening tools neatly stacked on the terrace, I quietly trundle them down the garden and start on the weeding. There's something raw and grounding about tackling a neglected garden, but there's also a magic to it, hidden treasures waiting to be rediscovered and nurtured back to life again.

In a garden as unloved as this one, the rewards are almost immediate and as I pull away nettles and other weeds, it's amazing how quickly I see a difference. After an hour or two, a quarter of the first bed is weed free, the herb garden pruned. The back door opens and Nathan comes out.

'I didn't hear you arrive. After you texted, I fell asleep again.' He's in jeans and a black T-shirt, his hair still damp from the shower.

'I thought I might as well make a start. I hope I'm not too early?' For a moment I wonder if I'd read him wrong.

He comes to join me. 'No, help yourself – any time. It's so much better already. I brought you some tea.'

I take the mug he's holding out. 'Thanks.'

He lingers for a moment. 'I have some calls to make this morning – but if you're still here when they're done, I'll join you?'

'Sure.' When he doesn't show any sign of moving, I smile at him. 'Go! I'm quite happy! You make your calls!'

Sitting on the grass, I drink the tea. It's a long time since I've ventured into unfamiliar surroundings and it's wonderfully peaceful here – while with some careful tending, the garden is going to be glorious again. There are established roses in need of pruning, a lilac, a clematis that needs cutting back and training over a wall, with no doubt many other secrets that will be revealed as the seasons pass.

I can already imagine planting hidden corners, maybe growing something up the outside of the terrace to tumble over the roof. Studying the house again, I frown. It's bizarre how similar it is to the one Liam and I nearly bought. But a whole lot of what's happened recently feels bizarre.

Inspiration strikes and I go over to a pile of gravel, scooping up a handful and taking it over to the newly weeded soil, spell out two words.

Nathan's house.

* * *

When he comes out much later on, I'm just about finished for the day. I'm also sweaty and covered in soil – not exactly attractive.

'I'm sorry, the calls went on longer than I'd thought they would,' he says apologetically, before looking around, astonished. 'I can't believe how much you've done.'

'Me neither.' I survey the vastly improved flower bed. 'You see, it isn't as difficult as it looks. You have to admit, it's going to look much nicer than concrete.'

He scratches his head. 'I suppose,' he says uncertainly.

'You promised,' I remind him. If he thinks I'm going to all this trouble just for him to rip it out, he needs to think again.

He smiles. 'Don't worry. Concrete is off the agenda.'

'Good.' Relief fills me. 'Anyway, I'm done. But I'm glad you think it looks a bit better.' I pause. 'How were your calls?'

'They were good, actually.' He pauses. 'Can I offer you a cold drink? Or a sandwich?'

I hesitate for a moment. 'I'd love a cold drink.'

He smiles. 'D'you want to come in?'

In his kitchen, I wash my hands before taking the glass he passes me. 'So how are you settling in?'

'Really well. It's kind of odd.' He looks nonplussed for a moment. 'I needed to make some changes in my life. Buying this house feels like part of that.'

'Oh?' I wonder what he's getting at. 'Did you break up with someone?'

He looks surprised. 'Not exactly.' He frowns. 'Or maybe I did.' His face clears. 'I suppose I broke away from who I was back then – and a way of life that wasn't good for me. But it isn't as easy as it sounds.'

'Change isn't.' As I know only too well, especially when it's change that's foisted on you. 'Doesn't mean it can't be a good thing, though.' I pause, wondering what made him reassess everything. 'So what was so bad about your old life?'

'Where to start.' He shakes his head. 'I suppose it was about always working harder and faster, always with my eye on the next big deal... It's kind of addictive, especially when you're surrounded by people who're exactly the same.'

'I get it,' I say quietly. 'My fiancé walked away from a job in the City. He decided he wanted a much simpler life.'

'That's what I'm seeking – well, at least, more of a balance, rather than a life that revolves around work.'

'You're in a good place for that.' I glance outside. 'Gardens are the perfect place to just sit.' I shrug. 'And be.'

'Just sitting is something I'm not very good at,' he says ruefully.

'It takes practice.' Finishing my drink, I put my glass on the table. 'Do you have a moment? Only I thought maybe we could go through some ideas for your garden.'

'Sure.' He puts his glass down. 'Lead the way.'

Going outside on to the terrace, I stand there for a moment. 'I suppose to start with, if I were you, I'd want to think about the view – not that it isn't already lovely,' I add hastily. 'But with all this space, you might want to think about letting areas of the grass grow long. It would be great for insects and you could still mow paths through it.'

He nods slowly. 'I like that.'

'OK.' Getting into my stride, I take the steps down on to the grass. 'In that case, you might want to think about where those paths are going to take you. To your vegetable garden, for example. Or maybe to a shady spot under a tree. There are so many places out here that would be lovely to just sit, or maybe read – if that's your thing.'

'I haven't read a book in months,' he says.

'Maybe you should,' I say mock-sternly. 'If you're serious about slowing your life down a bit. You could buy a book on gardening.'

'I like the idea of having a table and chairs somewhere out here. I mean, I know I have the terrace...' He tails off.

I nod. 'How about over there?' I point towards a gravelled area outside an old outbuilding. 'We could plant things like verbena bonariensis and asters and tall grasses.'

He looks baffled. 'I wouldn't know where to start.'

'They're all tall,' I tell him. 'And quite delicate. Imagine an ethereal kind of screen...' I glance at him, wondering if he gets it.

'Honestly? It sounds great, but I'm happy to leave it to you.' He pauses. 'Can I offer you some lunch?'

'No thanks, I'm going to head off. I may come back tomorrow – or the next day.' Not wanting to feel under any pressure, I'm intentionally non-committal.

'Whatever works for you. I'm just grateful that you're here at all.'

I start gathering my stuff. 'No worries.'

* * *

Back at home, after a shower and a slice of last night's pizza, I feel vaguely more human. But I feel something else, too. Distracted, I think the word is. Less focussed on my own little world for having something new to think about.

But no sooner has the thought formed in my mind than all the familiar emotions slam into me. The grief overwhelms me, along with guilt, that for one whole morning, I've dared not to think about losing Liam.

On cue, my mobile buzzes and Sasha's face appears on the screen.

'How's it going? I just wondered if you'd made your mind up.'

'I went,' I sob pitifully. 'And honestly, now I feel terrible.'

'Oh, Cal... I thought you might.' Her voice is sympathetic. 'Don't beat yourself up. It was always going to be a big step... There was bound to be an emotional backlash. Just take it easy for the rest of today, and see what tomorrow brings.'

'When does this stop, Sasha?' I say tearfully. 'When do I stop feeling guilty about even breathing?'

'Now, listen to me,' she says gently. 'Liam dying was never your fault. It was an accident of the worst kind, and you know he wouldn't want you to feel like this.'

'I feel like I'm betraying him...' I sob even louder. 'Doing this garden...'

Sasha's silent for a moment. 'So that's what this is about.' She pauses again. 'This guy... You like him, don't you?'

'*Yes*,' I cry. 'OK. So I do. But you know what? Even if he liked me back, it can't ever be more than that. *I can't lose anyone again. It hurts too much.*'

'I know you're going through a lot of pain... And I know all you want to do is run away from it.' Her voice is filled with kindness. 'It's what we do as humans – when the going gets tough, our instinct is to run. And for as long as we do, the pain is still there – just buried inside us. It isn't easy, but if you can just stop fighting it and let yourself feel it, it will pass, Cal. I promise you.'

If only it were that simple. If only grief were a straight line instead of a zigzag.

'You are doing so frigging well,' she says soothingly. 'Pour yourself a humungous gin and tonic, cry your heart out and ride this bloody storm. You're going to come out the other side – you do know that, don't you?'

'I hate frigging storms,' I sob.

'No one likes them. But they're part of processing what's happened – and when you've done that, there'll be nothing in your way to stop you flying.'

* * *

Flying terrifies the hell out of me, but I know what she's saying. After the call ends, I pour myself a small gin and tonic. Adding some ice and a chunk of lemon, I take it outside.

The light is changing, the sun sinking lower, the sky changing hue. Sitting on the grass, I watch a succession of tiny ants navigate around my feet before I look up at the wisps of cloud floating across the sky, thinking of what Sasha said. After stumbling through the motions this last year, for the first time since Liam died, I've started something new. Maybe the backlash isn't surprising. As for pain, I've lived with it for over a year, holding it close, suffering it gladly almost, knowing it's the flipside of my love for Liam.

10

NATHAN

After Callie leaves, work takes up the rest of my afternoon, and it isn't until evening falls that I go back outside. It's blissfully peaceful, the air alive with the sound of bees humming, as Callie's words come back to me.

Gardens are the perfect place to just sit. And be.

I breathe in a lungful of cool air, standing there for a moment. The flower bed she was working on has been transformed. Taking a closer look, I notice the sprawling plants she identified as herbs have been neatly trimmed, a couple of shrubs lightly cut back.

Seeing the stones spelling out my name, I can't help smiling. Taking out my phone, I photograph them. Then getting the wheelbarrow, I carry on where she left off, digging out tangled buttercup runners and nettle roots until the soil is clean and loose.

This gardening lark is definitely addictive – but it's killing my back, too. Even so, it's the most satisfying thing I've done in a long time. Taking another photo of the patch I've dug, on impulse I send it to Callie. Then collecting more of the stones from the pile of gravel, I settle down and started arranging them into the shape of a flower, as the germ of an idea comes to mind.

* * *

The next morning, I'm awake early and already making coffee when Callie turns up. Coming up to the house, she knocks on the back door.

'Hi. I saw you were up...' She hesitates. 'Do you have a moment?'

'Sure. Come in. Would you like coffee?'

'Could I have tea?' Getting a rolled-up piece of paper out of her basket, she spreads it across the kitchen table.

I glance at her with amusement. 'This looks serious.'

'It's only an idea.' She seems subdued this morning, as though there is something on her mind. 'Some nights I don't sleep much – last night, it was one of those. So I thought I'd draw up a kind of plan, but first I need some information from you.'

'Ask away.' I pass her a mug of tea.

'Thanks.' Sitting down, she turns to look at me. 'You see, I always think a garden reflects the life of its guardian. I call us guardians, because gardens are only ours for a relatively short time and eventually they're handed on to someone else. But each of us adds something of ourselves. Take yours, for example. Whoever planted the herbs, I think they were interested in healing – as well as more common ones, you have chamomile, fennel, hyssop, fever-few...' She pauses for a moment. 'My garden is a memory garden. The plants remind me of significant times – the empty space does, too. So... what I'm getting around to asking is what's important to you.'

I guess the empty space is representative of her fiancé's death. Sitting across the table from her, I start with the obvious. 'I want it to look nice – and be a relaxing space to enjoy.'

She makes a note on the plan. 'OK, so that's where scent comes in, too. Lavender and rose...'

I nod. 'I like both of those. And honeysuckle.'

'You have quite a bit of that. Go on.'

'I'm not sure.'

She leans forward. 'Can I be personal?'

A feeling of uncertainty comes over me. I have a feeling she's going to say it anyway. 'I guess.'

As she rests her chin in her hands to gaze at me, I have the strangest feeling that I've been here before.

'Where are you in your life?' she says softly. 'New home, a new interest, new beginning... We all have a story.'

I wonder how much to tell her. 'I'm healing.'

She's silent for a moment. 'Emotionally or physically?'

'Both, I guess.' It's as much as I want to say at this stage. 'Are you sure you have the energy for this? You did say you didn't sleep well last night.'

'I'm used to it. Back to your garden... I love the idea of it staying a healing garden.' She looks thoughtful. 'Just being in nature is healing. I know we talked about grasses yesterday. If you like them, we could use different varieties of them. When the wind picks up, they sound beautiful.' She pauses. 'So what kind of plants do you like?'

'I'm not very good on names,' I say slowly. 'I like all kinds of things. Tropical gardens and bright colours. I love bluebell woods, architectural plants, ferns, that kind of thing.' I glance at her. 'A bit of a mish-mash, I guess you'd say.'

She shakes her head. 'It's great, actually. The corner where we talked about putting a table and chairs, it's quite sheltered. It would be perfect for more tropical plants.'

'Also, I don't want it to look too perfect.'

'Don't worry about that!' Her smile reaches her eyes. 'You have all these corners, too. We could make quiet places to sit and just take it all in. There's so much we could do.'

I'm bemused at her enthusiasm for so much work. 'I can't let you do this for nothing. There's weeks of work here.'

She looks at me slightly sadly. 'But it's perfect for me, too...' She lingers for a moment. 'You see, it isn't just you that needs healing,' she says quietly. 'It's me.' Getting up, she finishes her tea, then rolls up her plan. 'I'll see you later.'

I feel a pang as she walks through the door; of all the gardens to channel her sadness into, for reasons I can't fathom, she's chosen mine. I watch from the window for a moment. As she gets to work, it suddenly makes perfect sense. Maybe the digging and weeding and discarding everything that's died is less about my garden and more a metaphor for her life.

At my desk, as I try to work, my mind is distracted. All I can think about is Callie out there in my garden, alone with her thoughts, working through whatever it is that she can't let go of. An hour later, unable to focus, I give up and go to join her.

Standing on the terrace, I watch her on her knees dealing with what looks like a particularly tiresome weed. With her hair twisted up under her wide-brimmed straw hat, her wrist adorned with multi-coloured bracelets, she looks ethereal somehow, her slight limbs belying her strength. Yanking the weed out, she sits back.

I walk over to where she's sitting. 'I have an hour to spare. Mind if I help?'

'I wish you'd asked five minutes ago.' She holds up the knotted tangle of roots she's been battling with. 'But yes, that would be great. Those nettles at the back need clearing. It's easier if you pull the stems up, before you start digging up their roots. Here.' She passes me some gloves and my garden fork. 'I'm going to deadhead some roses – if we're lucky, we might even get more flowers out of them.'

I like the way she uses *we*. As I start to dig, I realise the nettles have really bedded in, slowly encroaching on more and more of the flower bed. But by the time I've finished pulling up their knotted yellow roots, it's clean and weed free. Feeling oddly satisfied as I look at the patch of earth, I'm starting to realise I get this. Right here, I have my own little piece of nature that can either be a wilderness or a sanctuary.

Lobbing the last of the roots into the wheelbarrow, I go to find Callie. 'Fancy some lunch?'

'Is it that time already?' She snips a last rose. 'I don't usually bother much with lunch.'

She's so slight, I can believe it. 'In that case, you are in for a treat,' I say firmly. 'I'll be right back.'

Going inside, I examine the contents of my fridge, finding a cooked salmon fillet and some salad. After making us both a sandwich, I fill a couple of glasses with iced water and take them outside.

I find Callie sitting on the edge of the terrace. She drinks most of her water down in one.

'I'll get you another. Here.' I pass her a plate. 'I hope you like salmon?'

'I do. Thanks.'

When I come back out with her replenished glass, she's already devoured half the sandwich.

'I was thinking of doing some before and after photos.' I sit down next to her. 'I've done some already, but I thought it would be interesting to have them to look back on.'

'I did that with ours,' she says quietly. 'It didn't look anything like it does now – and it's amazing how much it's changed. There's so much of me in it – I think I'd find it really hard to leave there.' She pauses. 'But that's mostly because I think it's saved me.'

For the first time, I can understand how that could be a thing.

'Already I'm finding it therapeutic,' I say uncertainly. 'Honestly, if you'd known me before, you'd be amazed to hear me say that! My sister thinks I'm mad taking on something the size of this one – only because I don't know what I'm doing,' I add hastily, before changing the subject. 'What you were saying about this garden's history... I was looking in the shed – I found an old cartwheel and a broken statue... I was wondering if we could use them somewhere.'

Her eyes light up. 'Definitely.'

'Cool.' As I watch her finish her sandwich, I already know there's something about this girl – not just her internalised battle with her grief or the fragility that seems incongruous with her physical strength. It's the sense that she's forgotten how joyfulness feels.

'So are you converted yet? Into a gardener, I mean?' She looks at me hopefully.

'I'm definitely getting it.' I shake my head. 'Are you sure doing this isn't too much for you?'

'I only work three days a week. And I think it's good for me to be doing something different.'

It's the first time she's mentioned her job.

'Where do you work?'

'In a bookshop in Truro. I've worked there for years. I know them really well – and I guess it's easy. They've been really understanding.'

'Do you sell gardening books?'

'A few.' Her eyes turn to meet mine. 'I have one or two I can lend you, if you like. I'll bring them over with me, next time.'

'That would be great.' But I'm curious. 'So have you always lived around here?'

She nods. 'All my life.' Her face colours slightly. 'My sisters moved away when they went to uni. They have amazing jobs – I'm really proud of them. But I've always felt I have everything I want here.'

'Wow,' I say quietly.

'I know. It probably sounds weird that I've never moved away.'

I shake my head. 'I didn't mean that. I meant that some people go through their entire lives without ever being able to say that.' I'm as guilty as anyone else of wanting *more*.

'We're all different, aren't we?' Finishing her sandwich, she gets up. 'Are you going to show me the cartwheel?'

'What, now?'

'When you've finished eating! I thought we could walk around your garden again. I'll tell you about some more ideas I've had.'

* * *

When she sees the old cartwheel, she loves it. 'We could lean it against your house and plant tiny flowers around it – like violets and daisies. As for the statue... We could put it amongst the shrubs – or near the honeysuckle. If we buried the base, we could probably make it upright enough.' Stepping forward, she picks up a length of rusty metal. 'I think this is an old candlestick. You'll probably think I'm mad, but I love it.'

It isn't for me to question the eye of an artist. And I like the idea of incorporating some of the house's history. 'Whatever you say. I totally trust your judgement.'

'Good.' She looks pleased. 'There are other bits – but we can come back to them later. Now, there's this bit of garden I've been thinking about...'

Leading me around to the front of the house, she shows me a corner of lawn under the shade of a birch tree.

'There's brick under here.' Pulling up some of the grass, she exposes the worn terracotta underneath. 'If we dug up the grass, you could have a little table and some chairs here. You'd have a natural umbrella of shade from the branches – and different views...' She glances towards the house. 'And in between the bricks of whatever's under there, there are things we can plant from seed, like night scented stock. It isn't much to look at during the day, but at night the scent is intoxicating.' She turns towards the house again. 'Now... Your terrace.'

'What about it?' As far as I'm concerned, the terrace is perfect exactly as it is.

She glances sideways at me. 'You could always grow something up the front of it – climbing roses, clematis or something. It would soften it – and it would look really pretty when you're sitting outside.'

Lacking her imagination, I'm struggling to imagine how it would work. 'I can't picture it.'

A smile plays on her lips. 'I'll try to find an image of what I mean.'

Frowning, I look at her. 'Callie? If you don't mind me asking, why are you doing this?'

For a moment, her eyes hold mine, then she seems to crumble. 'I'm trying to move forward.' Her voice wobbles slightly, before she seems to take a hold of herself. 'It may sound mad, but coming here is a really big deal for me. You see... when I think of Liam, I feel this terrible pain.' She takes a deep breath. 'Sasha – one of my sisters – says we all go through life trying to avoid pain. And she's probably right – she's a therapist. But the problem is... unless you confront it, all you do is bury it. It means it hasn't gone away. It's still there.'

I frown. 'So what does Sasha suggest you do?'

Callie shrugs. 'Feel the pain. Realise I can survive it.' She shakes her head. 'Yesterday, when I left here, I felt terrible. I'd spent an entire morning doing something I enjoyed. I'm not supposed to do that.'

'Why not?' I say gently. 'The way I see it, life's a gift. Aren't we supposed to make the most of it?' Seeing a tear roll down her cheek,

I fish in my pocket for a tissue, passing it to her. 'Is that why you're here? You're hiding from it?'

'I don't know.' She blows her nose loudly. 'But I don't think so. I'm getting better at sitting with the pain. At some point, I have to imagine moving forward. But at the moment, I can only see as far as the end of each day.'

I know better than anyone how it feels when just as it seems you have your life in hand, the universe throws you a curveball. 'But that's OK,' I tell her quietly. 'We should probably all live much more in the moment. Beyond today, nothing's certain, is it?'

11

CALLIE

As always, it comes down to the simplest things. Someone's kindness and understanding; a tasty salmon sandwich eaten somewhere peaceful in easy company. But the trouble is it makes everything a hundred times worse.

Once I'm home my guilt comes flooding back. But as I sit in my garden, I don't fight it. Instead, I tell myself it's OK to feel like this as I try to breathe through the torrent of emotions I'm feeling, until very slowly they start to subside.

It's still painful. I'm aware, also, that it's different, though. But after a year of living such a stripped-back life, with even the smallest shift in my horizons I can feel something changing in me.

Thinking of my parents, I have a sudden desire to see them and later that afternoon, I drive over to their place. Parking in front of the house, I sit there for a moment. Even now, coming here reminds me of the day I was meant to marry Liam; of the happiness that was decimated by heartbreak.

But there are other memories, I tell myself fiercely as I go inside. Finding the house empty, I head outside again to where I know my father will be, pottering in his shed.

'Ah, Callie. I didn't know you were coming.' He envelops me in a hug. 'Your mother's out, you know. Something to do with the Neighbourhood Watch scheme she's got involved in.'

I'm guessing he means in the nearest village, as my parents don't really have any direct neighbours. But my mother's never happier than when she has a project in hand and this sounds right up her alley. 'That's OK. I just felt like coming over.'

My dad studies me for a moment. 'How are you doing?'

'I'm OK.' I nod. 'I mean, everything's raw still, but it's odd. I'm starting to feel as though something's changing.'

'That's a good thing,' he says gently.

'Is it?' As all my misgivings surface, I blurt it out. 'I can't work it out. It just feels wrong to start living again when Liam...' Hearing my voice waver, I break off.

'Liam wouldn't want you to be unhappy,' Dad says quietly. 'He'd want you to have a wonderful life. He'd want you to be happy, too. If I popped off tomorrow, your mother would have no qualms about getting on with her life – and I'd want her to. Life is a gift – one you can turn into something amazing, or alternatively waste. And before you say anything, I'm not suggesting you're wasting yours. You're going through a necessary process of adjustment, that's all.'

It's how it feels. It's also exactly what Nathan said earlier, about life being a gift. 'Some days I still can't think straight,' I say quietly. 'But more recently, I've been thinking I need to start doing something. So I'm helping someone with their garden.'

'Are you?' Dad sounds surprised. 'That's wonderful.'

'Is it? I can't tell. My instincts are out. All I know is, I can't carry on spending so much time at home.'

'No,' he says gently. 'But you shouldn't push yourself, either. When you've been through something of the magnitude you have, it takes time to let the dust settle. You'll know when the time is right.' He pauses. 'I should have said this before – I'm proud of you, sweetheart.'

I look at him in surprise. 'You are?'

'Yes.' His voice wavers slightly. 'You may not know it yet, but you're strong.' He puts down his tools. 'I'm parched. How about you let your old dad make you a cuppa?'

By the time we've had a cup of tea together, there's still no sign of my mother. But as I drive away, I'm thinking about what my dad said, about being strong. Most of the time, I haven't felt strong. I've felt helpless, my life out of control. But a year on, I suppose I am starting to put the pieces of my life back together – albeit a very unexpected life. If that means I'm strong, I'll take that.

Instead of going straight home, I drive to the beach. As I walk along the sand, I gather a handful of flat stones, skimming a couple of them across the sea, carefully arranging the rest into an uneven cairn.

In spite of the sun, there's a coolness to the breeze. Reaching the rocky headland at the far end of the cove, I stop. Ahead of me in the sand, someone's created a tree. It isn't exactly finessed. Made mostly of stones, the roots are a tangle of artfully arranged strands of seaweed.

A strange feeling comes over me as I gaze at it. The day we met, Liam was making a tree. There are words, too, traced with one finger into the sand. Staring at them more closely, I make out a message.

Will you go out with me?

Almost certainly, Nathan's done this. Startled, I gaze up and down the beach, wondering if he's here. But there's no one in sight. Instead, the tide is coming closer, but that's the beauty of transient messaging. You can say anything you want to in the moment, knowing its presence is finite.

He probably never imagined I'd actually read it – that's if it is for me. What would I say? It isn't a no, but I'm not sure it's a yes, either. Bending down, I trace letters that will soon be lost underwater.

Maybe.

The following day, I don't go to Nathan's house. Instead, I head down to the beach again. There's a late summer vibe, the warmth of the air tempered by a breeze that's strengthened, the sea restless with anticipation the way it is before a storm hits.

The tide is already coming in and, finding a rock, I climb up out of its reach, staying to watch its slow encroachment until the sand is submerged. On my way home, my phone pings with a message from Nathan. I wait until I'm back before I read it.

Hi, just hoping you've had a good day. Would you like to go for a drink this evening?

Yes. The answer is there immediately, before my guilt lashes out. How can I even consider this? Getting out of my car, I take a deep breath and rationalise with myself. Unless I'm going to be alone for ever, at some point in my life, there will be someone else to go for a drink with, maybe have dinner with. Why not Nathan? I text him back.

I'd really like that.

Five minutes pass before he gets back to me.

Cool. I'll pick you up at 8.

Going upstairs, I shower, then find a dress I really like. Mid-calf, it's a faded blue with short sleeves. Putting it on, I gaze at my reflection. Can I really do this? It's only a drink but it feels like I'm preparing for something of stupendous proportions and I find myself wavering.

I hear his car pull up in the lane, before there's a knock at the door. I've worked out what I want to say, but when I open it he hands me a bouquet of flowers. I gaze at them, distracted.

'These are gorgeous.' Wrapped in brown paper, they're tied with the coloured string that's the trademark of one of the farm shops. 'From Lily's?'

He nods. 'They're a thank you – for what you've done to my garden.'

'You didn't need to.' I bury my nose in them. Lily only sells flowers that are scented and locally grown. 'They're beautiful. Thank you.' I realise we're still standing on the doorstep. 'Want to come in?'

'Thanks.'

In the kitchen, I search for a jug for the flowers, trying to ignore how gorgeous he looks in faded jeans and a linen shirt that shows off his tan. When I'd been just about to tell him I'd had a change of heart, I'm doubting myself again.

He watches me arrange the flowers. 'They look great.'

When last time he came here I felt uncomfortable, it's a measure of how much has changed, as suddenly I like that he's here. 'It's easy with flowers like this. You can't go wrong.' Picking up the jug, I place it on the table, before turning to face him.

But he pre-empts me. 'I'm guessing this feels kind of strange for you. I was half expecting you might change your mind. I would have understood.'

A feeling of relief comes over me. 'To be honest, up until I opened the door, I had it all planned out what I was going to say to you. Then you gave me those...' I glance towards the flowers. 'For a few seconds, I forgot. And now...' I sigh. 'The truth is, it does feel strange. Part of me wants to go out with you, but there's another part of me that feels it's wrong – which, I know, doesn't make any sense...'

'But it's understandable,' he says. 'How about this for a plan? There's a pop-up bar in one of the coves tonight – about half an hour's drive from here. If going out for a drink is too much to get your head around, think of it like a business meeting – about my garden, over a drink or maybe two. I've been thinking about what you said – and I have some ideas to run past you.'

I'm silent for a moment. 'OK.' I pause. 'This isn't about you, by the way.'

He nods. 'I know. It's about coming to terms with what's happened to you.'

That he understands makes all the difference.

'Give me two minutes?'

Going upstairs, I put on some lipstick and find my favourite sandals and a cardigan. Then before I change my mind again, I go back downstairs.

'OK. I'm ready.' I hesitate. 'Thanks – for understanding.'

He smiles. 'You're welcome.' He nods towards the door. 'Shall we?'

* * *

The cove is one I haven't been to for some time, nestled between gently sloping cliffs. When we get out of the car, the sound of music drifts towards us, as does the smell of fish and chips.

A rush of nostalgia hits me as I remember another night,

another cove with a pop-up bar; but before it grows more vivid, I push it away.

'Are you OK?' Nathan looks concerned.

I nod. 'I think so.' Hesitating, I feel I need to try to explain. 'I've been to so few places over the last year. Coming here's bringing back memories.' I shake my head. 'I'm sorry. I really didn't intend to be so all over the place. Maybe I should have stayed at home.'

He seems unfazed. 'We're here now. Come on, I'll buy you a drink – and then if that's what you want, I'll take you back.'

We follow the narrow path that leads to the beach. The air is still warm, the sand soft underfoot as the path opens out. There aren't many people here but with the music and the setting sun, I can feel the ambiance soaking into me.

Reaching the bar, Nathan looks at me. 'What would you like?'

'I'd love a beer.'

He turns to the guy behind that bar. 'Hi. Make that two.' He looks around the beach, his eyes settling on the fish and chip bar, before turning to me again. 'Have you eaten?'

'No.' My eating habits have become somewhat irregular – pizza for breakfast, cornflakes for tea, that kind of thing.

'Do you like fish and chips?'

The smell of the food is irresistible. 'I do.'

Ignoring my protestations, he orders two portions before we take our drinks over to one of the tables. As we bask in the last of the day's sunlight, that we're sitting on a beach instead of in a pub puts me at ease.

'This is nice,' I tell him. 'Thank you.'

'You're welcome. I don't suppose there will be many more evenings like this. Summer's nearly up, isn't it?'

'I think there may be a storm on the way. I was watching the sea earlier. It gets kind of restless before the weather changes.' I pause, looking at him. 'You said you'd had some thoughts about your garden?'

'Yeah.' He smiles at me. 'You won't believe this, but I've been doing a little research. It was what you said about the healing properties of herbs... I like the idea of growing more of them, maybe in raised beds with gravel paths in between. And like you said, in corners. The other idea was to encourage wildlife. I'd like to give something back.'

As he speaks, I feel my enthusiasm growing for this project.

'I love it.' I pause, because he ought to know. 'I've been making a list of plants for your tropical garden. But you're going to need wood and gravel for your vegetable garden – maybe we should talk about costs.'

'It's OK – to a point, that is.' Fishing in his pocket, he gets out a folded piece of paper. 'I did this earlier.'

As he unfolds it, I see it's a carefully sketched plan. 'This looks quite expert,' I tell him. 'You've clearly done this kind of thing before.'

He nods. 'Except usually it isn't gardens.'

Just then, our fish and chips are delivered. As I unwrap them, I realise how hungry I am. 'So what is it you do exactly?'

'Property development – at least, it's what I used to do before my health problems got in the way. I'm in the process of negotiating the purchase of some land on the edge of Padstow.'

I find myself curious to know more about him. It isn't the first time he's alluded to his health. And he clearly isn't short of money. 'What are you going to do with it?'

'I'm not sure really. At first, I was thinking of holiday accommodation, but I'm considering building half a dozen high-spec homes.' Looking at me, he frowns slightly. 'Have I said something wrong?'

I feel myself tense, because I know the type of house he's talking about. They've popped up everywhere – ultra modern and glass-fronted; high-tech with minimalist interiors. Although he's talking about them as if they are different to holiday accommodation, these places are sold with holiday occupancy written into the deeds. And it's a dilemma. Their owners bring much-needed money in, but at the same time, local people are priced out of the market.

'Does Cornwall really need more top-end second homes that local people can't afford?' Realising how that sounds, I break off. 'I don't mean to sound rude, but more and more local people can't afford to buy a house around here. It's going to end up being a place only rich people can afford.'

He frowns slightly. 'There's a market for them – and if I don't build them, there'll be plenty of others who will.'

'I know you're right,' I say carefully. 'It's just that when there's already a shortage of housing for local people, I don't agree with it.'

'Fair enough.' He picks up another chip. 'I guess we'd better talk about something else.'

But I'm not giving up just yet. When he's been open-minded enough to reconsider his original plan fort his garden, maybe he might think again about his property development. 'Considering you've bought a fairly elderly house, and have all these wonderful ideas for your garden, have you thought you could apply the same principles to your property development?'

'If you bought a plot of land, what would you do with it?'

'Protect it,' I say promptly. 'Turn it into a conservation area.'

'I'm not sure there's a lot of money in that,' he says wryly.

'I suppose my angle isn't about money. It's like you said about your garden, it's about giving something back. I'd want it to be of benefit to the community in some way.'

'Hmm... I'm not sure my investors would go for that.'

I shrug. 'Unless you ask them, you'll never know, will you?'

'Actually...' He's frowning again. 'You might be on to something. The houses will be eco-friendly, made of local materials, using local craftsmen, set among grounds that could be a wildlife habitat. The two could exist alongside each other.' He looks at me intently. 'I could pay you to design the gardens.'

I'm still not sure what I think of it. 'At the moment, I have enough going on in my life.'

'Consider it,' he says quietly. 'That's all I ask. Would you like another beer?'

'OK.' I watch him get up and wander up to the bar, a strange feeling coming over me. All evening, it's as though I've stepped out of my life into someone else's; someone who seems unfamiliar. I'm not at all sure how that makes me feel.

Pulling on my cardigan, I gaze towards the water. On the horizon, dark clouds are gathering, the sea already changing colour, its movement picking up momentum, as I remember a dozen other storms Liam and I watched together.

'Looks like you were right about a storm coming.' Nathan puts a beer on the table in front of me.

'Thanks.' I'm silent, still remembering, but it's odd. Memories usually trigger a tsunami of nostalgia, but instead of wanting to leave, here with Nathan, I feel strangely at home.

'You'll probably think I'm crazy,' he says. 'I don't know this cove. But I keep getting the feeling I've been here before.'

'You mean déjà vu?' I used to have this theory that we lived hundreds of lifetimes, that were all part of our souls' evolution. 'Once, I would have said you'd probably come here in another lifetime... But now, I don't believe anything like that.' I take a deep breath. 'We're born, we live, we die... End of.' I shrug.

'Because of your fiancé?' he says quietly.

'Yes.' My voice wobbles slightly. 'Isn't love supposed to bridge the divide between almost anything? And since he died, I haven't had even the smallest of signs.'

'I don't know,' he says simply. 'Maybe there have been signs you've missed. I wouldn't give up just yet.'

When he reaches across the table and takes one of my hands, instead of pulling away, I let him. And it's nice, feeling the warmth of another human being, even if he does have some questionable principles. It's further proof that something's changed, because it doesn't feel wrong. But when I don't trust the feeling to last; it seems like the perfect time to end the evening.

'I've had a really lovely time tonight,' I say. 'But if it's all the same to you, could you take me home?'

12

NATHAN

As we walk back to the car, now and then our arms brush against each other while I fight the urge to take her hand again. I know how suddenly her grief can erupt, and she's told me how easily she slips into berating herself.

We don't say much as we walk. I guess already we've done more talking than Callie's become used to. When I arrived to pick her up, I fully expected her to back out at the last minute, most likely out of misplaced guilt. But by agreeing to come out, she seems to have surprised herself.

One thing's for sure. She isn't shy of voicing her opinions. I don't know her well enough yet to judge whether she's a speak-first, think-later kind of person, but I kind of suspect she isn't, that it's more a case of her wearing her heart on her sleeve.

'Look.' Beside me, she points towards an owl that's taken flight, its pale shape standing out against the rapidly darkening sky.

Hearing the wind pick up around us, I feel the first drops of rain start to fall, and it seems the most natural thing in the world to take her hand. 'We need to hurry!'

As we reach the car, the heavens open. Unlocking it, I climb in.

But seconds later, Callie's still outside. I wind down the window to see her face upturned towards the sky, her arms outstretched, as if she's celebrating the rain.

'Callie! You're getting soaked!'

For a moment, it's as if she hasn't heard me. But then she looks at me. 'I know... But you really should know how wonderful this feels!'

As she gets into the car, I worry her emotions will catch her out. But her eyes are luminous, and she smells of the rain, the sea, of the essence of what life is. Unable to stop myself, I do the only thing I can. I kiss her.

Almost immediately, I regret it, imagining it to be too much for her; too soon. As our lips touch, I feel her startle, but to my amazement, leaning towards me, she kisses me back.

I pull away gently. 'I'm sorry. I shouldn't have done that.'

'Sorry because you wish you hadn't?' Her voice is quiet.

'I don't wish I hadn't. I'm thinking that maybe it's too much – too soon.'

'Ah.' She's silent for a moment. 'I can understand why you've said that, to be honest. But just so you know, I'm not thinking that at all.'

Watching her sit there quietly, I'm starting to get worried. 'So what is it?'

Her eyes are troubled. 'I'm waiting for the backlash that always comes when I start to feel good about something. Tonight, this is literally the first time it hasn't happened.'

'Is that a good thing?' I ask cautiously.

'Maybe.' She shrugs. 'I think it's too soon to tell. Normally a part of my mind punishes me with guilt. My fiancé is dead and I've just kissed another man...'

'Come on.' Fearing the worst of her emotions is coming, I switch the engine on. 'Let's get you home.'

* * *

By the time we're back at Callie's, the rain is coming in sheets. As I get out of the car, the first rumble of thunder reaches my ears.

I wait with her on the doorstep as she finds her key and opens the door. Going inside, she turns to me for a moment.

'Thank you.' Her eyes are bright with gratitude. 'I had such a nice time.'

'Me too,' I say quietly. 'Go and put some warm clothes on. I'll see you soon.'

She nods briefly. 'Night,' she whispers.

It takes all my self-control to get back in my car. Raising a hand, I drive away. I have to admit that as dates go, it's one of the strangest I'd ever been on. But Callie isn't like other girls I've known. There's no guile, no game-playing, just an openness I find refreshing. She makes me think, too.

Back at home, I pull up close to the house. Then getting out, I stand under the downpour for a moment, inhaling the smell of damp earth, of grass, the faintest trace of honeysuckle. The rain is torrential, invigorating, too; but somehow, also, it's life-affirming.

* * *

After a night that's broken by lightning and thunder, I awake the following morning to a pale sun and a watery blue sky. It's as though the garden has been revitalised overnight. Green is already returning to the parched grass, while the trees have lost their dusty look.

By the time I'm up, Callie's car is pulling up. Going outside, I call out to her. 'Hi. Would you like tea?'

'Thanks.' The withdrawn, slightly wary look is back.

My heart sinks. Guessing she's had the backlash she'd been

talking about, I leave her to pull on her boots and gather her basket of gardening props. If she wants to talk, I have a feeling she'll make it known. I'm right.

Taking her a mug of tea, she looks almost slightly accusingly at me. 'I wish you hadn't done that – last night.'

Not sure where she's going with this, I play for time. 'Done what exactly?'

'Kissed me.' She sighs. 'Actually, that's not even true, which is exactly the problem I have. I should wish you hadn't – but I don't. As a result, I feel terrible.'

Hearing the angst in her voice, I try to reassure her. 'Don't you think at some point, you need to stop beating yourself up?' I say gently.

She freezes. 'If you'd lost someone you loved...' She pauses. 'I really don't think you'd ever dream of saying that.' Tilting her head, she looks into my eyes. 'Nothing about this is logical or predictable. There's no guide to dealing with grief. One day, it's like you're lost in a maze, the next adrift on a stormy sea. Now and then, there's a lull, but you can't even trust that, because you know it's a matter of time before the pain comes back.'

I have an idea of how grief feels – but more for the way of life I lost when I was ill, rather than the loss of a person. But I don't have any pearls of wisdom to offer, and I'm not sure Callie would want them from me.

Coming closer, she places her hand over my heart – a small gesture, the power of which she has no idea of. 'This is where it hurts,' she whispers.

But as I rest one of my hands over hers, she's already pulling it away. 'I'm going to start on the garden.'

'I'd help you, but I have to work this morning.' I have an investor to talk to, plans for houses to draw up.

Disappointment crosses her face. 'Of course. Your housing project.'

* * *

My tiny office space has no window, so I leave the door open. Now and then I catch a fleeting glance of Callie outside as I bring up the initial housing plans I've put together and study them again.

There's no doubt in my mind that Callie has a point about house prices around here. I also know for a fact that low-cost properties are hard to find because most of them have been snapped up as holiday homes.

I sigh. This is the reality of how the housing market works, with everyone maximising profit margins. But beyond creating individual wealth, it isn't contributing anything to communities. Quite the reverse – it's adding to far more serious social issues.

Resting my head in my hands, I sigh again. I'm not sure what else will work, but there's something about what Callie said that has got under my skin. I can't help thinking that maybe it's time to have a rethink.

13

CALLIE

After the rain, the earth is cool and soft as I finish tidying the first of the flower beds and start on the next. As I rip out encroaching grass and dig up dandelion roots, I think of Liam's mother.

Instantly it triggers a rush of guilt. Since Liam's death, on the few occasions I've seen her, I've barely been able to cope with my own grief. I haven't had it in me to handle hers.

But it's been a year – more than a year. I glance at the house. There's no sign of Nathan. I imagine him busy inside, working on his housing development project. I can't help but wonder if my words last night had any impact on him.

When a couple of hours later I still haven't seen him, I'm taken aback slightly. He kissed me, didn't he? And I kissed him back, didn't I? At the time, lost in the moment, it didn't feel like a mistake. But that doesn't mean he isn't regretting it, writing it off as a fleeting transgression. Maybe it would be as well, because even I'm not sure what to make of it.

I'm no clearer when he eventually comes outside.

'Hi.' In a faded sweatshirt and jeans, he looks distracted.

'One down, three to go.' Talking about the flower beds, I nod towards the one in question.

He glances at it quickly. 'That's great.'

Given the amount of work it's taken, it isn't the response I was hoping for. Sitting back on my heels, I look at him. 'Are you OK?'

'I'm not sure.' He's frowning slightly. 'You know the land I was telling you about? The sale's gone through.'

My response is guarded. 'That's good, isn't it?'

'It would have been – but one of my investors has pulled out.'

'Oh. So what happens now?'

'I either find someone else, or it's back to the drawing board and I'll have to think of something else to do with it.'

Which in my opinion would be no bad thing – but obviously he has to make some money out of it. 'You'll think of something.'

He looks distracted. 'I'll have to. Either that, or I'll sell it.'

I pass him the fork, nodding towards part of the flower bed. 'This bit over here needs digging next.' But I'm curious to know more about the land. 'Where is the plot, exactly?'

Getting out his phone, he brings up a local map. 'Here.' He passes it to me.

I study it. 'It's an amazing location, isn't it?' Close to the river and the cycle path, it's a little north of Wadebridge.

'It really is. Perfect for exclusive eco-homes.'

'Have you thought about a campsite? I mean a quiet, exclusive sort of place, with fixed tents.' As he starts to dig, my mind is whirring. 'That way, you could keep a lot of it wild – or plant as much as you can afford to – prairie-style with all these different grasses, with all these paths running through it...' Ideas were flooding into my head.

'Like you suggested for here?' He looks interested.

'Exactly. And you could have a café or restaurant – an eco- and plant-based one. More and more people are up for cutting back on meat. I really think you'd find there'd be a market for one. You could collect water and put up solar panels. And your philosophy could be how little damage you cause to the environment. I think people would really like that.'

As I'm speaking, I watch a smile flicker across his lips. 'You've got it all worked out, haven't you?'

'Honestly? It just came to me as I was talking.' I look at him. 'But I can imagine it – and it could work, couldn't it?'

He looks uncertain. 'I'm not sure I'm going to make much money out of a campsite.'

'But if the restaurant was a success, that would bring people in. You could employ local people, and you could host weddings. There are loads of people who like the idea of celebrating sustainably. It would be more profitable, too.'

But as he digs into a compacted piece of earth, Nathan doesn't look convinced.

* * *

That afternoon, I drive to Wadebridge to see Liam's mother. It would have been his birthday tomorrow and I know she'll be thinking of him as much as I am. On impulse, I take the long way around to look at the land Nathan's bought, hoping that seeing it for myself might trigger more ideas. Turning off the main road, I follow a narrow twisting lane for a mile or so, passing a farm and a handful of houses, until I reach a gate on my right into a field.

Pulling into the gateway, I get out. Standing there for a moment, I can see why Nathan decided to buy it. It's another of those magical places where the only sounds are the breeze, the insects and birds. Climbing over the gate, I start walking.

The site is huge, gloriously wild and peaceful. So much so, it surprises me that Nathan thinks he can get planning permission for housing here – though as I look around, noticing the occasional glimpse of roof obscured by trees, it's obvious other people have. And he clearly knows what he's doing.

Maybe eco-homes could sit at one with nature, but the process of building them would devastate the wonderful flowers and wild life here. Whereas camping... Closing my eyes for a moment, I imagine lying out here under a dark sky, gazing at myriad stars.

As I listen to the birds, the breeze caresses my skin and a strange feeling comes over me. With the sky above me, the grasses and wild flowers surrounding me, far from everything I know, I feel connected in a way that's been missing since before Liam died.

'*Liam?*' I whisper. But as I say his name, I know whatever I'm feeling isn't about him. It's about me. Holding out my arms, I start slowly spinning around, lost in the moment, in this beautiful, magical place, feeling a long lost part of me deep inside slowly stir back to life again.

* * *

It's an hour later by the time I drive to Wadebridge. I try to order in my mind what I want to say to Nathan when I see him next, my mind filling with images of what he could do with the land. If he wants my help, maybe I'll work for him. After a year of feeling removed, life is calling to me again.

Parking in the town, I walk the short distance to the narrow street where Liam's mother lives. It's cobbled; the deceptively narrow houses bely the generous proportions that lie inside. Knocking on the door, I'm slightly trepidatious as I stand there. But when she opens it and sees me, her face lights up.

'Callie, dear!'

'Hi, Marion.'

'This is the loveliest surprise.' After kissing me on the cheek, she stands back to let me in. 'You are coming in, aren't you?'

'If you're not busy?' As I go inside, I give her the flowers I bought on the way here, from Lily's farm shop.

'Not this afternoon. These are lovely, thank you.'

I follow her along the passageway to the large kitchen at the back of the house. It has a view on to her garden and large windows that let the light flood in, but there's an undeniable sense of sadness. I try to distract myself. 'Your garden looks pretty.' The borders are neatly kept and full of colour; the rose bush Liam and I gave her for her birthday one year is covered in soft pink blooms.

'Have you seen your rose? It's been flowering for months.'

'It's lovely.' Remembering the day Liam and I bought it together, I swallow the lump in my throat.

'Would you like tea?'

'I'd love tea.'

The house is filled with memories, memories that assail me: the stories Liam told me about his childhood here; the lunches we've had with Marion; how happy she was when we told her we were getting married.

Coming over to the table, she places two mugs on it. 'Still black no sugar?'

I nod. 'Thank you.' I hesitate before I ask, 'How are you?'

'There are good days and bad days.' Her eyes glisten. 'I'm sure it's the same for you. But on the whole, not so bad.'

'I miss him.' My voice trembles. 'I think no matter how much time passes, I will always miss him.'

'I know,' she says gently. 'We both will. But that's what happens when you love someone and they're not here any more.' She pauses. 'So how have you been?'

I'm silent for a moment. 'For the last year, I haven't done anything much except relive the time we spent together a thousand times over. It's been like trying to stay afloat in an ocean of grief. But... some days, at least, it's like the waves are getting smaller. And I've started something new. I'm helping someone with their garden.'

'That's a really good thing,' Marion says quietly.

Her face blurs as I gaze at her. 'I've felt so guilty – about being here when Liam isn't, or about doing anything new.' Tears roll down my cheeks.

'Grief does that to us.' She smiles sadly. 'It makes us hold tightly on to what we've lost – except we can't, because it isn't there any more. But going forward, you have a life to live, Callie. Liam wouldn't have wanted you to forget that.'

'Easier said than done.' I wipe away my tears. 'But I do know that.'

'Today was never going to be easy, was it?' This time, it's her voice that wavers.

'Today?' I stare at her.

She looks surprised. 'It's Liam's birthday.'

Shocked, I shake my head. 'Don't you mean tomorrow?'

'I don't think so, dear.' Marion looks puzzled. 'Today's the 17th. I'm sure it is.'

Checking my phone, I realise she's right; that with everything else that's been going on, I've lost track of time.

* * *

As I drive to the churchyard, a cocktail of emotions floods through my veins. Remorse is there, shame, self-blame, as I tear into myself for being too preoccupied, too selfish to remember what day it is.

On the way, I pay my second visit of the day to Lily's farm shop and buy a dozen red roses – not the stiff, imported variety, but irregular, softly scented blooms, most likely newly picked from Lily's own garden.

Reaching the church, I switch the engine off, sitting there for a moment. Bathed in late afternoon sunlight, St Enodoc's is surrounded by countryside, with views across fields towards Rock and the sea. Getting out, I walk over to the churchyard.

Today feels like a day of many days; one that's taken me from sadness to hope, before bringing me full circle as I find Liam's grave. Sitting on the grass, I place the roses one by one on his grave. 'Happy birthday,' I say quietly. 'I miss you.' Suddenly my emotions erupt. 'I wish you could hear me,' I say more loudly. Then, 'I really wish you'd bloody say something to me. All this time, Liam. And what have you given me? *Absolutely nothing.*'

Anger swirls inside me, anger that's inappropriate given that I'm sitting beside his grave. Or is it? I'm feeling it. I have every right to.

'How long's it been?' The voice comes from behind me.

Turning around, I see a woman about my age, with green eyes and long strawberry-blond hair. 'Just over a year.'

She looks at me curiously. 'Your husband?'

'Almost,' I say quietly, getting up.

'Mine died three years ago. The tosser got drunk and drove his car into a tree. Left me two toddlers and all his debts. Didn't stop me loving him, though.'

'Funny thing about love,' I say to her. 'Not at all logical, is it?'

'No. I used to come down here and beat his grave with my fist, calling him everything under the sun. One day, this old priest came over. I thought he was going to tear me off a strip, but he sat next to me while I effed and blinded. When I was done, he patted my hand. He said it was all part of it and that I should get it out of my system. Then he said at some point I'd remember the good days.'

I'm taken aback. 'Did you?'

She shakes her head. 'Shortly after he said that, the house was repossessed. I moved in with my parents. They've been a godsend, though it wears a bit thin, all of us cooped up together. Remembering the good times...' She shrugged. 'Fact was, there weren't any, if I'm honest.'

'Liam and I were really happy,' I tell her. 'We'd been together for five years. We were about to move into our dream home. Then on the way to our wedding, he was killed in a road accident.'

'Fuck.' She looks shocked. 'Sorry. But that's so sad.'

'Yes. I'd just arrived at the church when I found out.'

'Fuck.' She stares at me. 'And after, you feel so bloody guilty, don't you? Just for being alive. God. Mind you, I don't think we would have lasted. I thought having children might force mine to change his ways, but he drank too much – and he was weak.'

But Liam was none of those things. 'Liam was lovely. Kind, sensitive, always had time for people... He was a really good guy.'

'No one's that perfect,' she says drily. 'He must have had a skeleton or two hidden away.' She frowns. 'I'm sorry. Ignore me – I can't believe I said that. I don't even know you – or him. I'm just a cynical woman who finds it hard to trust people.'

I find myself liking her honesty. 'I'm Callie.'

'Tanith.' She holds out a beautifully manicured hand. 'We should start a club. The Graveyard Groupies, or Bereaved Bitches – what do you think? Shall I take your mobile number?'

14

NATHAN

I find it impossible to settle after lunch. That I'm having to rethink the development project is playing on my mind – but so is Callie. Maybe today is a significant date or something – an anniversary, or a birthday. But for some reason, this morning she seemed preoccupied.

In the end, I close my laptop. It seems pointless sitting at my desk when I don't know what I'm doing. Getting up, I go outside. The sky is a warm blue, a last blast of summer – before another storm hits, I can't help thinking.

Getting in my car, I set off for Callie's house, but then I decide to make a detour to Lily's to buy more flowers for her.

* * *

The bell jingles as I walk in and as the door closes behind me, the smell of freshly baked bread reaches me. Going over to the flowers, I peruse the bouquets. Drawn to one of mixed white flowers and what I now know to be herbs, I pick it up, then put it back. When

Callie's garden is filled with flowers, I want to give her something simple, elegant, different.

Another bouquet catches my eye, of soft-petalled red roses. Lifting it up, I breathe in its fragrance, deliberating over them for a moment, before deciding I'm as certain as I can be that Callie would love these.

* * *

It's twenty minutes later when I pull up outside her house. Picking up the flowers, I knock at her door.

'Coming!' I hear her call out, before the door is flung open.

'Hi.' She seems to freeze for a moment. 'Um, do you want to come in?'

'If it's convenient.' I try to explain why I've come here. 'You seemed preoccupied this morning. I wondered if today was a significant day or something. Anyway, I brought you these.'

As I hand her the bouquet of flowers, her face turns pale. 'How did you know?' she whispers.

'Know what?' I frown at her, puzzled.

'These.' She looks at the scented roses I've just given her, then at me again.

Not sure what she means, I follow her into the kitchen. On the side is a tomato and olive tart dusted with herbs. 'That looks good.'

'Have some, if you like. I felt like cooking something, but now it's done, I'm not hungry.' Before I can reply, she's already cutting me a huge square of it. Handing me a plate, she passes me a napkin and a fork. 'Tea? Or a beer?'

'I'd love a beer.' As I watch her, she seems matter-of-fact. But as I've come to realise, Callie can be a conundrum of different people: elfin girl, grieving woman, and slightly lost, almost as if she doesn't know what to do with herself. 'Thanks.' I take the can she holds out.

Unwrapping the flowers, she puts them in a vase, arranging them so that they appear to tumble effortlessly over the sides, before turning to me. 'Shall we go outside?'

I follow her through the doors that open on to the garden. 'I could do with doors like that.'

'You should have them opening on to your terrace.' Sitting down at the wooden table, she sips her beer. 'Sorry – about the flowers just now... They're beautiful. They really are...' She frowns. 'I've had quite a strange day.' Going on, she tells me about going to see her fiancé's mother and realising she'd got her dates wrong. On her way to his grave, she'd stopped to buy some flowers. 'You'll never believe this, but they were the exact same ones you gave me.'

'Red roses?' Sitting opposite her, I feel thrown. The thing is, I'd picked them up and put them back again, at least twice before deciding – and given all the bouquets in the shop, it seems bizarre that I've chosen the very same ones.

'Exactly the same. Soft and scented, just like yours.' Her eyes search mine. 'They're one of my favourite flowers, which also seems kind of odd, don't you think? Anyway, at the church, I met this woman. I was sitting by Liam's grave having a bit of a rant and she heard me. It turns out she'd lost her husband a couple of years ago. She told me she'd done a lot of ranting – she was funny, actually.'

'Kind of like gallows humour?' I pause between mouthfuls of the tart.

'Kind of. We talked for a while. She told me about her husband and I told her about Liam. Then she said no one was that perfect.' Callie's silent for a moment. 'It got me thinking. People aren't perfect, are they?'

'Not in my experience,' I say wryly. 'But Liam... maybe he was one of the good people in the world. After all, he fell in love with you.'

Her cheeks flush slightly. 'I suppose I can be a bit of a rose-tinted-spectacles kind of person. I always look for the good in people.'

If only more of us could do the same. 'That's good, isn't it? I think too many people tend to do the reverse.'

'I've always believed part of loving someone is accepting everything about them – not just the good.' She pauses. 'Do you like the tart?'

'It's delicious. You should have some.'

'I might do later, if I'm hungry.' She looks at me. 'The other thing that happened was I went to see your land today.'

I wince. 'That project is fast becoming a headache.'

She raises an eyebrow. 'Do you want to know what I think?'

'OK,' I say guardedly.

She's off again, regaling me with her ideas, which to her credit, are relatively wildlife-friendly. For the first time since I've come here, her troubles seem to lift. 'You could call it wild camping. I know you're not convinced and I was going to find you some pictures but I haven't had time yet. But I will before tomorrow. Then I was thinking, maybe we could go and see it together.' Pausing, she brushes a flake of pastry off my sweatshirt. 'What do you think?'

I shrug. I have nothing to lose – though possibly not a lot to gain either. But given her enthusiasm, I owe it to her to at least listen. 'Tomorrow morning?'

* * *

As I drive home, I'm still undecided as to what this is between us. Friendship, definitely, but from where Callie's standing, I'm not sure it's any more than that. It's as though the kiss never happened, but from everything she's said, it's been a day of weirdness for her. It's also her fiancé's birthday. And in all this, there's still so much we haven't told each other.

When I get home, I pick up the post that's lying on the doormat, hesitating as I recognise one of the letters, putting it to one side to open later, before getting a plate for another piece of the tart Callie insisted I take.

Carrying the plate outside, I sit on my terrace. The temperature has dropped, enough to consider lighting the wood burner. I've always liked the turn of the seasons, as one fades into the next and it's already starting, the dulling of green to burnished autumn shades; the cooling of the air; the forming of mist in the valleys.

As I finish eating, my phone pings with a message from Callie asking for my email address. No sooner have I sent it to her than an email arrives, with a Callie-esque message in the subject line.

This is what I wanted to explain!!

It's followed by a whole lot of links, to camping suppliers, eco-campsites, prairie gardens, while the last is a link to a Pinterest board.

As I scroll through the images, I start to get what she's been talking about. The idea of tents set amongst huge swathes of natural planting is stunning. The only question is if it is worth the investment.

As if she reads my mind, another email arrives.

You could host weddings...

There are more photos, one of a huge tepee-style tent, in which there's a firepit and trestle tables that could host far more than weddings. Suddenly I find myself getting interested. Camping would only work for the summer months and I need to explore how big the market is. People are becoming more conscious about limiting their damage to the environment, but basing a business on it? I wasn't sure.

If you don't like the idea of camping, how about shepherds' huts?

More pictures follow, though I happen to know that these come with a hefty price tag. But there's plenty here for me to think about.

I send her a reply.

Thanks. These are really great! And so was your tart.

I hesitate before adding:

I have an appointment tomorrow morning, in case you were thinking of coming here. But make yourself at home.

By the time I go to bed, she hasn't replied. But I wake up to a message the following morning.

Thank you x

I stare at the x, before getting out of bed. A feeling of trepidation fills me as I think about the appointment. I can't afford to be late.

* * *

'It's all looking really good.' After running the usual tests, my consultant sounds positive.

'Thank goodness.' Relief washes over me.

'Whatever you're doing, keep doing it. Your blood pressure is good, nothing out of range in the test results...' She smiles at me. 'I wish it was the same for everybody.'

'So...' I pause. 'Is that it?'

'Sure is. You're free to go. We'll be in touch before your next appointment.'

'Thanks.'

As I walk out of the consulting room, it's like a weight has lifted. Not so long ago, I'd never have imagined I'd ever feel well again, let alone get my energy back. But thanks to modern medicine, I've been granted a reprieve.

As I drive home, I feel the strangest mixture of euphoria and gratitude. My illness has taken the spontaneity out of life. Since then, I shouldn't be taking even a single day for granted. I feel something fire up inside me. Having been given another chance, I need to stop letting time pass and do something with it.

Suddenly I'm thinking about the land I've bought. My work is the only link to my old life, but that's a life I want to change. I'm lucky that, in the short term, money isn't an issue. And Callie's right, I can't help thinking. Instead of making even more money, maybe this is my chance to give something back.

Putting my foot down, I feel excited. I can't wait to talk to her about it. But as I turn into the drive, my excitement fades. Getting out of my car, I notice the wheelbarrow full of weeds, abandoned in the middle of the garden. But there's no sign of her car here. Callie's gone.

15

CALLIE

By mid-morning, Nathan still isn't home, when with another wheelbarrow full of weeds pulled up, I'm distracted by my mobile buzzing. After taking the call from my mother, I put the gardening tools away as quickly as I can, before grabbing my things, my heart racing as I hurry to my car.

I drive as fast as I dare – since Liam died, I'm wary about driving too fast. But today, given what's happened, it's different.

As the miles pass, I replay my mother's words, fear gripping me. *Your father's been having chest pains. He's been taken to hospital...* All my life, my father has been there for me, through thick and thin. Until now, he's been strong and healthy. The thought of losing him has never crossed my mind before.

A sense of panic fills me. I can't lose him – not after losing Liam. Pulling into the hospital car park, I get out and run towards the entrance. As the doors open then close behind me, I follow signs for the Acute Cardiac Care Unit.

Reaching the reception desk, I glance at one of the staff.

'I think my father's here – Stewart Miller. Can you tell me where he is?'

As she glances at her screen, I'm terrified. What if something's happened? If I'm too late?

'One of the nurses will take you to him.'

As she finishes speaking, I notice a nurse coming towards me. 'Are you Callie?'

I nod. 'Yes. Is he OK?'

She looks concerned. 'He's had an ECG and he's stable – but we'll be carrying out more tests. It's standard procedure after a heart attack.'

I feel lightheaded. 'A heart attack?'

'You didn't know?' Stopping at a door into a small room, the nurse turns to me. 'He's in here.'

Going in, I take in my mother's anxious face.

When he sees me, my father tries to smile. 'You didn't have to come, love. I'll be home in no time.'

'Hi, Dad.' I kiss his cheek, trying not to show how frightened I feel. 'Hi, Mum.' I do the same to her, before looking at them both. 'Will one of you tell me what's going on?'

'Your father had a heart attack. Only a small one, thank God.' In a rare display of affection, she pats his hand. 'Shouldn't be too long before we're out of here.'

She's talking as though it's trivial.

I pull up a chair. 'When did this happen?'

'He started having pains last night. Then this morning...' She glances at my father. 'It started getting worse.' She sighs. 'Of course, I called the GP, who called an ambulance... And here we are.'

I feel another of rush of fear. 'You should have told me before.'

My parents glance at each other.

'We didn't want to worry you, love,' my dad says quietly.

I know they think they're protecting me; that after Liam's death, they don't want to frighten me.

'Do my sisters know?'

'Don't call them,' my dad says weakly. 'I don't want them rushing over here. I'm going to be OK.'

'Dad, if it was one of them, wouldn't you want to know? Alice's job is caring for people with heart problems.' I get up. 'I'll give them a quick call. I'll be right back.'

Going back outside, I try Alice first. When she doesn't answer, I leave a voice message, then do the same after trying Rita. The only one who picks up is Sasha.

'Is he going to be OK?' She sounds shocked.

'I haven't spoken to a doctor yet. I'll try to find one when I go back in. They've done an ECG but they're going to do more tests.'

'Keep me posted, won't you?' She sounds anxious. 'I'd come over but I have a client due any minute.'

'Don't worry. I'll call you later on.'

Ending the call, I stand there for a moment. The sky is pale, the sound of passing traffic relentless. The morning in Nathan's garden feels a world away. My father has always seemed invincible, but as I know too well, none of us are.

It seems unfathomable how quickly so much has changed. But as I know from experience, it can happen to anyone. When I go back into the hospital, there's a doctor with my parents. After introducing herself, she explains that they'll be keeping him in; that the next forty-eight hours are critical.

'I'd really rather go home,' my father says stubbornly.

'Dad, I think you'd better do what they say. Hopefully you won't be in here for long,' I say gently, trying to hide how frightened I feel. Glancing at my mother, taking in the paleness of her face, I realise how scared she is, too. 'Mum? Maybe later on, I could drive you home to pick up some things for Dad?'

Her eyes widen. 'I hadn't even thought about getting home. I came in the ambulance with your father.'

I'd guessed as much. 'That's OK. We can go together.'

* * *

A couple of hours later, I persuade her to leave Dad for a while and as we walk out to my car, she's silent. Only as we're driving away does she let on how worried she is.

'I mean, I know we're not getting any younger. And none of us go on for ever. I suppose you never expect something like this to happen.'

'No. But at least he's getting the care he needs,' I try to reassure her. 'They said they were keeping him in for a few days... With any luck, he'll be home after that.'

'But life's going to have to change a bit. They were talking about cutting down on alcohol and eating healthily – he isn't going to like that too much.' She pauses. 'Thank God he doesn't smoke.'

'One thing at a time, Mum. The hospital will give him all the info he needs.'

She turns to me suddenly. 'I'm so sorry, Callie. I know how difficult this must be for you.'

I shake my head. 'No more than for any of us.'

'Confronting your mortality is pretty brutal, isn't it?' Her voice wavers.

'I know.' I'm just coming through an entire savage year of it. Just then, my mobile buzzes. I pass it to my mother. 'It's Alice. Can you talk to her?'

* * *

Back at my childhood home, I let the dogs out into the garden while my mother goes upstairs and gathers some things together. The air is cool, the birdsong vibrant, as for a moment I contemplate a world without my father in it before pushing the thought away. He's going to be OK. He has to be.

For the next couple of days, I drive my mother to the hospital, staying with them, scrutinising him for signs of change, relieved when slowly the colour comes back to his skin.

The second evening, Sasha comes to visit. When she walks in, I can see from her face how worried she is.

'I wish I could stay,' she says anxiously.

'You mustn't worry,' my dad says. 'I'm going to be out of here before too long – everything will go back to how it used to be.'

Sasha glances at me, then at Mum. 'I don't think it's quite that simple – I mean, you're going to have to make some changes, aren't you?'

'We'll see.' My parents exchange glances, before my mother says, 'Don't you two worry yourselves. And you can tell your sisters I have everything in hand.' Her voice is reassuringly firm, the way it always is when she makes up her mind about something.

* * *

After booking some leave, Rita promises to come down at the weekend for a few days. But Alice is unable to get away from work, though she has been in contact with his doctor here. She's also given my mother pages of information on what to expect when Dad comes home, as I count my lucky stars that we are all able to support each other; that my parents aren't going through this alone.

While we're sitting there one afternoon, my phone pings with a message from Nathan.

Hey, haven't seen you for a while. Hope you're OK? x

'Who's that?' My mother's eagle eyes never miss anything.

'A friend,' I reply nonchalantly as I text him back.

Sorry, I've been meaning to get in touch. My father had a heart attack. He's OK, I'm with my parents in the hospital.

Pressing send, I add a line.

How is your garden?

As I type, my phone pings with another message.

Graveyard Groupies meet up at Charlie's Fish Shack 8 p.m. Friday.

Smiling, I reply, *yes*, just as Nathan gets back to me.

I'm sorry Callie. I hope you're OK. My garden misses you. I do, too.

Reading it, I get a warm feeling because I miss him, too – and his garden. When I look up, both my parents are watching me. 'I'm just texting – I met this woman when I went to Liam's grave. She lost her husband – so we're going to meet up on Friday.'

'That's good, dear.' My mother turns back to my father. 'Has anyone said when they're letting you out of here?'

'Early next week.' My father raises his eyebrows. 'Bit of a bloody long time away, isn't it?'

'You won't believe what Alice has sent me.' My mother shakes her head. 'Pages about diet and gentle exercise...'

'She's told me.' He looks glum. 'But I suppose it's a small price to pay for a few more years.'

* * *

The following morning, knowing my father is on the up, I drive to Nathan's, savouring the prospect of some solitary hours in his garden, though there's a part of me that's looking forward to seeing him again.

When I turn into his drive, there's a small red car parked outside his house. Getting out, I hesitate, not sure I'm up to meeting someone else. Glancing towards the house, through the window I catch sight of a girl – or more the side view of her. She has shoulder-length dark hair and is talking animatedly. Then as Nathan comes into sight, going over to her, he hugs her.

It's as though I've been electric-shocked. Getting in my car, I reverse out of the drive, before turning around and driving away. If Nathan has a girlfriend, why did he kiss me? Logic kicks in. It's possible, of course, that she isn't his girlfriend – she's just a friend, I tell myself. But that isn't the point. What bothers me most is that I care – too much.

When I get home, I'm restless, as for the first time ever, the walls of my home feel claustrophobic. Picking up one of my favourite books, I take it outside. It's a book I've read dozens of times over the last year and sitting on the grass, I start leafing through it.

The world is full of small things. Tiny ants; the individual petals on a flower; blades of grass that are a million shades of green; the molecules of air and water that together make up the oceans and the sky; the ether in between...

I love that it reminds me about what makes up this world; how small we are, our lives no more than a bubble around us. It was why I was so determined to walk the coast of northern Spain. I wanted to break away from everything I knew; to push myself out of my comfort zone.

The idea of doing it with Liam was less daunting than doing it alone. But as I sit here, I realise I still want to do this. Moreover, it feels like something I need to do. Getting up, I go inside again and search for the reference book I bought when Liam and I were planning to go. Sitting on the grass again, I find the route we planned to take, the Camino del Norte, reading the familiar names of the places we researched.

My eyes turn to the space in the flower bed that was destined to hold memories of our walk there. But as I gaze at it, I know what it's become. It's empty; symbolic of everything I've lost, as suddenly I realise, that empty patch of soil is my roadblock.

16

NATHAN

Watching Callie's car reverse down the drive, I can only guess it's because she's seen another car here and is still wary of meeting strangers.

'Who's that?' Robin gazes out of the window.

'The girl who's helping me with the garden. She's probably forgotten something.' I don't allude to Callie's history.

'Shame. I want to meet her.' Robin's eyes are teasing as they meet mine. 'I mean, it's a while since my brother's had a woman in his life.'

I shake my head. 'You're jumping to conclusions. It isn't like that.'

But she doesn't let it go. 'So what is it like?'

'She's an amazing gardener. I asked her if she'd help – and she agreed.'

Robin tilts her head on one side. 'So she works for you.'

I shake my head again. 'Not exactly. She won't let me pay her.' I pause. 'She's also very anti my development project.'

'A bit of an eco-warrior? Not your usual type, then.' Robin sounds amused.

'I don't have a type,' I object. 'And it's more she objects to local people being priced out of the property market. She thinks I should use it to benefit the community in some way.'

'She has a point,' Robin says briefly. 'By the way, you so do have a type – blond, athletic, into adrenaline sports, a bit of a foodie...' She pauses. 'In a nutshell, an Emily.'

'Emily is ancient history. You really don't know me at all, do you?' I pretend to sound wounded.

She looks at me oddly. 'I used to think I did – but I have to admit, you have changed – in some ways.'

'Hardly surprising, is it?' I say quietly.

After Robin leaves, I try to get down to some work, putting together some figures to see if a campsite is actually viable – assuming I'm able to get the relevant permissions, stopping to send Callie a quick message.

Sorry to have missed you this morning. How is your dad doing?

But even a couple of hours later, she hasn't replied.

Wanting to know if she's OK, that evening, I get in my car and drive over there. When I knock on her door, she opens it seconds later. In a loose-fitting T-shirt and frayed denim shorts, she's barefoot.

'Hi!' She doesn't meet my gaze.

'Hi. I saw your car arrive this morning, but when you left so suddenly, I was just wondering if you were OK.'

'I'm fine! Why wouldn't I be?' Her voice holds a trace of brittleness.

'No reason.' I study her face. 'I also wondered how your dad was doing.'

Relief crosses her face. 'He's OK. He should be coming out after the weekend.'

'That's great news.' I hesitate. 'If you're not busy, could I come in for a moment?'

Standing back, she opens the door wider, before closing it behind me. 'Can I get you anything?'

'No – I'm fine. I've been thinking about you. It can't have been easy, your dad being taken ill like that.'

'It's not been the best time. Alice, one of my sisters, is a cardiologist. She's been great talking to his consultant. But life isn't going to be the same any more.'

When something comes out of the blue, I know too well how frightening it can be. 'No, I guess not. But he'll be kept a close eye on, won't he?'

She smiles faintly. 'By all of us.'

'Anyway... I don't know if now's a good time, it's just that I've been thinking about what you said about my development project. I've had an interesting day putting some figures together.'

She looks surprised. 'For a campsite?'

'That was my initial plan.' I pause. 'It was what you said, about locals being priced out of the property market. Camping wouldn't exactly be helping with that, but .'

She looks slightly less wary. 'But you'd be creating jobs, at least.'

'That's true. I suppose I was wondering if you'd had any more ideas.' I'm distracted as I glance at the table on which she's spread out a map. 'Going somewhere?'

'At some point.' She tells me about the trip she'd planned with her fiancé. 'I'm thinking it's something I need to do,' she says quietly.

'It would be some adventure.' I'm impressed.

'I need to prove to myself that I can do it.' There's determination in her voice. 'But also, I have this feeling it will be good for me.'

'That's great, then.' I pause, not sure whether to ask her why. 'Where will you start from?'

'I'll show you if you like.' Going over to the table, she points to the eastern end of the northern Spanish coast.

It isn't a part of Spain I've ever been to before. 'So where will you fly to?'

She shakes her head. 'I won't be flying. I'll get the ferry to Spain.'

In my book, that takes courage. 'You're brave. The Bay of Biscay can get pretty rough,' I tell her. 'I did that crossing – only once. I swore I'd never do it again.'

'I'm not at all brave. I'm terrified of flying.'

'Oh.' I'm not sure what to say. 'As in you won't even consider it?'

She shakes her head again. 'Not ever. It's the fact that if something goes wrong, you're thousands of feet in the air.'

'It's pretty safe.' I look at her. 'And you are brave, you know. Planning this walk on your own.'

She's quiet for a moment. 'It doesn't feel like that. It feels more like something I'll always regret if I don't do it. And, I don't know... maybe it's an adventure?' She went on quickly. 'I'm not really an adventurous person. And I've never done anything like this before. Maybe that's why it's become so important to me.'

'It sounds like an amazing trip.' Part of me is envious of her.

'I think so. But also...' She hesitates. 'I'm hoping it's going to help me move on.'

In my eyes, that makes her even braver. 'Are you busy this evening or can I persuade you to come out for a drink?'

She hesitates. 'It's been a funny few days,' she says softly, meeting my eyes. 'I think I need a little time alone.'

I'm taken aback. 'Of course. No problem. I understand.'

'Do you?' She sounds sad. 'I like you, Nathan. I thought you liked me, too.'

When she uses the past tense, I wonder what's changed. 'I do.' Stepping closer, I reach out and stroke a strand of hair off her face. 'I like you a lot,' I say quietly.

There's angst in her eyes as she looks at me. 'It should be simple, shouldn't it? But I think I've realised that losing someone hurts so much, I can't risk it happening again.'

Standing there, I try to work out whether she's saying no to tonight, or no for ever. 'I know you've been through the worst kind of heartbreak,' I say to her gently. 'But it doesn't mean it would happen again.'

For a moment she doesn't speak. 'I think it's easier right now if I'm alone.'

There's more I want to say to her, but for whatever reason, it isn't the time. 'Maybe I'd better go.' I linger, wanting her to change her mind, but she clearly isn't going to. 'I'll see you.'

As she nods slowly, there's a sadness in her eyes I don't understand.

As I drive away, I'm confused. It's the turnaround in her; her use of the past tense. *I thought you liked me, too.* I don't understand what's changed – unless maybe her dad being ill has shaken her up.

I think back to what she said. *I like you, Nathan.* When she clearly feels something for me, it doesn't make sense. In the end, I come to the conclusion that it's simply too soon; that when you lose someone you love, a year is nothing.

* * *

I've started to wonder if I'll see her again, but a couple of days later she surprises me. When I step out on to my terrace with a mug of coffee, Callie's already hard at work, the wheelbarrow piled high with weeds.

'Morning,' I call out. 'Can I get you some tea?'

'Thanks.' She carries on with what she's doing.

'I didn't expect to see you,' I tell her, when I take her tea over to her, 'after what you said the other day.'

Her cheeks flush slightly. 'I thought about it. The thing is I told you I'd help you – and I don't like going back on my word. Hopefully it won't be long before it's manageable enough for you to take over.'

'You really don't have to do this,' I say. 'I could always find someone else to help.'

She freezes momentarily. 'If that's what you want.'

'Not especially.' I'm taken aback. 'I like you being here. But as long as you know I appreciate you doing this.' With this conversation going nowhere, I change the subject. 'How is your dad?'

She looks at me properly. 'He's doing OK, actually. The hospital is happy with him. He's just going to have to watch his diet, and exercise more than he used to. But it could have been much worse.'

'Yes.' But I'm not giving up on her. 'I wish you'd let me buy you dinner – to say thank you.'

Her eyes are wistful. 'I had it all planned out what I wanted to say to you. It's true what I said the other day. I like you.' As she steps closer, the strangest feeling comes over me. 'But then the other day, when I came here, I saw you.'

I frown at her. 'What do you mean?'

She glances up at the window. 'The girl who was here? Who you had your arms around?'

Breathing a sigh of relief, at last I understand. 'That wasn't what you thought it was. My sister came over.' I watch surprise flicker across her face. 'I'd had some good news and she was happy for me.' I shrug. 'That's all it was, I promise you. And that really isn't the kind of thing I'd do to someone I like.'

Instead of laughing it off, she's silent. 'When I saw her, I just felt so horrible. I mean, it's crazy – I hardly know you. But spending time with you has felt like such a huge step for me. So has letting myself like you – and then, I thought I'd read you wrong. I've had too much pain in my life to go through any more.' She bites her lip. 'I suppose I came around to thinking it would probably be best if we were just friends.'

It clearly makes sense in Callie's mind. But hearing her tell me she likes me, yet we can't be any more than friends, is tying my brain in knots.

I gaze at her. 'Don't you think some things are worth taking a risk on?'

'Of course.' She's quiet again. 'I suppose I might as well say it like it is.' She pauses. 'The thing is, it would be nice – for a while, but at some point, we'd have to go through the awfulness of breaking up – because in the end, that's what happens to everyone.' She shrugs. 'It's painful.'

I've never heard such a negative assessment of relationships. 'Not necessarily. We might turn out to be the love of each other's lives...' As I watch her face, too late I realise how crass I've been; that she's already met the love of her life, and lost him. 'I'm so sorry, Callie. I know what Liam meant to you. I didn't mean that to come out the way it did.'

She shrugs again. 'It's fine.'

But from the look on her face, I can see it's far from fine.

'I really didn't mean to upset you. Can't we just backtrack a bit? Like you said – be friends?'

She hesitates. 'OK.'

Finishing her tea, she turns back to the garden as I go inside. But as I sit at my desk and started working, I'm thinking of Callie. In truth, I want us to be more than just friends, and in her heart, I suspect she feels the same. I sigh loudly, wondering how this has become so complicated.

When she's finished, instead of leaving without saying goodbye as she usually does, she comes to the door.

'You said you wanted to talk about the campsite? I have a few minutes now if you're not busy.' She's less troubled than earlier.

'OK.' This is the last thing I've been expecting. 'Come in. I'll go and get my laptop.'

Going over to the sink, she washes her hands. 'Do you have anything cold to drink?'

'In the fridge,' I call out. 'Help yourself.'

When I come back in, she's opened a can of coke. Coming over, she sits next to me as I bring up the sketch I've made.

'This is my original plan. I've based it on your ideas – low density of tents, high percentage of wildness. If I went ahead with this, I'd test the soil and see if it needed nutrients. Then what I'd like is a mixture of wildflower meadows and prairie planting that would mean each plot felt secluded.'

She nods slowly. 'I really like it.'

I go on. 'I was thinking there needed to be gravel paths, in case of rain... but other than that, most of the land would be undisrupted. I'd put in solar panels, collect rainwater...' I have to stop myself from getting carried away. 'I've asked for some quotes for the tents and building materials. Once I have them, my plan is to do my sums and apply for planning.' But I'm optimistic about that, too. With the eco-credentials of what I'm proposing as well as its low environmental impact, I'm hoping it will sail through.

Callie looks thoughtful. 'My dad knows someone who works for the council. They've been friends for years. I could probably put you in touch if you'd like me to.'

'That would be amazing.' I can't believe my luck. 'You've no idea how much it helps to talk to someone who knows the ins and outs.'

'This is way better than your housing idea.' Her eyes linger on me for a moment.

'I'll definitely employ local people. My only concern is how much money it will generate.' I pause. 'I'm trying to think of something that can run in parallel with it – the camping season is short. Ideally, I need it to make money all year round.'

She nods. 'If it isn't going to be about housing, there must be something else that would be community-based.' She frowns slightly. 'I'll think about it.' Then her frown clears. 'And I've been thinking about it – what you said outside just now.' Gazing at me, she smiles. 'About being friends – it's good.'

17

CALLIE

Having told Nathan we can only be friends, a feeling of relief settles over me. Until this sea of grief calms, being friends is simpler, undemanding; something I'm comfortable with.

That afternoon, after a shower and a change of clothes, I drive over to the hospital. Inside the small room where my father is, my mother's latest obsession has taken root. Taking in the bags of wool and knitting needles everywhere, as I look questioningly at my father, he shakes his head at me.

My mother barely looks up. 'I'm knitting you a sweater.'

Just then, Rita comes in. When she sees me, her face lights up. 'I didn't know you were coming.'

I hug her. 'Are you staying long?'

'For a couple of nights – just to keep an eye on these two.' She says it affectionately, her gaze turning to our parents.

'Someone needs to.' I watch our mother busy with her knitting.

She frowns up at me. 'You look nice. Are you going somewhere?'

I'm aware of everyone's eyes on me. 'I'm meeting a friend,' I tell her, leaving them to wonder. 'How are you Dad?' Going over, I kiss his cheek.

His colour has returned and he sounds much more like his old self. 'There's nothing wrong with me. They need to send me home and give my bed to some other poor bugger.'

'I'm sure they will when you're ready. What's this?' I pick up the list that's on the table next to his bed.

Rita raises her eyebrows. 'That's Mum's list of knitting orders from some of the nursing staff.'

'There's nothing wrong with that. Young people these days don't knit, do they? Perhaps I should teach them.' My mother sounds businesslike.

'Your mother's set up quite a little cottage industry in here.' My father rolls his eyes. 'Still, keeps her out of trouble.'

'Honestly, Stewart.' She sounds disapproving. 'You know how I feel about wasting time. At least I'm doing something practical with it.'

Catching my eye again, wisely my father remains silent.

'I wish you were staying longer,' I say to Rita.

I wonder if there's something she isn't saying when she asks me, 'Why don't I come to yours on Sunday night?'

With all the confusion in my mind, an evening with one of my sisters is just what I need. 'I'd love that.'

Just as I'm about to leave, Sasha turns up. Noticing her eyes are troubled, I wonder if she's worried about dad or if it's the man in her life.

'Hey!' Coming in, she hugs me and Rita, then our parents. 'How are you both?'

'They're fine,' I tell her, nodding towards a bag of wool. 'Mum's taking orders from the nursing staff.'

'Anyone would think there was something wrong with that,' my mother says crisply.

'There's nothing wrong with it, Mum.' Leaning down, Sasha kisses her on the cheek.

I glance at my watch. 'I'm sorry to leave you all so soon, but I have to go.'

Sasha fixes her eyes on me. 'So where are you off to?'

'I'm meeting a friend,' I say airily, taking in her look of surprise. 'I am now a fully fledged member of the newly formed Graveyard Groupies. We're meeting at Charlie's Fish Shack.'

My mother looks at me as if I'm mad, while Rita splutters and Sasha looks approving. 'Good for you. Are you around tomorrow?'

I nod. 'Come over any time.'

* * *

Inside Charlie's Fish Shack, Tanith is sitting alone at a corner table. In a black dress, her strawberry-blond hair cascading over one shoulder, she looks suitably bereaved – and stunning.

She's pleased to see me. 'Hi! Glad there's going to be at least two of us. White wine? I have a bottle.'

'Thanks.' Sitting down, I watch as she reaches into the ice bucket and pours me a glass. 'So how many other bereaved bitches have you roped in?' I ask her.

'Three. One probably won't come. She's still in the "all over the place" phase. Fluctuating emotions, tidal waves of survivor guilt... we both know how that goes. Here's Freya.' She looks up as another woman comes in. A little older than us, when she sees Tanith, she raises a hand in greeting. 'Ten years on, still not over him. But you and I are not ever allowed to be like that, OK?' Tanith mutters. 'Hi, Freya! So pleased you could join us. This is Callie.'

'Hi.' I hold out my hand.

'You're so young.' Freya looks sad. 'Both of you. It's so terrible.'

While I'd been guessing we'd share our experiences, the last thing I need is someone telling me how terrible it is. Glancing at Tanith, I wonder if this is going to work.

'Have a glass of wine.' Tanith pours her a glass. 'Oh, good. Here's Joey.' As a thin woman in an orange dress comes over, Tanith introduces us all. 'Now that everyone's here, why don't we tell each other a little about ourselves? I'll go first.' She gives them a potted version of what she's already told me about her husband dying. 'So there you are. I suppose realising I would have divorced him by now has been quite helpful overall. But the fact is I married the wrong man. Callie?'

I look from Freya to Joey. 'I lost my fiancé just over a year ago. He was killed on the way to the church on our wedding day. It's been the worst year of my entire life.' I hesitate, before going on. 'But now and then, I'm starting to believe I'll be OK again.'

After Freya tells us about the husband she lost ten years ago, my heart goes out to her. To be so encumbered by grief so many years later is desperately sad, while Joey's story is something else.

'I found out after he died, he'd been living a double life. He had another wife, more kids...'

'Fuck.' Tanith looks horrified. 'You had no idea?'

Joey shakes her head. 'He was a pilot – I just thought he was away a lot. Of course, once I knew, I wanted to kill him...'

'I'm not surprised.' Tanith sounds shocked as she looks around at us all. 'I suppose the point is, we're all in the same boat – well, almost,' she adds, glancing at Joey. 'But apart from mourning what we've lost, I think we should celebrate – being alive; and being strong, vibrant women.' She raises her glass. 'To us.'

Freya holds her glass firmly on the table. 'I'm not strong at all – that's the point.'

'You've made it through ten years,' Tanith says kindly. 'Don't you think you should feel a little proud of yourself?'

In Freya, I can't help but see something of myself. She's reluctant to let go of the past, to accept that life could be worth living again. It isn't a comfortable feeling. We both have a life to live, as

I'm finding out. All of us do. Joey, however, has channelled her anger at her husband into strength.

'When I found out he'd been leading a double life, I realised how little he must have thought of me. And our children.' Her voice trembles. 'So I told myself, I'm better than that. If he hadn't died, he probably would have gone on deceiving me for years. How awful is that?'

'You deserve so much better.' Glancing at Freya, Tanith tries to draw her out. 'Don't you think?'

'Yes, but...' Freya looks uncertain.

'No one needs a man who lets them down,' Tanith says quietly, but firmly.

An hour or so later, Joey and Freya make their excuses, leaving me and Tanith alone.

'What did you think?' she asks.

I finish the last of my wine. 'That you are an awesome if slightly random bereavement counsellor – and that everyone really does have a different story.'

'Ha! You could say. I was a bit worried that Freya would bring us down. But she was OK. Hearing Joey's story might even have done her good.'

I shake my head. 'The trouble with Freya is she's a widow rather than a woman – at least, that's how she seems to see herself.'

'Very astute.' Tanith drains her glass. 'She truly is a woman defined by her past.'

'I've been one of those for over a year,' I tell her soberly.

Tanith looks sympathetic. 'It's hardly surprising. It's massive, isn't it? Losing someone you love? All that time passes when you can't think about anything else.'

'Until somehow you stop feeling guilty about wanting to be happy again.'

'But you're not stuck, are you?' Tanith asks. 'Not like Freya is?'

'No.' Shaking my head, it's a revelation to realise I'm not.

'Listen to us.' Tanith rolls her eyes. 'Fancy another one?'

Over another glass of wine, I have a question for Tanith. 'So, since he died... has there been anyone else?'

She shakes her head. 'Other than a quick shag with an ex, no one. You?'

I decide to tell her about Nathan. 'I have kind of met someone – just recently. But it's too soon. I got scared off. I thought I saw him with someone else – who turned out to be his sister, but it brought back that horrible feeling of not knowing where I stood. All I knew was I couldn't go through losing anyone again.' I hesitate. 'We're friends, though.'

'Friends is good.' Tanith looks confused. 'Maybe it is too soon. But if you like him... maybe you need to get braver.'

'Braver?' I shrug, thinking of what Nathan said: *you are brave, you know*; mentally, I add it to my grief vocabulary. 'I'll figure it out. Eventually.'

'A word of advice. Whether it's too soon or not, everyone's going to have an opinion on the next person you meet – not that it's any of their business.' Tanith becomes more serious. 'You and I, we have a lot of life left – hopefully. We both know how nice it is when you think you've found the right man to share it with – even if mine did turn out to be an utter scumbag.' She rolls her eyes. 'I have terrible judgement. But if you really do like this guy, I wouldn't leave it too long.'

* * *

Her words stay with me as I drive home that night. I might be stronger, but mostly, I don't feel brave. And while I know I've confused Nathan. I've confused myself. But when so much is about timing, friends is fine. For now, it doesn't feel right being more than that.

The next morning Sasha comes over. 'Rita's taken Mum to the hospital.'

'That's nice of her. Dad's doing really well, isn't he?'

'Thank goodness.' Relief washes over her face. 'I've been so worried about him.'

'I think we all have.'

We take our cups of coffee into the garden.

'We're lucky aren't we – Alice being a cardiologist. She's so good at explaining everything.' I frown. 'But when it comes to hearts...' Sitting down, I try to explain about Nathan. 'It isn't about him. He's a really nice guy, Sash. When I met him, I felt like I was being disloyal to Liam. But when I saw him again, we just got along so easily.'

'This is the gardening guy?' Sasha sits opposite me. 'So what's the problem?'

I hesitate. 'Everything was fine until I thought I'd seen him with someone else – who, as it turned out, happened to be his sister. But it was like something closed up inside me. I think the memory of how I felt when I lost Liam came back. I don't ever want to feel that kind of pain again.'

'Maybe it's too soon.' Sasha looks sympathetic. 'What does your gut tell you?'

'That's a very good question. It keeps changing.'

'It will come to you, Cal. Sometimes it takes a little time.' Sasha's eyes wander towards the empty flower bed. 'Do you think maybe it's time you planted Santiago de Compostela?'

'I've been thinking a lot about that.' I tell her about my plan. 'I've decided I'm doing the walk – on my own.'

Sasha's eyes widen. 'The whole north coast? That's frigging awesome, Cal!'

Now that I've decided, I know it's the right thing. 'I think I have to. I need to prove something to myself – and it's like there's this unfinished chapter in my and Liam's lives that I need to complete before I can properly move on. I know it probably sounds bonkers, but it makes sense to me.'

'Not as bonkers as the Graveyard Groupies.' Sasha giggles.

Remembering last night, I shake my head. 'Actually, it wasn't. You know, it made me realise other people go through just as much – if not worse.' I tell her about Joey. 'I actually came away from there feeling relatively normal.'

'Well hooray for that.' Sasha's silent for a moment. 'You know, this walk... depending on when you're planning to go, I could come with you.'

'You?' I look at her in surprise. 'It's miles, Sash. You don't walk.'

'That's why I should do it. Let's face it, I could do with a change of scene.' A shadow crosses her face.

I remember how preoccupied she looked when she arrived at the hospital. 'Is everything OK?'

She sighs. 'Not really.'

So I was right, there is something. I wouldn't mind betting I know what it is. I shake my head slowly. 'Not that man again.'

A shadow crosses her face. 'I've told him it's over – but he refuses to stay out of my life. He hangs around waiting for me to finish work, sends me all these texts...' She sounds wretched.

'Sash, that's stalking.' I'm outraged. 'You have to tell the police – or his wife. Or even better, both.'

'I know,' she says miserably. 'I suppose, under it all, I did love him.'

'Listen to yourself,' I tell her firmly. 'You might be a flipping brilliant therapist, but you're missing what's under your nose. He's a rat – and you don't need him. As long as he hangs around, there isn't space in your life for anything better. Tell him to fuck off and if he doesn't, call the police.'

Sasha blinks at me. 'You're so right. I'm pathetic, aren't I?' Right on cue, her phone vibrates. After clicking on the message, she looks at me. 'It's him again – this is what he does. All the time.'

'Well, not any more. Tell him. Now.'

After typing a response, Sasha shows it to me.

This is over. If you get in touch or try to see me again, I'll call the police. And your wife.

'Good.' I watch her send it. 'Now block him.'

She looks startled. 'Why didn't I think of that?' Sending it and blocking his number, she puts her phone down. 'I feel better already. Now about this walk... If I start training, what do you think about me joining you?'

'I haven't imagined anything other than doing it alone. But you need it, just as much as I do. I'd love you to come with me!' As I look at my sister, I feel a jolt of something akin to excitement. 'I've got it all planned. We can get the ferry to northern Spain, then a train to where we start from.'

She looks uncertain. 'A ferry? Do you have any idea what the Bay of Biscay can be like?'

'It has to be better than flying,' I say firmly.

Sasha doesn't look convinced. 'I doubt that very much.'

'Please don't even think of changing my mind. You know flying absolutely terrifies me.' I change the subject. 'Are you going to the hospital later?'

'This afternoon.' Sasha rolls her eyes. 'I need to go to the shops first. Mum wants me to pick up more wool. She's utterly obsessed.'

'She was the same with the wedding,' I say quietly, remembering.

* * *

After Sasha goes, I find my jacket and pull on my trainers before driving to one of the beaches that Liam and I loved. It's an hour away, along narrow country roads through a landscape where the first signs of autumn are showing in the turning of the leaves, the newly ploughed stubble fields, before I take the flint track that leads down to the car park.

Getting out, I breathe in the salty freshness, remembering the first time Liam and I came here. It was a cold winter day, the light giving the beach a magical quality so that the water sparkled, the sand seeming almost to glow. It's a memory we later immortalised in a part of our garden, in a piece of driftwood bleached almost white surrounded by stones and shells from the beach. The air was crisp that day, stinging our cheeks, and as we walked, we collected a whole range of sea treasures, revelling in having the whole place to ourselves.

Today the water is green, swirling with an energy that feels amplified by the breeze. But as I stand here, it isn't the same any more. Gazing out to sea, I realise why it can never be the same. The magic Liam and I found was only partly about this place. It was more about what existed between the two of us.

* * *

On Sunday evening, when Rita comes over, she arrives carrying wine and takeaway pizzas.

'I'm famished,' she says. 'The hospital canteen had virtually nothing in it.'

'Are they OK?' I'm referring to our parents.

'Mum's up to her ears in wool.' Rita pauses for a moment. 'And Dad...' Her eyes fill with tears.

Going over, I hug her. 'He's going to be OK,' I say gently.

'I know.' She wipes her eyes. 'It just got me thinking about *what if he wasn't?* I can't imagine him not being around.' Her voice wobbles.

'Hey, you don't have to.' I pass her a box of tissues. 'I know – it's been really scary, for all of us. But he's on the up.'

'Sorry.' She blows her nose. 'I suppose it's not a great time right now.'

Alarm bells start ringing. Not Rita too? 'Your student?'

She nods. 'Can we open the wine? I could murder a glass.'

Over pizza and wine, she tells me what's happened. 'We'd just spent a Saturday night together. He got up quite early, which was unusual. I asked him where he was going. He told me he had a date. I was shocked – wouldn't anyone have been?'

'Absolutely,' I say strongly. 'Shocking of him.'

'You haven't heard the best of it.' Rita pours another glass of wine. 'He laughed. He said our relationship was just sex and that I was too old for him. Of course, we could still shag, as long as I understood he was seeing this other girl.'

'Fucking bastard,' I say furiously. 'I hope you told him where to go.'

'I told him no way. Then I asked him to leave.' She hesitates. 'The thing is, I know this girl he's seeing. She's beautiful and smart – and young...' Her voice wavers.

'Oh, Rita.' I say. 'You're beautiful and smart. And...' Pausing, I frown. 'Ages ago, you said it was just sex between you.'

'I know I did.' Rita's cheeks redden. 'But it was more, Cal. I didn't want to, but I fell in love with him.'

'Oh...' My heart twists in anguish for my sister. 'Oh, that's so sad.' A thought comes to me. 'You're not going to... just shag him, as he put it?' When she doesn't speak, I stare at her. 'You are?'

'I did,' she says miserably. 'Just the once. Please tell me how ridiculous I am.'

'You're not ridiculous,' I say softly. 'You're wonderful and lovely, and you deserve someone who can see that. Anyone else just isn't worthy of you.' I pause. 'The Ancient Greeks must have had something to say about such things.'

A smile flickers briefly on her lips.

Throw moderation to the winds, and the greatest pleasures bring the greatest pains.

That's Democritus. I think we've both seen how that works.'

'It's so true, isn't it?' I'm silent for a moment. 'How loving uninhibitedly can cause so much pain?'

Rita goes on. 'There's another one I like to think of as slightly more optimistic.'

I nod. 'Optimistic is good.'

It's not what happens to you, but how you react to it that matters.

'That's from Epictetus'

I'm quiet, thinking. 'Quite wise, weren't they?'

'It's what I love about them.' Rita's eyes light up. 'The Greek philosophers knew so much. And it's still relevant. They understood how it's our own toxic beliefs that cause us to suffer, but also that we have the power to change them.' She sounds more positive. 'So I have to change my thoughts – and I have to look forward.'

But she's missing something. 'Sometimes I think we dwell too much on the future. I mean, what happens is often completely unexpected.'

'Go on.' Rita listens intently.

'Well, there isn't a lot of point in living in the past. It's been and gone. You can't get it back.' I pause, frowning slightly. 'And we both know I'm not much good at planning.' Suddenly it comes to me. 'Maybe what we all should do a little bit more of is live *now*, in the moment.'

18

NATHAN

On Monday morning, I get up to find Callie's car parked outside. Through the kitchen window, I watch her work, focussed and methodical, oblivious to everything else. Making her a cup of tea, I take it out to her.

'Hi.' Her eyes light up. 'Is this for me?' She takes the mug. 'Thanks.'

'How was your weekend?'

'It was good. I went to a Graveyard Groupies meeting – and two of my sisters came over. In fact, Rita's only just left – she stayed last night. My mother...' Frowning, she shakes her head. 'It's not worth explaining. But my father's coming home today.'

'Graveyard Groupies? Sounds gothic.' I wonder what she isn't saying about her mother. 'But that's really great news about your father.'

'It is. We've all been so worried. Oh – and the Graveyard Groupies... we're just a few women who have lost someone. I know it sounds morbid but it wasn't. It was nice, actually. Some of them have really been through it.' She changes the subject. 'Have you got any further with your plans for your land?'

'Kind of. But I've been having a bit of a rethink – largely thanks to you.'

'Oh.' She looks anxious. 'Is that a good thing?'

'I think so – good for my conscience, at least. I'm quite sold on this campsite idea. The next stage is planning.' I hesitate. 'I have a couple of ideas I'm hoping will work for the local community, too.' I pause again. 'But you do know, don't you, that if I'm going to do this, I'll need your help.'

She looks surprised. 'I'll help with the planting – if you like.'

'Not just that.' I look at her. 'I was going to ask you to help me list all the eco-credentials that the site would have – including a café. And this time, I want to pay you.'

She's silent for a moment before she replies. 'OK.'

Having prepared myself for her reluctance, her answer takes me by surprise. 'You're sure? I mean, that's great. I just wasn't sure you'd want the commitment.'

She smiles. 'Someone needs to keep you – I mean the project – on track. It may as well be me. You might regret it, though. I am a purist – and you should probably know there's an obsessive streak in my family.'

I study her closely. In the days since I've last seen her, something seems to have changed. She seems lighter, more free.

'Thanks for the tea.' She passes the mug back. 'I thought I'd start pulling up the grass that's grown over the brickwork – under the tree.'

'Before you do, could we make some notes about eco-credentials?'

'Sure.' Pulling off her gardening gloves, she walks beside me towards the house.

We sit at the kitchen table. 'I was thinking with the café,' I say, 'about it being zero plastic. I know it's a commitment, but it would prove it's possible. I want to keep chickens there and grow vegetables – there's more than enough room.'

Callie listens intently. 'You could focus on seasonal veg – and you could consider serving mostly home-grown food,' she added. 'Maybe bring in bread from a local bakery, and employ local staff and tradespeople? You could also look into upcycling furniture for the tents.'

Her enthusiasm is infectious. 'This is exactly what I need. Keep going.'

'Composting loos, natural fabrics, wood burners...' She stops. 'Are you going for the giant tepee?'

'I haven't decided.' I'm still weighing up whether the cost is worth it or not. 'I've had another idea, too, because I want someone on site to run everything. So I'm thinking of building a small house – an eco-friendly, one,' I add hastily. 'And whoever I employ will be a local person. I have a friend who's an architect. He's already agreed to draw up a detailed plan. I should also talk to the neighbours.'

'I really like the sound of that.' she says.

'This is great,' I say softly. I put down my pen. 'I hope you don't mind me saying this, but you seem... I'm not sure how to put it.'

Her cheeks flush slightly. 'Different? I feel it – like I'm taking all these little steps forward. Facing my fears – some of them, at least. Why don't you sketch your plan and show me what you're thinking?' She stands up. 'If you're not doing anything tonight, would you like to come for dinner?'

She goes back outside, leaving me sitting there, utterly confused. Far from taking little steps, it seems that Callie's taken a gigantic leap. I'm not going to crowd her. I'm going to let things take their course, but maybe there is hope that we could be more than friends – one day.

* * *

That evening, I pick out a nice bottle of wine and, armed with the sketch I've been working on, set off for Callie's house. When I pull up outside, the door is open, the sound of music coming from inside.

I knock. 'Hello?'

'Hi! Come in.' She's wearing a calf-length dress, her hair clipped back so that some strands have escaped. She takes the bottle of wine I'm holding out. 'This looks nice.'

'I hope so. I've brought the sketch, too.'

'I'll just pour us drinks.' As she goes to the fridge, I glance around the kitchen. Evening sunlight beams through the open window, while from state of the worktops, it's clear she's been busy cooking. She shows me a bottle. 'Will this do? It's quite similar to yours, actually!' She pours the wine into a couple of glasses before passing me one. 'Cheers!'

'Cheers.' I chink my glass against hers.

She sips her wine. 'Can we look at your sketch?'

'Sure.' I follow her over to the table where I unroll it.

Her eyes dart around it, taking it in. 'This is really good – the drawing, I mean.'

'And the plan itself?' I watch her slightly anxiously.

'It works,' she says slowly. 'It's just, if it were mine, I'd probably do it a little differently.'

'Such as?' I'm curious.

She's silent for a moment. 'I have a better idea. Why don't we go down there and I'll show you?'

I frown. 'What – now?'

She shrugs. 'Why not?'

I wonder if her show of spontaneity is another of those little steps forward she's taking. But with no real reason not to, and with the food on hold, we go out to my car.

'I'm really pleased you changed your mind,' Callie says quietly. 'When you were talking about those houses you wanted to build, you sounded like all the other property developers around here, targeting the second home owners, not caring about anything other than making money.'

'That's a little harsh,' I tell her. 'We all have to make a living somehow – and those houses would have been environmentally friendly.'

'This is much better,' she says firmly. 'When I next see my dad, I'll ask him to contact his friend. Hopefully you can meet up with him.'

'That would be great.' I turn off the main road into the lane.

'I really love it here,' Callie gazes out at the passing landscape. 'It's like you have the best of the Cornish countryside, with the river and the sea and the cycle path.'

'I just hope it gets approved.' Reaching the gateway, I pull over.

Getting out of the car, I open the gate and follow Callie into the field. 'OK. Tell me what you're thinking.'

As she turns around, her eyes are sparkling. 'I would build your café here.' She gestures to the nearest part of the land. 'It's more accessible and would mean less impact on the grassland. You'll need a car park, obviously. I'd probably screen it from the rest of the site with fruit trees and maybe mixed hedging, with a path through the middle.' As she starts walking, she indicates to the left. 'Then here, I'd plant your vegetable garden on this side where it's more open, and build your chicken run on the other – it's more sheltered.'

Turning, I take in the line of trees. 'Noted.'

'Beyond that...' She walks a little further. 'This is your campsite.'

I smile. 'I was imagining each tent in its own little plot, around which we – or you – would plant grasses and herbs. Then the rest would be left as a wildflower meadow, with paths mown through it, just like you suggested for my garden.' The thing is, I can already imagine it, a haven with glorious views and minimal impact on the environment.

Callie's eyes are shining. 'You're right. That's exactly how it should be.' She's quiet for a moment. 'Listen.'

As the breeze ripples through the long grasses, I stand beside her, mesmerised. I've never seen this place at this time of day. Suffused in low sunlight, the field seems to sparkle, the wings from a dragonfly glittering gold as it flits past us, while the only sound is an orchestra of insects. Suddenly I get everything she's been talking about.

'Magical, isn't it?' Her voice sounds distant. 'There's all this life here, all around us.'

Transfixed, I watch some tiny, iridescent moths hover above the grasses. 'I understand,' I say quietly.

* * *

Back at Callie's, while she effortlessly puts together a tortilla, I wander out to her garden. There's a chill in the air, the colours there beginning to turn to autumn's rich shades.

Reaching an empty part of the flower bed, I can't help frowning. When every other corner is crammed with planting, it seems incongruous. At that moment, she comes to join me.

'Another project?' I ask.

'Ah.' She looks hesitant. 'The idea was that when we came back from our honeymoon, we were going to plant it with memories of the walk in northern Spain. I suppose if I'm honest, the emptiness has felt symbolic, but that's going to change. I've decided I'm doing the walk early next year. My sister, Sasha, is coming with me.'

'Wow.' But I'm starting to understand how a garden reflects the person who cares for it. Right now, this patch represents loss and grief to Callie, but that she's already planning to remedy that speaks volumes. 'Then after, when you plant it, your garden will be full.'

'Something like that.' Her voice is husky all of a sudden. 'Are you hungry?' As she gazes at me, something flickers in her eyes.

Lightly stroking back a lock of hair that's fallen across her face, I fight the urge to kiss her. Instead, I nod. 'Shall we go inside?'

* * *

Callie produces a loaf of bread she baked earlier, and we sit at her table. She serves up the tortilla with a crisp green salad. As I eat, I become aware of her eyes on me.

'I've talked a lot about me,' she says shyly. 'But you haven't told me much about you.'

I put down my fork. 'What do you want to know?'

'I suppose I'm curious.' She gazes at me intently. 'About who you used to be – before I met you.'

Generally I like her candour, her way of getting to the point, but suddenly I feel under scrutiny. 'Well, for quite a few years, I lived in London. I used to buy up potential sites and build houses. Then when I wasn't working, I used to have rowdy nights out with friends, or long holidays in exotic places.' I fold my arms. 'And yes, I suppose I was all about making money. But as you know, that's changed.'

'Can I ask why?' she says quietly.

I pause. 'I had a health scare. Let's just say it made me rethink almost everything – about how I want to live and what's impor-tant... I hit the rowdy nights out on the head and opted for a quieter, simpler life.' It's a simplification but that's the essence of it.

'No regrets?'

'None whatsoever.' I wait for the question I know is coming.

'You said you had a health scare...' she says tentatively. 'What happened?'

'It's a long story. I have a heart condition – quite a rare one. For years, I was completely unaware, but once it was diagnosed, I didn't know how long I might have. Everything changed.'

Callie looks shocked. 'I can't imagine how scary that must have been.'

'It was.' Our eyes meet. 'I'm OK now, though I still have to go for check-ups.'

'I'm really glad you're OK.' She reaches out to touch my arm. 'So that's the reason you've decided to change your life?'

'Yes.' It's more than I'm comfortable saying to most people; I change the subject. 'This food is great – exactly the kind of thing we could serve in the café.'

* * *

As I get in my car, I'm no less confused. There have been too many moments where our eyes meet, where we understand each other in a way that feels instinctive. Yet for some reason I've been holding back; I gave her the abridged version when she asked about my illness – probably because it brings back too many difficult memories. Then when I left, I kissed her on the cheek before walking outside; a kiss I'd wanted to be so much more.

Driving home, several times I think about turning around and going back. I want to tell her I won't hurt her, that I've never felt this way about anyone else. I want to hold her in my arms, to gaze into her beautiful eyes, to kiss away her sadness; I want to remind her how magical life could be, how wonderful it could be to share it with someone.

But something tells me the time isn't right. And I'm still coming to terms with the health scare I've had. Maybe after Callie has done this walk, after she's planted the last empty corner of her garden, she'll be ready to move on. But while she's still working out whatever it is she's working out, all I can do is give her however long it takes.

19

CALLIE

After Nathan leaves, I pull on a jumper, before pouring another glass of wine and taking it outside. After sunset, my garden becomes a magical place for night creatures, and I watch a moth, its delicate wings perfectly camouflaged as it comes to rest on a tree; little bats that flit about silently.

Sitting there, as I think back over the last year, I conjure a memory of the day I should have married Liam, as vividly as if it happened yesterday. Yet at the same time, it feels a long time ago.

I listen to the hoot of a distant owl as Tanith's words come back to me: *no one's that perfect.* As I said to her, I'm a bit of a rose-tinted-glasses person. But there's something I've never told her or anyone else.

Under this night sky that's brilliant with myriad dazzling stars, my mind wanders back to a week before the wedding. The minute Liam walked in, I knew something was very wrong. As he looked at me, I felt cold all of a sudden.

I don't know if I can do this, Cal.

Do what? I remember the shockwave that hit me. Our wedding was just days away, everything booked and paid for by my parents. Unable to believe he was doing this, I asked him why.

It's so final. He couldn't meet my eyes. *It's a big step, marriage. And...* When he hedged, I knew there was more he wasn't saying. *I know you want kids. And I've gone along with the idea – I didn't want to upset you. But if I'm really honest, I'm not sure...*

Shock after shock had kept coming at me. Whenever we'd talked about having a family, Liam seemed to love the idea. But clearly, he hadn't been straight with me. This man I loved with all my heart, who I believed was my once-in-a-lifetime love, was threatening everything I held precious. I had to know. *Why now?*

If not now, it'll be too late. He sighed. *Untangling a marriage is so complicated.*

I remember staring at him, feeling nauseous. We weren't even married and he was talking about divorce. Panic-stricken, I asked him if he'd met someone else. His pause told me everything.

We talked, that's all. Nothing happened, Callie. I swear I would never do that to you. But it got me thinking: what if we get married – if we're not right for each other? If one of us meets someone else?

I told him that if we loved each other, we'd weather our storms, build a future together. But if he wasn't sure how he felt... When he stood there in silence, I asked him to leave.

I never knew where he went that night. Rocked, I lay awake in bed gazing into the darkness, even after my tears stopped, unable to sleep. The following morning, I got up early, taking a cup of tea out into the garden. Looking around, I took in all the flowers and herbs I'd grown, timed perfectly to reach their peak for the wedding – except now, it didn't look like there was going to be one.

Unable to face telling anyone, I sat there all morning, imagining dismantling our lives, splitting everything in this house; in the cold light of day wondering what the future held, until just after midday,

I heard a car outside before the kitchen door was opened. When Liam came outside to find me, he looked terrible.

I'm so sorry, Callie. I honestly don't know what happened to me. Crouching down, he took my hands in his. *I think it was last-minute nerves. I was awake all last night. I couldn't stop thinking how different my life would be without you. I want to marry you, more than anything in the world. I want to have children with you, too... If you can forgive me?*

As I listened, tears filled my eyes, tears of relief. But underneath it, I was shaken. When I'd trusted him enough to marry him, he'd gone back on his word. There was fear, too. He might be over whatever was dogging him last night, but what if six weeks, six months, six years down the line, it happened again?

For the rest of that day, we talked, honestly, about our feelings, our desires for the future in a way we should have long before we'd decided to get married. But the truth was I'd been too naïve, too swept away by the romance of it all to think beyond that.

That evening, we went for a walk on the beach. There on the sand, for the second time, Liam had traced the letters in the sand before going down on one knee.

Please, Callie, marry me...

Knowing in my heart it was what I wanted, too, there was only one thing I could say. Over the next few days, I mentioned our blip to no one, telling myself that it was better we'd cleared the air, got things out in the open. Maybe we were even stronger for it. I asked nothing more about the woman he'd met, just threw myself wholeheartedly into the final days of planning before our wedding.

The honest truth is that things between Liam and me were far from perfect. But no relationships are perfect; nor is it realistic to expect them to be. I loved Liam the only way I knew – unconditionally.

Suddenly I realise how much stronger I've become, because if it happened again, I'd postpone the wedding until we were sure. And if we weren't, I would believe there would be something, someone better for me. The girl I am now wouldn't want to be with anyone who had doubts.

Maybe it explains why my grief has been so intense. Having come close to losing Liam a week before the wedding, my emotions were already on a knife-edge. On our wedding day, when I found out he wasn't at the church, I genuinely believed he'd changed his mind. I'd been beside myself. Then after I found out he was dead, I fell apart.

But as I gaze up at the night sky, I realise it isn't wrong to want to live, to love, to be happy again; it isn't wrong to start again, with something sweet and new. Fighting the urge to call Nathan, I want to tell him I do like him, that I don't mean to be confusing. That yes, right now, I am scared, but it won't always be that way.

* * *

The following morning, I feel lighter as I get up early and set off for Nathan's house. When I get there, to my surprise, he's up and about earlier than usual, sitting on his terrace drinking coffee. Getting out of my car, I wave to him.

'Hi!' I call out.

'Morning! Tea?'

'Please.' As he disappears inside, I finish getting my things out of my car before going to join him. As I reach the terrace, he comes back outside.

He passes me a mug. 'Thanks for last night.'

'You're welcome. It was nice.' I pause. 'You're up early.'

'I've been up since five. I've been sketching what we talked about. Can I show you?'

He goes back inside and returns carrying a massive sketch pad.

Sitting down and opening it, he looks slightly anxiously at me. 'What do you think?'

He's drawn everything that we talked about, with the addition of a large outside kitchen in the camping part of the site, and solar panels, too. As I study it, I'm blown away. 'This is awesome,' I say quietly, as our eyes meet, lingering for a moment before he glances away.

'Thank you. I hoped you'd like it. I'm going over to see my friend tonight – the one who's an architect.' He gets up. 'Meanwhile, I'm going to finish putting costs together. If he's happy with it, I'm pretty close to applying for planning.'

I open my mouth and close it again. 'Wow. You get things done, don't you?'

He looks surprised. 'Best way.'

'I can give you some links to websites about plants, if you like? It would help you cost that side of things, too.'

'That would be great.' He glances around, before picking up a notebook. 'I'll add that to my list.' He pauses. 'You mentioned weddings... Do you know of any outdoor venues around here?'

I shake my head. 'Not really – it's why I think it would work. The only downside would be the increase in traffic, but you could keep the weddings small - or lay on a bus and get around that.' I look at him. 'You're going for the giant tepee?'

He nods. 'I think I'd be mad not to. It will make the site so much more versatile.'

I feel a flicker of excitement. 'I don't think you'll regret it.' Suddenly I remember. 'I'm going to see my parents later. I'll talk to Dad about his friend at the council.'

'That would be great.' He glances at his watch. 'I should get on. I have a phone meeting about to start. Catch you later?'

'Sure. Thanks for the tea.' I watch him go inside, slightly disappointed.

I finish pruning a lilac tree, oblivious to the clouds gathering overhead, my mind wandering back again to the week before my wedding; how Liam's last-minute nerves had left me walking on eggshells; the way my smile had been brighter, so that no one would know how on edge I was. But I'd tried to understand before forgiving him, because I knew in my heart I loved him.

* * *

Three hours pass before the rain starts. Gathering up my things, I head towards the house to tell Nathan I'm leaving, but when I see him through the window talking on his phone, I wave at him before hurrying to my car.

As I drive home, the cloud gradually lowers, the rain coming in sheets as the weather sets in. Not sure I want to spend the rest of the day alone, when I get home, I text Tanith.

You free tonight? x

When she doesn't reply, after changing into some clean clothes, I drive over to see my parents. Pottering in his workshop, my father looks much more like his old self.

When he sees me, his face lights up. 'Callie! What a nice surprise!'

In one of his old sweaters, he seems content to be in his own world. Going over, I hug him. 'Hi, Dad. How's it going?'

'Pretty good, really, sweetheart. Can't complain. Could do without this rain, though.' He looks perplexed. 'Your mother wants me to make a box for her to keep all her wool in.' He shakes his head. 'I expect by the time I've done it, she'll be on to the next thing. But she was quite insistent.'

'Hmm. Sounds like Mum.' I watch him measure up a piece of wood. 'But don't take on too much, will you? How are you feeling?'

'Not bad at all. I think they've sorted me out. Of course, your sister's on my case, about diet and exercise.'

Alice has been great, coming down by train from London whenever she can. I can just imagine her laying it on the line.

'I hope you're listening to her. She knows what she's talking about.' I pause. 'Actually, I wanted to ask you a favour.'

'Yes?' He looks up.

'A friend of mine has bought some land. He wants to develop it. His original plan was to build high-end eco-houses, but he now wants to build an eco-friendly campsite and café – low impact, zero plastic, etc. I wondered if there was any chance you could ask Nick if he could spare half an hour – just to run ideas past him, and get some advice, really.'

'I'm sure he'd find the time. So who's this friend?' My dad raises an eyebrow.

'He is just a friend.' I feel my cheeks flush. 'His name is Nathan. If I give you his mobile number, could you pass it on to Nick?'

He looks amused. 'Of course I can.' He pauses for a moment. 'So, this chap Nathan... Just a friend of yours?' His eyes twinkle.

'He is.' I sigh. 'He's really nice – and I do like him. It just feels too soon after Liam...' I tail off.

'Only you know the answer to that,' he says gently. 'But you'll know when the time is right.'

'Sometimes I think it never will be.' It bursts out of me. 'When Liam's gone, it doesn't feel right to think about being with someone else.'

My dad is quiet for a moment. 'It's probably one of the hardest parts about moving on, isn't it? The guilt?'

'Yes.' Tears prick my eyes.

'But Liam wouldn't want you to be alone. You know that, don't you? He'd want you to have a happy, fulfilled life... To have a family.' He pauses. 'There will come a time when you meet someone else – who's more than a friend – at least, I hope you will. Maybe it's this Nathan – or maybe it will be someone else. But when you do, it will be OK.'

'I know. I'm figuring it out.' Swallowing the lump in my throat, I hug him. 'Thanks.' Getting out my phone, I send him Nathan's number. 'OK. You have his number. I'll let him know.'

While I have a cup of tea with my mother, my phone pings with a text from Tanith.

I so need to escape! Pleeeeease! There's a pub near mine, The White Horse. See you at 6? xx

Texting back that I'll meet her there, when I look up, my mother is watching me.

'How much longer are you going to stay in that house?'

I'm astonished. It's the first I've heard that she has an opinion on my house. 'I've no idea. Why?'

She shakes her head. 'I just don't think it's healthy, a young woman spending all that time on her own.'

'I'm fine there. It's my home. And actually, I have quite a busy life just now. I have friends, Mum. I'm not alone all the time.'

'Well, I suppose that's something.' But she sounds disgruntled. There's obviously something on her mind. 'What are you trying to say?'

'I suppose I was wondering if you'd thought about going to live with one of your sisters – just for a while. It might help you to get your life back on track – and you'd see a bit of the city. Get away from all those memories.'

'Oh no,' I say firmly. 'Incidentally, was this their suggestion or yours?'

'All of us, really.' She at least has the grace to look slightly awkward.

'So you've all been discussing me?' I sit back. 'Look, I know you mean well. But I'm perfectly happy where I am.'

My mother is silent for a moment. 'The thing is... Don't you want a home of your own? And a job? I know you have the book-shop, but wouldn't you like something a little more challenging? You know what it's like around here. Nothing happens.'

'As it happens, I have been offered another job,' I say loftily. 'Quite an interesting one. I'll tell you more about it once it's confirmed.'

* * *

'They all gossip about me,' I tell Tanith when I get to the pub. 'Not in a horrible way, because they care – just in a *they know best for me* kind of way.'

She rolls her eyes. 'Tell me about it. Every frigging day, my mother has something to say about the boys. I'm either too strict or too soft, I feed them the wrong food, I let them watch too much TV...'

'If I win the lottery, I'll buy you a house,' I reassure her.

'Thanks, Cal. But that's not bloody likely though, is it?' She glances towards the bar. 'Shall I get us another?'

When she comes back, I have an idea to run past her. 'Early next year, I'm going away for a while. If you want, you can house-sit for me.'

'Really?' Her eyes widen. 'Where are you going?'

I tell her about the walk and the reasons I'm going. 'I'll probably be away about five or six weeks. On one condition, though – you'll have to look after the garden.'

'Anything,' she says immediately. 'Six weeks away would be utter bliss.'

'That's sorted, then.' I pause for a moment. 'There's something else, too. You know, I miss Liam. I'll always miss him.' My voice wavers. 'But it really does feel like something's changing – like I'm less stuck, is probably the best way of describing it.'

'That's a good thing, isn't it?' Tanith sounds sympathetic. 'If you're slaying the demon that guilt is?'

'Weird, isn't it? You get so used to living with guilt, that when it starts to fade, you feel guilty about that, too.'

'It's a pointless emotion,' Tanith says sternly. 'But I think you've worked it out. It isn't wrong to want to live. Just a bloody shame it takes us such a long time to get there. But love makes fools of us,' she says savagely. 'Complete bloody useless, simpering fools. God, I hated myself when I lost my husband.'

'That day...' I think of the day Liam died. 'It was a coinciding of so many variables that meant the crash happened. I've thought so many times that if Liam had left the house earlier – or later, or if the other car had been driving just a little slower, or even if we hadn't been getting married.' I gaze at Tanith. 'If any one of those things had been different, Liam would probably still be alive.'

'You can't think like that.' Tanith shakes her head. 'I mean, given the traffic, pollution, the crap we put into our bodies, it's more of a miracle that any of us survive. If his time was up, it would have happened one way or another.'

I stare at her as though she's mad. 'Tanith. We're talking about an accident.'

'I know.' Picking up her glass, she sips her wine. 'But think about the bigger picture for a moment. Our lives are everything to each one of us. But in the context of the timeline of the planet... Unless we do something remarkable, we don't make any significant difference to anything – at least, most of us don't.' She shrugs. 'Our lives are soon forgotten about.'

I frown. 'That's a little bleak. Don't you like your life?'

Tanith pauses. 'Of course I do. I bloody love it. I love my kids even more. But if you believe – as I do – that before we come to earth, we choose our lives, beyond the day-to-day stuff, it's about experiencing what needs to happen in order for us to fulfil what we came here for. I don't know – but maybe Liam had achieved what he'd set out to.'

But she's got it wrong. 'Liam had plans. He wasn't done. It's just so sad he ran out of time.'

She frowns. 'In one way, of course it is. There's another possibility.' Tanith looks at me.

'What's that?'

'He gave you what you needed,' she says quietly. 'Because of him, you know what love is. And I know it's been really tough, but losing him and everything else that's happened this last year, has made you the person who you are now.'

But it's too much for me. 'That's fine if you believe that we live a number of lifetimes. Personally, I don't. We're born, we live, we die. That's it. There isn't anything else after that.'

Tanith looks outraged. 'Now who's being bleak?'

I stand my ground. 'Actually, I'm being a realist. Do you have any idea how many times I've sat at Liam's grave and asked for a sign?'

Tanith sounds interested. 'And did you get one?'

'I got nothing,' I say defiantly. 'In well over a year, not a single thing. That's how I know how final death is.'

'What were you hoping for, exactly?'

'I don't know.' I'm cagey. 'The sound of his voice, an image or something. Anything really.'

'Like a religious vision of our lady in Lourdes, you mean,' she says sarcastically. 'For what it's worth, I don't think it happens like that.' She pauses. 'Maybe your head is too full of other stuff and you need to tune out the noise of this world. When I want to, I find somewhere wild. I close my eyes and listen to the birds, or the wind in the trees. I feel connected. I can't explain it any other way. It takes me way out of my tiny little bubble of a world.' She flicks her hair back. 'We should all do it. We're just too bloody busy rushing through our days to make time.' She goes on. 'This last year has really shaken up your life. And now there's this new guy – and incidentally, if you find love twice, you're far luckier than most of us.' She shrugs. 'Call it coincidence, if you like. But there's clearly a synchronicity in the way things are turning out.'

I look at her, baffled. Yes, I can see how different I am. 'You're not suggesting there was a point to Liam dying?'

Tanith looks horrified. 'Of course I'm not. All I'm saying is sometimes things happen that are out of our control. And they change the choices we make going forwards.'

20

NATHAN

'I spoke to my dad yesterday,' Callie says the next morning when she turns up at mine. 'He's going to ask his friend to call you – his name is Nick.'

Since we've been starting to pull ideas together for this camping project, so far it seems to be happening seamlessly.

'Thanks for doing that – and please pass on my thanks to him.'

She nods. 'I will. Right. I'm going to finish pulling up that grass.' Sounding purposeful, she points to the area of partly exposed brickwork that she's suggested should become a seating area.

'I have half an hour before I need to start work. I'll help you.'

The satisfaction of the feel of damp earth on my hands is becoming familiar, as is the way the grass comes away in tufts, exposing the old bricks beneath that are another part of this house's history. There's something about being with Callie, too: her quiet resolve, her calmness.

'You're enjoying this, aren't you?' Her eyes twinkle as she looks at me.

'I never thought I'd say this, but I am.' Sitting back on my heels, I hold up my hands. 'The old me wouldn't have contemplated doing anything like this. But something about it feels therapeutic.'

'Sounds like it's working,' she says mysteriously.

'What is?' I gaze at her blankly.

'You thinking less about the future, and being more in the here and now.'

'Some of the time, maybe.' I smile at her. 'I have to admit, though, there are normally far too many things rushing through my head.'

Coming over, she sits on the grass next to me. 'Close your eyes.'

Frowning slightly, I do what she says.

She goes on. 'OK. Take a deep breath, and hold it for a few seconds. Then very slowly, let it out.' She pauses. 'Keep doing it.' A minute or so later, she says, 'Let yourself listen to the sounds around you – the breeze, the birdsong and whatever else comes to you. Think about how many scents there are in each breath of air.'

As she talks, I feel my mind empty and a sense of calm come over me, as I forget about everything else except being here with Callie.

'You can open your eyes,' she says softly.

I open them to find her watching me curiously.

'How do you feel?'

'Quiet. Deeply peaceful.'

'Good.' She nods. 'That's what I mean about being in the moment.'

Aware of the time passing, I stand up, stretching. 'It's the last thing I feel like doing right now, but I really should work.'

'You should do this more often,' Callie says quietly. 'Just sit and be peaceful.'

'I will,' I promise. 'This is looking so much better.' I glance at the newly revealed bricks.

'Cool, aren't they? Next year, you could sprinkle some seeds into the gaps in between them,' she says. 'I'll tell you what to buy – you only want tiny things, like daisies, or miniature herbs... Plants that will smell nice – as well as look pretty.'

'Are you doing anything later? Or would you like to go out – maybe for dinner?' I watch something – regret, maybe – flicker in her eyes.

'I can't tonight – I have plans.'

Given she's hidden herself away for a year, I'm curious. 'The Graveyard Groupies again?'

'Not this time – though I saw Tanith last night.' Callie frowns slightly. 'She said something that made me think.'

I look at her quizzically. 'Oh?'

She shakes her head. 'I'm thinking out loud, really. We talked about loads of things – but one thing she said was how most people's lives aren't important because they don't do anything significant with them.'

'What?' I look at her incredulously. 'Isn't it enough to be there for the people you love?'

'I think she meant on a more global scale,' Callie says vaguely. 'I mean, she sort of has a point.'

'Yeah, but it's not like we're all born an Einstein or an Aristotle or a Shakespeare. Most of us lesser mortals are destined to live much quieter, humbler lives.'

'It got me thinking, though,' she persists. 'We all have innate potential and creativity. So what makes the Einsteins of the world different? It can only be that for some reason, they constantly pursue more. They must think in a different way, really use their time. But most of us aren't driven that way.'

'I agree with you on that.' When I was ill, it had amazed me how easy it was to let hours drift by.

She frowns. 'Anyway, after talking to Tanith last night, I didn't sleep for ages. So I started reading about creativity. I've always linked it to books and art and architecture – gardens, even. But it's more than that, isn't it? It's about a way of thinking.'

I'm getting left behind. 'So why don't we all use this creativity we have?'

She shrugs. 'Habit? And because we're so used to being told what we should do, we never question it.' She stops. 'A bit like you – doing what everyone else around here does, building more high-end eco-houses for second home owners.'

'Until I stopped and thought about it,' I say quietly. 'Thanks to you.'

'But you have thought about it.' Her eyes meet mine. 'I haven't – not really; not until now. I mean, look at me. I have a part-time job in a bookshop, a garden I love, but that's about it. Meanwhile my sisters all have amazing careers...'

'We're not all cut out to be cardiologists or therapists. And you've been through a tough year,' I remind her. 'It might not be the best time to make far-reaching decisions.'

'Maybe not. I just feel like I'm re-evaluating things.'

'Because you've lost someone,' I say quietly. But I understand how an upheaval in your life can make you re-examine all kinds of things.

'Probably.' She's silent for a moment. 'The thing is, I've always loved my simple life. I still do – and it used to be enough. But now, I'm not so sure.'

* * *

She doesn't tell me if there's anything in particular she's considering, but it's clear she's having a rethink. I see it as another sign that she's working through her grief, imagining what to do with the rest of her life. And that's how it goes, I contemplate, as I sit at my desk. We go through our lives in our own slightly blink-

ered way, until something happens that challenges the way we
think, as Callie has me – though I still have to find a way of building
a campsite that will benefit the lives of local people.

After speaking to Callie's father's friend and fixing a time to
meet for lunch tomorrow, I drive over to Robin's.

'I haven't seen you in ages.' She looks mildly disapproving as
she hugs me.

'I've had quite a lot going on,' I say vaguely.

'The housing project?' She raises an eyebrow. 'How's it going?'

'I've had a change of plan. A major change, as it turns out.'

'Tell me.' Robin's eyes are on me. 'Oh – but first a drink. Tea,
coffee, beer?'

'A beer would be great.'

Going to the fridge, she gets out two bottles and hands one of
them to me. 'Cheers, big brother. Now, tell me all about it. I'm
assuming you've been talked out of it by the eco-warrior gardener
you don't pay?'

'Kind of...' I hesitate, not sure where to start. 'It's just that she
has all these ideas and it got me thinking. She was completely right
about how building houses would ruin acres of land. We went over
there a few evenings ago. It was alive, Rob – with insects, moths,
birds and goodness knows what else. Places like that should be
preserved, not dug up for stupidly priced houses.'

Robin looks perplexed. 'This girl... She's really got to you, hasn't
she?'

'Before you say anything else, there's nothing going on,' I say
firmly. 'We're friends – good friends – but that's all.'

'Fine. OK.' Robin backs off. 'I believe you, by the way! But I must
admit, it would be nice to see you happy with someone.'

'Everything is fine as it is,' I tell her.

'So go on telling me about your project.'

'It started out as a campsite with a café. The idea was to produce our own eggs and grow vegetables – there's a lot of land. Each pitch will be set in its own garden. The rest of the land will be left as wildflower meadow.'

'It sounds amazing. But is it going to make you enough money?' Robin sounds doubtful.

'I'm still working on that. I'm thinking of investing in a huge tepee. That way, we could offer eco-friendly weddings. It could also serve as a centre for community events.'

'How likely are you to get planning?'

'There's a good chance.' I tell her about the conversation I had with Nick. 'I'm having lunch with him tomorrow. I want to focus on the eco-credentials and the community angle. As far as possible, everything would be sourced locally. Employees would be local, all the materials natural...'

Robin frowns. 'It sounds as though you're going to have to spend a lot.'

That's the only downside. 'It'll be a long game – unless I set it up and sell it. But to be honest, that's fine. I can afford to buy myself some down time – and I'm ready for something different.' It's true. I've had enough of chasing suppliers, pinning down costs, working under the pressure of a rapidly dwindling time scale. 'I'm not getting any investors involved. I'd be answerable only to myself.'

She stands there. 'So where does this girl come in?'

'She's going to help me – at least, I hope she is. My plant knowledge is still pretty poor.'

Robin looks resigned. 'Then isn't it time you did something about that?'

I'm not sure what she was getting at. 'Like what?'

'Go on a course – online, even.' She rolls her eyes. 'If you're going to do this, why not learn as much as you can?'

I'm taken aback. As the project manager, I don't need to be an expert. 'I was going to hand that part over.' In the past, I used to

oversee every part of whatever project I was working on. This is
another change I need to make – trusting other people to make
decisions. Ignoring her as she raises her eyebrows at me, I change
the subject. 'How's Max?'

Her smile returns. 'He's good. He's out this evening, meeting up
with an old friend. Do you want to stay for dinner?'

* * *

After discussions with Nick, some days later I get around to
submitting my planning application. Meanwhile, as the blustery
winds and heavy rainfall of autumn set in, I see less and less of
Callie.

'Your garden is preparing for winter,' she tells me one morning.
'The leaves need raking up, but we need to leave the seed heads on
the flowers for the birds.'

Guided by her nature-friendly philosophy, I do as I'm told. 'I
suppose there isn't much to do over the winter.'

'There's less,' she says thoughtfully. 'You still need to keep an
eye on weeds, though. If your veggie garden was up and running,
you could still be planting things.' She shrugs. 'Maybe next year.'

* * *

A Saturday morning arrives, one that's mild, the valleys filled with
mist, the air laced with the scent of bonfires. It's too lovely a day to
spend inside. Pulling on a sweater, I step outside just as Callie's car
pulls up.

She's dressed in a long grey sweater and loose-fitting jeans.
Seeing me, she calls out. 'I've brought you something!'

Coming over, she passes me a paper envelope. 'There are some
seeds in there – and I've had another idea. We could build you a

cold frame, so that you could start things off now to plant next spring.' She pauses briefly. 'I'll help you if you like – if you're not busy?'

Her cheeks are flushed, her eyes alight as they meet mine. She's the first girl I've known who could make building a cold frame sound exciting and I can't help smiling. 'OK!'

We stand there in silence for a moment and I take in the light catching her hair, the hazy blue of the sky, the tang of autumn in the air, realising this is what it's about – being in the moment. 'How about we start with a cup of tea?'

We take our tea out into the garden, and Callie shows me where she thinks we should build the cold frame. 'Last time I was here, I told you there wasn't much to do during winter, but actually, there's loads you can do – like finishing clearing your veggie garden for one thing. But also, it's a really good time to do the invisible stuff – like digging in compost and planting seeds.'

Her enthusiasm injects me with new motivation. 'Do you have time to go shopping?'

* * *

After a couple of hours mooching around a garden centre and buying far more than I'd intended to, we load up the car and drive everything home.

'This is amazing,' Callie says happily as we unload it all. 'I know where I want these to go.' She's talking about the half a dozen pots of what I now know to be hellebores, their delicate petals a dusky pink.

'I'll see what I can do putting this cold frame together.' I carry it over to a sheltered corner near the outbuilding. 'And please, feel free to plant anything wherever you think.'

The cold frame comes together surprisingly easily and by late afternoon, Callie is planting the last of the bulbs as the light starts to fade.

'I love this,' she says quietly. 'Early in the new year, you'll see their shoots start to show. When the soil is so bare and the air so cold, winter flowers always seem miraculous, somehow.' She turns to look at me, her eyes searching mine as she speaks softly. 'I've had the best day. Thank you.'

Coming closer, her arms go around me. Leaning against me, she's still, somehow peaceful in a way that touches my heart, as putting my arms around her, I just hold her.

* * *

As Callie and I slowly grow closer, life feels more settled. I dare to dream – of a different life, one that maybe we could share. But only a couple of weeks later, as November starts, my plans suffer a setback when my planning application is rejected. From everything Nick had led me to believe, because I've included a base that could function for the community, I've been counting on it being approved. I haven't considered it wouldn't be.

Maybe it's simply a case of not knowing the right people – though Nick says it isn't.

'They cite impact on trees and restricting road access,' I say to Callie. 'Plus some local fly in the ointment has described it as a vital wildlife habitat that I'd be damaging.'

'They're trying to protect wildlife – but you are, too. And this is far more wildlife-friendly than a housing development,' she said crossly. 'So fricking frustrating. Some of these people are so small-minded. You should appeal.'

But aware of my stress levels going up, I have to be mindful of how much of a battle I'm prepared to take on. 'I'm going to sit on it for now. I'll talk to Nick again – see if he has any advice.'

It's possible we can redesign the site so that it's further from the trees. I don't tell her that I've been having second thoughts about the project; that maybe building eco-houses would be simpler – they'd be well away from the trees and they'd create far less traffic. Plus it's familiar territory.

That evening, I have a call from a builder I've worked with before – just once. After he missed the brief in one or two ways, we ended up falling out. But he's amicable enough as he goes on to explain he's looking for a piece of land on which to build some housing – maybe a business partner, too. After the call ends, I'm suspicious, though. I can't help thinking he must have been tipped off. The timing is too coincidental.

When I talk to Callie about it, she's angry.

'You can't give up at the first hurdle.' Her eyes flash. 'Anyway, if you didn't get planning for a campsite, what makes you think you'll get it for houses?'

I sigh. 'There would be far less traffic down that narrow lane for one thing. Also...' This is the tough bit. 'There are precedents.' I shrug. 'It's how it works.'

'If you build houses...' She looks mutinous. 'You know how much life you'd be destroying.'

I feel torn. If I'm honest, it feels like a backwards step, one I'm not entirely happy with. 'I haven't made any decisions. And I'm going to appeal the planning decision.'

'Good.' She looks at me. 'Do you remember that conversation we had, about most of us not doing anything meaningful with our lives?' When I nod, she goes on. 'With that piece of land, you have a real chance to prove there's a truly environmentally friendly way to run a business. Wouldn't that be great?'

'Maybe.' I admire her dedication. But now I'm confronted with problems, and knowing the amount of money building the houses will make, it isn't straightforward.

After that conversation, I don't see her for a week. I guess she's busy planning her walk in Spain. But I have a feeling it's about more than that – that having thought I'd changed my mind about building on the land, she feels disappointed in me.

At a routine check-up with my GP, it transpires my blood pressure is up. Given my condition, I know I can't ignore the significance of this. The GP advises me to reduce my stress levels and prescribes some pills. As I walk away I'm uncomfortable. It's all very well Callie having principles, but I have health concerns to consider. If the campsite is going to turn into a battle, it's one I don't need. But it's an opportunity, too, to change the way I've always worked; to maybe do something that's about more than money.

And if I don't take it on – I sigh – I'm not sure Callie will want any more to do with me.

21

CALLIE

As I drive to my parents' house, the rain is unrelenting, the countryside sodden, a reminder of what Cornish winters can be like.

When I turn into their drive, there's an unfamiliar car parked outside. As I go into the kitchen, the dogs don't move from their slumber beside the aga but apart from a half-drunk cup of tea, there's no sign of my parents. Going out into the hallway, I call out.

'Mum? Dad? Are you there?'

My mother appears at the top of the stairs. 'Callie?' She looks surprised to see me. Coming downstairs, she kisses me on the cheek. 'Your father's in bed. He hasn't been feeling so good. The doctor's with him.'

A feeling of fear grips me. 'Is it his heart again?'

My mother hesitates. 'The doctor thinks it might be related. He's been feeling breathless. He's had some oxygen delivered.'

My heart starts to race. So this clearly hasn't just happened. 'Mum, you should have told me. When did this start?'

'Yesterday. And I know I should have called.' She pauses. 'You know what he's like, though. He doesn't like any fuss.'

But as I stare at her, I recognise the classic signs of denial, of wanting an unpalatable truth to be anything other than what it is, because I've been there myself. 'Shouldn't he be back in hospital?' I say quietly.

'Possibly.' Her voice wavers.

Just then, an unfamiliar man comes down the stairs. When my parents have been registered with Doctor Reynolds for years, I'm guessing he's the out-of-hours GP.

'How is he?' I say immediately.

He looks at me. 'You are?'

'This is Callie, our youngest,' my mother introduces me.

The doctor nods. 'He's comfortable. I've tried to persuade him he'd be better off in hospital, but he refuses to go.'

'In that case, I'll talk to him.' Leaving the doctor with my mother, I go upstairs, knocking quietly on the door of my parents' bedroom, before pushing it open. 'Dad?'

'Hello, love.' He tries to sound bright.

But as I take in the lack of colour in his face, alarm bells start going off. Reaching the bed, I kiss him on the cheek. 'What are you up to, Dad? The doctor says you should be in hospital.'

'I know. But I don't want to go.' He looks stubborn. 'I was there for days last time.'

'You needed to be,' I remind him. 'Dad, please, do what the doctor says.'

He shakes his head. 'I don't think so.'

A feeling of frustration takes me over. I understand why he'd rather stay at home, but this is serious. He needs to be properly checked out.

'Listen, Dad, if this is about your heart, you have to go in. You're worrying me.' My eyes well up. 'You're worrying Mum too. This is serious. I don't want to lose anyone else.' Tears start to trickle down my cheeks.

Lying there, he's silent for a moment. Then reaching for my hand, he grips it weakly. 'OK.'

* * *

When I call Alice to let her know, she's relieved.

'Thank goodness you're there. They'll run some tests and see what's going on. I'll call them later and get the lowdown.'

'Thanks, Al. He didn't look good at all.'

'He probably wasn't oxygenated enough.' She pauses. 'Try not to worry. They'll sort him out. I'll let Sasha and Rita know.'

But Alice's words are only mildly reassuring and I can't shake the feeling of fear that hangs over me. I know from what she's said before, that when it comes to hearts, it isn't always possible to fix them.

While we wait for an ambulance to arrive, I help my mother pack a few things for my father to take with him. I offer to drive her, but after the ambulance leaves, she decides to follow in her own car. 'It makes sense. I don't know long I'm going to be there. Oh.' She looks stricken. 'I haven't fed the dogs.'

I touch her arm. 'Don't worry, Mum. I'll do it.'

After she's gone, I go to the kitchen and let the dogs out into the garden. As I wait for them to return, I glance around the room, taking in the familiar furniture, the carefully framed photos of me and my sisters. My eyes settle on one of me and Liam and I study it closely, frowning at how much younger and freer I look.

But a lot has happened in a year. When the dogs come in, I feed them, leaving a light on in case it's dark when my mother comes home, before setting off for the hospital.

By the time I get there, my father is already being assessed. As I wait with my mother, she surprises me. 'Funny how when you're young, you think you have for ever. And I know we all expect to lose grandparents. It's more natural, somehow. But you somehow never think of it happening to you.'

It's as though she's talking to me woman to woman, rather than mother to daughter. 'Dad's going to be OK,' I say anxiously.

It's impossible to tell what she's thinking as she falls silent for a moment, before she turns back into my mum. 'Of course he is. Why don't we get a cup of tea?'

After carrying out some tests, they keep him in. But as I drive home, my mind runs away with me. Having lost Liam, the thought of losing my father is unimaginable, but when he'd seemed so well after coming home the first time, this sharp decline is worrying.

Back at home, I call Sasha.

'I'm really worried about him.' My voice wavers. 'He doesn't look at all good, Sash. I keep thinking...' My voice breaks.

'I know. I'm worried too.' Her voice is anxious. 'All we can do is take each day at a time. He's in good hands. But I hate not being able to be there.' She pauses. 'I spoke to Rita earlier. She's stuck with work commitments – she feels exactly the same.'

'Like you said, it's each day at a time.' I try to feel more hopeful, grateful at least that I can be there.

That evening, in an effort to distract myself, I study my map of northern Spain. The route I'm planning to take is known as Camino del Norte. At 825 kilometres long, it usually takes around thirty-five days. I've chosen it because it's the coastal route. But as I sit there, I can't focus. When all I can think about is my parents together in the hospital, planning this walk seems trivial.

Picking up my phone, I call my mother. 'Mum? How's Dad doing?'

'Not too bad,' she says quietly. 'They're looking after him. You mustn't worry.'

'OK.' But as I end the call, I can't shake the feeling that hangs over me. He may be OK tonight. But I can't help worrying about what tomorrow might bring.

* * *

The following morning, after an update from my mother, I have a sense of being in limbo. It's an overcast day, and as I step outside, the countryside is veiled in mist, the damp clinging to every leaf and blade of grass.

After my shift at the bookshop, on the way home, I drive over to Nathan's.

'You're just in time for a cuppa,' he says as he opens the door. Studying my face, he frowns. 'Are you OK?'

'Yes and no,' I say. 'Could I come in for a moment?'

'Sure.' He holds the door open. 'You look like you could do with something stronger than tea.'

'Tea would be lovely.' Then for no reason, my eyes fill with tears.

'Hey,' he says gently. 'Has something happened?'

My shoulders start to heave, and I can't speak. Coming closer, he puts his arms around me. Leaning against him, I can't help but breathe in the scent of him – wood smoke mixed with aftershave, my tears falling unstoppably as I feel one of his hands stroke my hair.

After a few minutes, I pull away. 'I'm so sorry.' Wiping my face, I take in his shirt, wet with my tears and smudged with my eye make-up. 'I've made a mess of your shirt.'

'The shirt doesn't matter.' He asks me again: 'What's happened?'

'My dad is back in hospital.' I say through my tears. 'He was taken in yesterday, by ambulance.'

Nathan looks startled. 'I thought he was doing well.'

'He was.' Wiping my face again, I gaze at him. 'We all thought so. It's why this is so frightening.'

He's silent for a moment. 'Do you think it feels worse because of losing your fiancé?'

My emotions get the better of me as I whisper. '*I think so.*'

After he makes us a cup of tea, we talk more, about life and how you think you have for ever, when as we both know for reasons of our own, there's no way of knowing what the future holds.

When I get up to leave, he hesitates at the door.

'I know how tough this must be for you. But I'm always here, you know – if you need someone to talk to.'

Reaching up, I kiss his cheek. 'Thank you.'

* * *

The last of the leaves fall as autumn rolls into winter and my father comes home. When his weekly check-ups confirm he's doing OK, only then do my fears slowly start to dissipate. Meanwhile, as my mother starts planning Christmas, I think back to last year. Other than going through the motions and leaving early, I remember little of it. But this year... With all my sisters coming, with Dad's health not so good, I know we have to make this a special one.

This year it's me who helps my mother decorate the house. My father is under strict instructions to take it easy. Lugging in a huge tree between us, we set it up and decorate it. As we hang the familiar baubles, my mother hands one to me.

'I remember the day you chose this. You were about five – and you loved anything and everything with glitter on it.'

It's rare for my mother to be sentimental. I take it from her. It's a Barbie pink unicorn from which most of the glitter has worn away.

'You should keep it.' She carries on decorating the tree. 'Goodness knows, we have enough of the things.' She sounds more like her old self.

Going over, I hug her. 'Thank you.' I feel emotional all of a sudden.

'It's only a bauble,' she says briskly.

'Not just for that.' I hold her hands for a moment, grateful for everything she's done for us over the years. 'For all the Christmases. For the wedding that never happened. For everything.'

'Oh, Callie...' Her eyes are misty as she looks at me. 'You girls have been the greatest joy in my life.' She pauses. 'All I really want is for you to be happy again.'

'I'm starting to believe I will be.' I swallow, because it isn't easy to say. 'It's just that when you lose someone, it makes everything so complicated.'

'Of course it does. It turns your life upside down.' She smiles wistfully. 'I'm proud of you, you know, for how you're dealing with this.'

Tears fill my eyes. 'Thanks Mum. I'm not sure I did, to start with. But I think I am now.' I hesitate. 'Are you OK? What with Dad and everything?'

'I won't say it hasn't been a shock.' She's silent for a moment. 'I suppose these things make you think about what's really important in life.'

* * *

The week before Christmas, I call round to see Nathan with the gift I've chosen for him. When he opens the door, he looks tired.

'Callie. I wasn't expecting you.'

I smile. 'It's OK. I won't stay.'

'No, come in. Please.' Standing back, he opens the door more widely, closing it behind me.

'OK. I can't stay long, though. I came to give you this.' I pass him the tray of primrose plants I'm holding. 'You can have them in your house over Christmas. Then after, you can plant them outside.'

Peeling off the paper, he looks pleased. 'Thank you. I hope you're going to tell me where I should plant them?'

I shake my head. 'That's for you to work out.'

He glances around. 'I have something for you, too. I was going to wrap it, but seeing as you're here...' Going over to the table, he puts down the tray of primroses and picks up a book. Coming back, he passes it to me. 'I saw it in town and it made me think of the walk you're doing. I hope you don't have it?'

I feel a flicker of warmth as I gaze at the cover, taking in the title. 'I don't. It's perfect.' It's about the Camino del Norte. 'This is the exact route I'm planning to walk. Thank you.' Reaching up, I kiss him on the cheek. 'That's a really cool present.'

Our eyes meet. 'So are primroses.'

I smile again. 'Ha! I bet you wouldn't have thought that a year ago.'

He pulls a face. 'A year ago, I wasn't up to anything much.'

He's clearly alluding to his illness again, but as always, he doesn't explain.

Instead, he changes the subject. 'Can I get you a drink?'

I hesitate. 'A glass of wine?'

After he pours us a glass each, we sit on the sofa. 'It's nice being here again. You've made it really cosy.' Glancing around, I take in the Christmas tree in the corner, the seasoned logs stacked either side of the wood burning stove.

'It's nice you being here,' he says quietly. 'The house is great in summer, but it makes a good winter house, too.'

Studying him, I realise he doesn't just look tired. His face is pale and there are circles under his eyes. I frown. 'Are you OK?'

'I'm fine. I've just been busy.' But it sounds like there's something he isn't saying.

'You haven't been overdoing it out there, have you?'

'Not really. But it's looking good, though.' Nathan smiles. 'The hellebores we bought have dozens of flowers, and there are shoots coming up that I think are snowdrops...'

'Wow.' My eyes widen. 'I'm impressed.'

'My sister told me I needed to educate myself. So I have been.'

I wonder what's happened to the planning appeal for the campsite. 'So have you got any further with your plans for the land?' When he stiffens, I know it isn't good.

'Nothing's certain yet, but I'm talking to that builder I told you about.' He sighs heavily. 'You're not going to be very pleased with me, Callie. I'm not exactly pleased with myself, but I've been finding it all quite stressful – and stress is one thing I'm supposed to avoid. The easiest solution is to build houses. They'll be as environmentally friendly as it's possible to be. I'm sorry. I know it's far from ideal. But...'

'It's what you do.' As I finish his sentence, disappointment wells up inside me.

'The thing is, I don't know what else to do.' He looks troubled. 'I agree with all your principles. It's just that right now, I can't find a way to make them work in practical terms.'

'It's OK.' I shrug. 'At least you tried.'

Getting up to leave, I'm aware of an awkwardness that wasn't there before as I linger a moment. 'Happy first Christmas in your new home.'

'Happy Christmas,' he says gently. 'Come over sometime. I'll show you what I think I've found in my garden, and you can laugh at me when I get it wrong.'

I hesitate before nodding. 'OK.'

* * *

As tradition dictates, my sisters and I convene at our parents' house. Rita and Sasha arrive the night before Christmas Eve, armed with bags of beautifully wrapped gifts. Their presence brings light to the house. With my mother busy in the kitchen, I catch a moment with them.

'Mum's a bit different,' I say quietly. 'Can't quite put my finger on it. A little bit sentimental, I think you'd say.'

'Mum sentimental?' Sasha frowns. 'Maybe she's worried about Dad.'

I nod. 'I think she's more worried than she's letting on.'

'I'll go and help her.' Picking up a bag, Rita heads for the kitchen.

'Where is he?' Sasha looks troubled.

'Resting,' I nod towards the stairs. 'He does a lot of that these days.'

* * *

When Alice joins us on Christmas Eve, her presence is calm and reassuring – more so when I spot the medical bag she's brought with her. 'Just so I can keep an eye on his blood pressure.'

The four of us are more subdued than usual, our chatter more muted, our eyes anxious as we glance between each other and our parents. Meanwhile, Alice has an eye on everything, it seems, including the food. But my mother's clearly done her homework.

'This is non-dairy,' she tells Alice as she serves up dauphinoise potatoes. 'It's made with plant milk and a plant-based spread. I've made it before and believe it or not, he really likes it.'

'Bravo, Mum.' Alice tastes a spoonful. 'It's delicious.'

As the six of us sit around the kitchen table, it's reminiscent of the Christmas Eves of our growing-up years, yet it's different, too. There are moments I think of Liam, wishing he was here, but mostly I'm thinking of my family and how grateful I am to have each one of them.

Christmas Day is as it always has been in our house. A lazy morning in pyjamas as we open some presents, followed by us getting dressed up in our Christmas finest for a late lunch.

Having been banished from the dining room by my mother, I am amazed to see, when at last we're allowed in, that the table's beautifully dressed in green and silver, the room lit by dozens of candles. It's the first time my mother's done anything like this.

'This is beautiful, Mum.' I take in the candles on the table and on the windowsills, the effect enhanced by stands of fairy lights.

She looks pleased. 'I saw the idea in a magazine. I'm glad you like it.' She glances at my father, her eyes slightly anxious.

He takes her hand. 'You've done us proud, love. But you always have.' He kisses her cheek.

'Come and sit down everyone.' Letting go of his hand, she's businesslike again. 'Callie? Could you help me?'

As we're dishing up, I can see that even with the food, there's a twist on the old favourites.

'We have to think of your father's health – and I thought it would be good to change things up a bit.'

I can't help wondering if this is about me as well as my father. But when my mother's gone out of her way to make this a different kind of Christmas, I don't allow myself to wallow in the past. Instead, I focus on everything in the here and now: on this day with my wonderful family, because, these days, we're not together often enough.

* * *

On Boxing Day, after coffee and toast, as my sisters and I prepare to walk off yesterday's lunch, my parents come into the kitchen.

'Ah. Glad I've caught you all together.' My father sounds jovial, but when I look at him, his expression is serious. 'If you have a few minutes, your mother and I would like to talk to you.'

* * *

'I can't believe they're going to sell.' As we walk up the lane, the four of us are stunned.

'It's a huge place,' Rita says sympathetically. 'A lot of work, too. It's probably sensible.' But she doesn't sound convinced.

'It's just that it's our home.' Sasha's voice wavers.

'Can we agree that whatever we say out here, we keep to ourselves?' Alice says. 'Dad's heart isn't in a good way. I've seen his medical notes. Between you and me, I don't think he believes he's going to get better.'

As Rita gasps, I have a strange feeling inside. It's what I've been feeling, too, subconsciously, but until now, I haven't known how to put it into words. I turn to Alice. 'I think you're right.' I go on, 'I've spent quite a bit of time with them lately. There have been small changes – and bigger ones, the main one being that Dad does very little these days, and we all know how active he used to be.'

'So what do we do?' Rita sounds shaken.

'Say nothing,' Alice says gently. 'They're dealing with this in their own way. And of course, medical diagnoses can be surprising. Dad could have years ahead of him.'

But when none of them speak, I know they're as worried as I am. 'I know what we do,' I say quietly. 'We make the most of today, and tomorrow, and the next day... We tell them we love them. That we know how lucky we are.' I look at them all. 'I know we'll all be sad to see the house go. But look at what they've given us: our child-hoods, the freedom to be ourselves; the beauty of the Cornish coun-tryside. The support and sense of security we've always had... Not everyone has that – and every part of that is down to them. And now...' I shrug. 'However we might feel about it, they have to do what's right for them.'

'Wow,' Rita says, linking her arm through mine. 'I completely agree.'

'Me too,' Alice and Sasha say quietly.

We carry on walking and I take in the familiar surroundings that I've known for as long as I can remember, but the sense that Dad might not have long is growing stronger. It could mean that this is our last Christmas together; that everything we've always counted on could be about to change.

22

NATHAN

After spending a quiet Christmas with Robin, the day after Boxing Day I drive home. The roads are quiet, people presumably at home with loved ones. Opening the door, as I go inside, my eyes settle on Callie's primroses.

I'd resisted Robin's efforts to persuade me to stay longer. I'd found myself restless to get back here. I place the book she gave me on the table. It's on the basics of vegetable gardening and already, having started reading it, I'm inspired with ideas to put into practice.

But it's more than that. I'm craving some time alone, to soak up the peace here. Going outside, I stand on the terrace for a moment. The air is still, laced with the faintest hint of wood smoke. I gaze towards the area I've designated to become my vegetable garden. Right now, it's still a jungle of weeds and brambles, rather than the neat rows of vegetables I'm envisaging. But having given myself a break from work for a few days, it's the perfect time to make a start.

After sitting in Robin's house eating too much, I welcome the fresh air and exercise as I start to dig. It's hard work; the sodden earth sticks to my spade as, fuelled by my fantasy of neat rows of vegetables, I carry on. But when in the past I used to fantasise about beautiful women or exotic holiday locations, as I stand there caked in mud, I can't help laughing at myself.

* * *

The next day, after another back-breaking afternoon of clearing weeds, I text Callie.

Hope you had a good Christmas. Are you doing anything New Year's Eve?

I hesitate. Last time I saw her, I admitted that I actually am one of the low-life property developers she despises; I'm not at all sure she wants to hear from me. But knowing I'm risking rejection, I send it anyway.

The following day, I still haven't heard back from Callie. Disappointed, my mind turns to something else I've set myself to do. It's a letter of thanks to an anonymous stranger who came to my rescue when my health was at its worst and I was close to dying.

It's something I've been thinking about for a while now, putting it off only because I prefer not to dwell on that time. But the selfless act of a stranger has altered the course of my life; there is so much I want to say to them.

There's a protocol to follow to uphold anonymity: I should use first names only, or no names at all; I can give no details about locations. But those are irrelevant, as far as I see it. What really matters is the message.

Sitting there, I start writing, finding it surprisingly difficult to put into words. When I was weeks away from dying, when treat-

ment was failing me, I was acutely conscious that the life I so
desperately wanted to hold on to was slipping away from me.

Thank you isn't enough... Without you, quite simply I wouldn't be
here. Not a day passes I'm not aware of that, or...

I'm interrupted by a knock on the door. Taken by surprise, I get
up. I haven't heard any cars pull up outside. Going to the door, I
open it.

'*Emily*?' I do a double-take.

'Don't look so surprised.' Her green eyes are catlike as she
smiles at me. 'Merry Christmas, Nathan. Aren't you going to invite
me in?'

Speechless, I stand back to let her in.

Brushing past me, Emily glances around. In skinny jeans and
wearing perfect make-up, holding a bag that's clearly expensive,
she's exactly as I remember her.

'Nice place you have here – though I have to say, not at all what I
expected.' She turns to look at me. 'Is it your next project?'

'No. This is it – my home.'

Surprise flickers through her eyes. But much has changed since
we last saw each other. Last time was when I wasn't well. She kindly,
but quite brutally, ended our relationship at a time, if I'm honest, I
most needed her.

Turning, her eyes rest on me. 'You look well,' she said softly.

'I am.' It comes out more curtly than I mean it to. 'Would you
like a cup of tea?'

'I was thinking more of something along the lines of this.'
Reaching into her bag, she produces a bottle of champagne with a
flourish.

'It's a bit early in the day for me.' I have a feeling I know where
this is going. 'But I can pour you a glass.'

'Maybe later,' she says smoothly. 'I'll put it in your fridge.' She pauses. 'Unless you're busy?'

Glancing at my letter, I pick it up before she can read it. 'Emily, what exactly are you doing here?'

'I've just spent Christmas with my folks.' Shaking her sleek brown hair back, she rolls her eyes. 'It was getting a bit too much – Father droning on about the Boxing Day shoot, while Mother's planning her New Year's Eve party... Deadly dull. I'll probably head back to London. But as I was at a loose end, I thought I'd look you up.'

'You won't find any excitement around here,' I tell her. 'My life these days revolves around work and my garden.'

'That's all?' She arches one of her eyebrows.

'Tea?' I say pointedly.

'Sure.' She wanders across to the window. 'It's quite a view. But don't you get lonely here?'

'Never,' I say firmly. 'It's the kind of life I've needed for a long time.'

'It would make a nice weekend bolthole.' Coming over, she rests a perfectly manicured hand on one of my arms. 'We had such fun, didn't we, Nathan? Don't you ever think about us?'

There's no apology, no, *how are you,* or, *I'm sorry for letting you down.* As she speaks, alarm bells are going off. Stepping back from her, I pass her a mug. 'Not really. Life's moved on. And let's see – it's been, what, eighteen months? What have you been up to in that time?'

Going over to the sofa, she sits down. 'I've been busy. Work has been sending me all over the place – Dubai, the States, Milan, Paris...' Emily works for an exclusive jeweller, hence the large, intricately designed ring she wears on the middle finger of her right hand.

I perch on the other end. 'Sounds nice.'

'It is.' She pauses for a moment. 'But what I've realised is how much more it means when you have someone to share it with.'

Seeing the look in her eyes, I feel uncomfortable. Emily has never been subtle and having seen it all before, I know exactly what her game is. She's come here because she wants something. 'I'm sure there have been plenty of guys in your life since you and I split up.'

'One or two, maybe,' she says casually. 'But none of them were like you.' Edging closer, her hand is back on my arm.

In the nick of time, I hear my phone buzz with a text. 'Excuse me a moment.' Getting up, I go to find my phone.

The message is from Callie.

It was good, but a bit strange... Not sure about New Year's Eve. I'll text you.

At least non-committal is better than an outright no. Switching off my phone and putting it down, I glance across at Emily. 'Would you like a tour of the garden?'

She glances down at her pale pink boots with stiletto heels. 'I'm afraid I'm not really dressed for it.'

Those few words symbolise everything that's changed. As she speaks, I find myself yearning for Callie, who with her windswept hair and off-beat clothes, her honesty and outspokenness, could never be contrived about anything. Going back to the sofa, I sit down, fixing my eyes on Emily's. 'What is this really about?'

She holds my gaze, then she looks away. 'Fuck it, Nathan. You were always able to see through me. OK – so I had a row with the folks. They've said they're stopping my allowance. Just like that. They said 'I should be able to manage' , is how they put it. I'm beyond furious. It's completely unreasonable of them. I've no idea what they expect me to do.'

'Maybe stand on your own feet like everyone else?' Taking in her shocked expression, I go on. 'You earn a decent salary, Emily. There's no reason you can't survive on it.' When she looks uncomfortable, I frown. 'Is there?'

As she drops the act, there's angst in her eyes. 'I have debts, Nathan. My own stupid fault, of course. I thought if you and I got back together...'

'I'd bail you out?' I can't believe how outrageous this is. 'Em, the world doesn't work like that. You need to pay your way, not suck other people in to solve your problems.'

'Ouch.' She shoots me a look.

'It really isn't complicated. Sell your flat and find a cheaper one – or move slightly out of town. Then with the rest of your money, start repaying your debts.'

Her gaze is beseeching. 'But if we...'

'There is no *we*,' I tell her firmly. 'There never will be. You made it perfectly clear when I was ill. We were over a long time ago.'

She sighs. 'Can I ask one favour?'

'You can ask.'

'Can I stay? It's just for one night. I want my parents to know how pissed off I am.'

Against my better judgement, I say, 'OK.' Instantly I regret it. 'But in the spare room.' I pause. 'Can I be honest with you?'

'I'd expect no less,' she says wryly.

But she needs to know how lucky she is. 'Your parents have funded your lifestyle for as long as I've known you. Have you ever thanked them? Because if you haven't, maybe you should. You've treated your salary like pocket money. It isn't like that for most people. I don't think you know how bloody lucky you are.'

I'm hoping she's listening, but my words seem to fall on deaf ears.

'Now you've said yes, I'm having a drink.' Going to the fridge, she gets out the bottle of champagne.

Watching her, I feel myself tense. Once, I would have given in to her, shared the bottle of champagne before opening another, allowing myself to get drawn back in to her cat-and-mouse games, mildly flattered. But I have no desire to do that now. I feel nothing for her. It's yet another example of how much I've changed.

23

CALLIE

The day before New Year's Eve, there's an atmosphere in the house I can't put my finger on. A sense of expectancy, perhaps. The kind of hush that comes before something momentous happens. While Sasha's in the study speaking to one of her clients and Rita goes for a run, I pull on my boots and go outside.

It's the same out here. The air is cold and still. Even the birds are quieter than usual. Glancing down at the ground, I take in the first needle shoots of wild daffodils, the clusters of snowdrops that over the years have colonised the lawn. I hope whoever lives here next loves it as much as we have.

But as I walk across the grass, instead of savouring the peacefulness, the strangest sensation comes over me. I put it down to the thought that this is our last Christmas here, that this time next year, my parents will be living somewhere else. As long as my father is OK...

No sooner have I formed the thought than I'm distracted by a shout from Alice.

'*Callie... Quick... You need to come.*'

As I run towards the house, my heart starts to race. I know why

I've been feeling like this. Something's terribly wrong. I throw the back door open just as Alice comes into the kitchen.

Her face is pale. 'He's almost certainly had another heart attack. I've called an ambulance. Mum and Sasha are with him... Where's Rita?'

'Gone for a run.' I hurry towards the stairs.

'I'll call her. The ambulance should be with us in minutes. I'll wait downstairs.'

Alice picks up her phone just as the back door opens and Rita comes in. Flushed from running, as she looks at our faces she instantly knows something's up. Leaving Alice to explain, I hurry upstairs.

As I creep into our parents' room, my stomach turns over as I take in my father, unconscious in bed. His face is grey, his breathing shallow. Beside him, Sasha's face is ashen.

Tears fill my eyes as I crouch down next to the bed. 'Hey, Dad... It's me, Callie. I love you, Dad.' I take one of his hands. 'We all love you.'

'I've been telling him.' My mother's voice is dry and husky, her eyes wide with fear.

Just as Rita comes into the bedroom, there's the sound of a vehicle pulling up outside, then the front door opening; a brief hesitation before there are footsteps on the stairs. When the paramedics walk in, they're calm and focussed, but there's no hiding their sense of urgency as they check him out, wasting no time before gently moving him on to a stretcher and taking him to the hospital.

* * *

At the hospital, Christmas is forgotten as we wait, but Alice is right. After tests, the doctors establish he has indeed had another heart attack.

'You should go home,' my mother says quietly. 'There's nothing you can do.'

'We're not going anywhere, Mum,' Alice says immediately.

'She's right.' Sasha crouches down next to Mum. 'We're staying.'

We sit in silence, each of us lost in our thoughts. Now and then I glance at Mum. She's always so organised, so matter-of-fact; but tonight it's clear how frightened she is.

Some hours later, a nurse comes to find us. Her expression is grave, leaving us in no doubt how serious this is, but she tells us he's stable, at least for now.

* * *

After driving Sasha and Rita back to my parents' house, I can't settle. 'I'll leave you here while I pick up some things from home,' I tell them. 'I won't be long. Call me if you hear anything, won't you?'

'We'll come with you,' they say in unison.

But I tell them to stay put. 'I'll be fine on my own.'

It's dark and I switch my headlights on, as I drive, thinking of my father, overwhelmed by this strange sense I can't shake, an entrenched fear that we're going to lose him. Tears fill my eyes, the road in front of me blurring, as suddenly I'm filled with a desire to see Nathan.

Slowing down, I turn around and head towards his house. I don't know what I want to say, just that when all of us are so worried, I want a few minutes of the comfort his presence brings, the peacefulness his garden has.

When I turn into his drive, an unfamiliar car is parked outside. It's a new BMW convertible – definitely not his sister's. Telling myself I'm not going to jump to conclusions again, I park and switch the engine off. As I get out, the door opens and a woman comes out. Tall, with glossy brown hair, she's wearing skin-tight jeans and ridiculous boots – actually not ridiculous at all – just the kind of boots I'd break my ankle in if I tried to walk in them.

In the doorway, I make out Nathan saying something to her before she tosses her hair over her shoulder and kisses him, full on, on the lips.

Shock knocks the breath out of me, before I feel a deep twisting sensation inside me. This is what Tanith warned me about. I've left it too long to tell him I like him. Now, he's met someone else.

Tears fill my eyes as I hear Nathan's voice call out through the darkness.

'Callie... *Wait...*'

'I'll see you another time.' I'm already stumbling back to my car, ignoring him as he hurries towards me. I start the engine and drive away.

I'm a fool, I tell myself, for even coming here when my father is seriously ill in hospital. I should be with my sisters, or with my mother. But as I drive back to my parents' house, it feels like my life is falling apart around me. My father being ill, my parents selling up, Nathan meeting someone else... all happening at the same time. And I'm powerless. There's nothing I can do about any of it.

When I see Sasha and Rita, as they take in my tear-stained face, they embrace me in a sisterly hug.

Sasha lets go first. 'Come on. I'll make you a cuppa. Alice called while you were out. She and Mum will be home in an hour or so.'

* * *

Ignoring Nathan's texts, that night, alone in my old bedroom, I don't sleep. I'm partly on alert for the sound of a phone call from the hospital. But also, I'm doing some serious soul-searching.

When Nathan and I are only friends and he's free to see whoever he wants to, I don't understand why seeing him with someone else hurt so much.

Lying there, I wish I could bring my trip to Spain closer. But with my father so ill, it isn't an option. I have no choice but to stay in Cornwall and wait this out.

* * *

On New Year's Eve, my father's condition is no different. After spending the afternoon at the hospital, my sisters and I drive home.

'Not exactly one to celebrate, is it?' Rita says feelingly.

'At least he's stable,' Alice tries to reassure us. 'And Mum's with him.' Our mother has refused to leave his bedside.

'Maybe we should have stayed.' Sasha sounds anxious.

'He needs to rest,' Alice says gently. 'We can see him tomorrow.'

'But what if...' Hearing my voice tremble, I break off.

Alice's hand touches my shoulder. 'One day at a time.'

* * *

We're a sober group that evening. Raiding the fridge, we put together a meal of sorts from the food my mother so thoughtfully amassed and open some wine.

'All I can say is, I'm so grateful we're all here together.' Rita raises her glass. 'To you guys. You're the best.'

We chink our glasses together as the wood crackles in the fireplace.

'Makes you think, doesn't it?' Sasha says. 'How quickly things can change?' She turns to me. 'We haven't really talked about Liam, Cal.'

'It doesn't mean we're not thinking of him,' Rita says gently.

'I know. There are still days it feels like he could walk back in through the door.' But they're getting fewer. 'When I think back to last Christmas, then the one before...' I swallow, taking in the sympathy in their eyes. 'It's really weird how in many ways, it feels like a lifetime ago.'

'You're doing so well,' Alice says gently.

'Am I? I feel like I've been drifting. I look at you three and everything you've achieved in your lives. I'm kind of thinking I need to find my thing.' I watch them glance at each other. 'I was asked to go out tonight,' I say suddenly, watching the surprise on their faces. 'By Nathan, the guy I'm helping with his garden.'

'Maybe you should have gone,' Sasha says quietly.

'Right now, I want to be here with you three.' I don't tell them about the girl I saw at Nathan's. However shocked I felt at the time, it doesn't ring true that Nathan would ask me out if there was someone else in his life. 'So what's happening with you guys?' My eyes turn to Sasha. 'Married-man – has he gone?'

'Well and truly.' She looks relieved.

'That's great news.' I raise my glass and chink it against hers. 'Your turn, Rita.'

'Completely over him.'

'Hallelujah. He was a real piece of work. So,' I hesitate, 'is there someone new?'

'Maybe.' Rita's cheeks flush pink. 'I'm not saying a word until I know if it's going anywhere.'

'Don't leave it too long, please...' I look at Alice. 'And?'

'And what?' She tries to keep a straight face.

'Come on, out of all of us, it sounded like you'd found someone... You have to tell us!' Rita rolls her eyes.

'OK.' Smiling around at us, Alice relents. 'It's really nice, actually. We're thinking of moving in together.'

'OMG.' I stare at her. 'You have to bring him here. We need to meet him. How about tomorrow?'

She's laughing as she shakes her head. 'He's staying with his family – in Edinburgh. But yes, I'd love you all to meet him – as long as you don't do this to him.'

'Do what?' I say innocently.

'This frigging inquisition, or whatever you want to call it.'

'You have our word. It's brilliant, though.' Sasha's eyes are bright. 'I'm really happy for you.'

The mood changes as we lapse into a silence that's broken by the tick of the grandfather clock.

'It's kind of weird to think of another family living here.' Sasha sounds emotional. 'I mean, all our lives, it's been our house.'

'Things change,' I say simply. 'Not always the way we want them to. And there's not always anything we can do about that. After they've moved out, I won't want to come back.'

'Me neither,' Rita says.

At that moment, a sense of urgency grips me. Trying to hide how uneasy I feel, I get up. 'You know, I might pop back to the hospital. I don't like to think of Mum on her own.'

My sisters look alarmed. 'We'll come with you.'

'It's OK.' I hesitate. 'You stay here. I'll bring Mum back with me and we can all go over there tomorrow.'

I don't tell them I have the strangest sense that time is running out. Knowing I have to be there, I drive as fast as I dare, my eye on the clock, willing time to slow down; berating myself. We should have stayed at the hospital. We shouldn't have gone home. It's shortly before midnight when I arrive there. Parking, I sprint across the car park, through reception and up the stairs to where my father's ward is.

Slowing down as I walk along the corridor, I feel slightly removed. Outside the small room where his bed is, I see my mother. As I take in her tearstained face, her defeated look, a feeling of dread fills me.

'Mum? Is Dad OK?'

There is no flicker of surprise as she sees me, just unbearable sadness in her eyes. When I take her hands, I notice she's shaking.

'He's had another heart attack.' She seems frozen.

Fear floods through me. 'Are the doctors with him?'

She nods. 'Callie...' Her grip on my hand tightens.

I get out my phone. 'I should call the others.' But after the wine they've shared, none of them are in any fit state to drive.

My mother shakes her head. 'There's no point. By the time they get a taxi over here...' She shakes her head again.

I see then that she has it, too. The sense that time is running out. And she's right. Finding a taxi at midnight on New Year's Eve is nigh on impossible. I text my sisters.

Dad isn't at all good. I'm staying with Mum for a bit. Will keep you posted.

Alice replies straight away.

We'll come over. I haven't had that much to drink.

I get straight back to her.

You can't risk it. The police are all over the place.

It's true. The closer I'd got to the hospital I'd noticed more and more drink-driving checkpoints.

An eternity passes as we wait, each minute spun out so that it feels ten times as long. When eventually a doctor comes towards us, I don't need to ask how my father is. I already know from the way my heart is racing, from the empty feeling I have inside, how bad this is.

'We've done everything we can. He's still with us,' she says quietly. 'His breathing is very shallow. We need to see what the next few hours bring. Would you like to see him?'

I hold my mother's hand as we make our way to my father's bed. His eyes are closed, his face slack and as I look at him, my eyes fill with tears. Sitting on the chair next to the bed, my mother takes one of his hands, before leaning across and kissing his cheek.

On the opposite side, I crouch down and take his other hand. 'I love you, Dad.' Tears are pouring down my face and I wipe them away with my sleeve, before glancing at Mum, knowing all we can do is wait.

24

NATHAN

I'm hoping to see Callie, wanting to explain about Emily to her. I still can't believe the timing of that – Callie arriving just as Emily was leaving, witnessing that inappropriate, unwanted kiss. But ever since, I haven't seen her.

After seeing in the New Year alone, a week later I drive to Truro to meet the builder I'm thinking of working with. As I walk along a narrow street, just ahead of me a door to a café opens and Callie comes out. Her face is pale and she seems to have shrunk somehow.

When she sees me, her eyes widen. 'Hi.'

'Hi. I'm sorry about...' Seizing my chance, I start to explain. But then I realise she isn't alone – two other women are with her. Seeing the similarity in their faces, I realise they must be her sisters.

'This is Sasha and Rita. This is Nathan,' she says to them before turning back to me. 'Dad had another heart attack. We didn't think he was going to make it but he's turned a corner.'

Shock hits me as I try to imagine what she's been through. 'I'm so sorry.' I don't know what else to say. 'But I'm glad he's getting better.'

'Thank you.' Her eyes shine with tears. 'We should probably get on.' As Callie glances at her sisters, they look at me quizzically.

'Take care,' I say quietly.

'Nice to meet you,' one of them says – I'm not sure which is which. Her worry shows clearly in her eyes.

* * *

I can't stop thinking about Callie as I walk away. I remember how I felt when my father was ill; my mother passed almost exactly a year after he'd died. When we'd always been close, their deaths left me rootless, bereft, as for the first time I'd realised how much family meant, that, apart from Robin, I was alone in the world.

I know Callie will be going through shades of the same, especially now, when she's only starting to get over losing her fiancé. My heart twists in anguish for her. But when one of your parents is seriously ill, as I remember well, it takes over absolutely everything.

* * *

The meeting with the builder leaves me uneasy. He's too cocky, too sure of his ground, already mentioning shortcuts, when what I want to build are genuine eco-houses.

'There are much cheaper alternatives, mate.' He grins at me. 'Apart from you and me, no one will know.'

'That's not the point.' I try to keep him on track.

'Yeah, but think about the money, mate. If you can save a bit here and there, you can't argue with that. There are plenty of potential buyers out there, wanting fancy holiday homes. So what if this or that isn't quite right? They're hardly going to notice.'

Not liking the direction this is taking, in the end, I draw the meeting to a close. 'Let me think about this,' I say firmly.

On my way back to my car, on impulse I stop to buy a card for
Callie. But as I drive home, my mind is all over the place. I despise
working with people like this builder. I have a feeling the planning
application would be dodgy, too – a backhander to the right person
in order to get what he wants. Right now, it feels unjustifiable.

* * *

When I get home, I take out the card I bought, thinking for a
moment before starting to write.

> *Dear Callie,*
>   *I just wanted to say again how sorry I am to hear your dad is*
> *ill. I hope he's better soon – and I'll be thinking of you. I'm always*
> *here if you want someone to talk to.*
>   *Take care of yourself.*
>   *Nathan*

I add a PS.

> *I've planted the primroses.*

Sealing the envelope, I put it to one side. I'm guessing Callie will
be spending most of her time with her family, but at some point I'll
drive it over to her cottage.

Getting up, I go over to my desk and switch on my laptop. The
building project is playing on my mind. It isn't too late to pull the
plug on it – we haven't gone past the discussion stage and I'm a long
way from being ready to sign anything.

There's one thing the guy said that has stuck, however. But I
need to do some research and check it out.

* * *

In the afternoon, I drive over to Callie's house. As expected, when I arrive, there's no sign of her car. Getting out, I stand there for a moment. It's a quiet January day, a chill to the air as I notice a few wild primroses growing in the hedgerow, reminding me of the ones she gave me.

After posting the card through her door, I drive home, deep in thought. When I was ill, it struck me how weird it is, that when death is one of life's certainties, most people are reluctant to talk about it. When I thought I was running out of time, I wanted to talk to Robin about it. But she was evasive. *I don't want to think about you not being here.*

I tried to impress on her that, in the position I was in, it would help me just to talk. In the end, one of the nurses sat with me and listened, her voice reassuring as she made it clear that if it came to that, I wouldn't be alone.

Our avoidance of talking about death is cultural, I suppose, driven by fear of the unknown, leaving people walking on eggshells around it. My own close shave was a stark reminder of that – though actually it was more a much-needed wake-up call: not to let time go by, to fully live this life while I still can.

I sigh. I know it's part of the reason it isn't working out with this builder. Living life fully means believing in what I'm doing, being true to the person I want to be. And whatever else is uncertain, if there's one thing I am sure of, being a liar or a cheat isn't part of it.

25

CALLIE

My parents' house feels strangely quiet, filled with the weight of our combined worry about our father, the shared fear that we could lose him. It isn't helped when my sisters go back to work, coming and going as often as they can.

'I really don't want to leave here,' Rita says tearfully. 'But I have to go back to work.'

'I know.' Going over, Alice puts her arms around her. And this is how it goes – each of us there for each other as these moments engulf us.

'I keep trying to tell myself that he's going to be OK,' Sasha wipes her face. 'I'm just so worried about him.'

While my father takes tiny steps forwards, we're all worried. It feels like we're hovering at the end of a chapter that's lasted all our lives. Without our father, the future would feel shaky, uncertain, until I realise what's got me through the last year or so of my life, what my father's far-reaching legacy is, that will always be here. It's this family.

'I know we have Mum. But even though Dad's ill, we still have each other,' I say fiercely, drawing on the strength I know I have;

looking at my sisters. 'We all know that, don't we? That whatever happens, none of us need ever feel alone.'

* * *

My sisters promise to return whenever they can. Though my mother holds up heroically, in quieter moments it's clear how frightened she is. But like last time, my father keeps making progress until suddenly we're looking at him coming home.

My mother switches into another gear. 'Now, I think we should move a bed downstairs – at least to start with. I don't want him worrying about the stairs. And once he's home, we need to think about putting the house on the market.'

My jaw drops. 'You're still doing that?'

'I think the sooner the better.' My mother frowns. 'With your father not well, we really do need somewhere much easier to look after.'

The day my father comes home, we breathe a collective sigh of relief. He's noticeably frailer after his time in hospital, but his relief at being home is palpable.

The following day, Tanith texts me.

New Year's Graveyard Groupies bash this Saturday. We start this year as we mean to go on! You up for it? xx

I text her back.

I'll pop in, but I won't stay. It's been a bit chaotic. My dad's been ill xx

Almost immediately, my phone buzzes.

'Shit, Callie. I'm so sorry.' Tanith sounds shocked.

'Thanks.' My heart warms at the sound of her voice. 'He's better than he was, but it hasn't been the best time.'

'Of course not.' She hesitates. 'I really understand if you give it a miss. But I'm here if you need me. Any time.'

* * *

In the evening I go home for the first time in ages. When I go inside, I find a card delivered by hand. Opening it, I read the message, then the signature, touched that Nathan took the trouble to come here; I smile as I imagine him planting the primroses. Getting out my phone, I text him.

Thank you.

Pausing, I'm struck how things happen that cut through the banality of life; that's become apparent these last days and weeks. And it's the value of the people in our lives, the important ones, who touch our hearts; who in the smallest ways, show us they care. Whatever we are or aren't to each other, Nathan's definitely one of them. Adding an *x*, I press send.

One morning, I take a drive on my own to one of the beaches. But this isn't one that Liam and I found. It's one I remember from my childhood. The spell of calm weather has passed and the beach is empty, the sea wild, a cold wind gusting on to the shore.

As I stand there, my head fills with memories of coming here as a child with my parents and sisters. I can almost hear the echo of our voices, picture the blanket laid out on the sand, my mother's picnic basket of delicious food; my sisters running ahead of me towards the sea... Maybe it's because my father's been so ill, but as the picture fades, it comes to me. The essence of who Liam was can't just disappear.

I'm aware of the wind swirling around me before, thinking intently, I tune it out. When it comes to life and death, there is still so much we don't know. What if I've been looking in the wrong place? If, somewhere I can't reach, he is out there?

'Liam?' I whisper. For a moment, nothing happens. Then as the faint scent of his cologne comes to me, I gasp, as I hear the echo of his voice.

I'm proud of you.

It's as though he's standing beside me. I spin around. 'Are you here, Liam?' I whisper.

I'll never know if I imagine the word that comes to me, but I do know it's true.

Always...

It's a moment I keep to myself, trying to make sense of it before giving up. But I'm left with a profound sense of gratitude for the conviction that while Liam may have gone from this life, he is still with me.

* * *

I've still been spending most of my time at my parents' house. At some point I know I have to go home, but I'm worried about leaving my mother with too much to cope with. When I go to find her, she's in the kitchen sorting through a mountain of paperwork.

She looks up as I come in. 'Ah, Callie. Isn't it time you thought about going home?'

'What about you?' I say anxiously.

'You mustn't worry about me. I'll be fine,' she insists. 'I have plenty to do before we put the house on the market.'

I've been wondering if they've changed their minds about moving, but they clearly haven't. 'I'll come back tomorrow,' I tell her. With my father able to do little to help, there's too much for her to do alone.

'There's really no need. You have your life to live,' she says firmly. 'We'll be absolutely fine. I can always call you if I need you.'

Gazing at the paperwork, I think about the cupboards and drawers full of a lifetime's worth of possessions. 'Mum, there's a lot to do here.'

'Well, I'll do what I can, then maybe you girls can help me with the rest.' Her no-nonsense manner is back.

'Are you sure you're going to be OK?' I say quietly.

'Of course I am.' She stops for a moment. 'We both are. Your father and I have had a long and wonderful life together. We've been lucky that until now, we've both had our health. But as you get older, these things happen. You know, I'll always be grateful to him.' She hesitates, an odd look crossing her face. 'Do you know he saved me from a dreadful man?'

Astonished, I sit down opposite her. 'I had no idea. What happened?'

'A very good question.' She frowns. 'I suppose at the time, I was a little deluded, really. I was engaged to this chap. Completely smitten.' She rolls her eyes. 'Anyway, just before our wedding, I found out he'd been having an affair. It was quite shocking at the time. Your father was one of his friends – well, that was until he found out. He came to see how I was. Of course, I was utterly hopeless. I told him how in love with Magnus I was...'

'Magnus?' I can't help but giggle.

My mother looks surprised. 'That was his name, yes. Your father proceeded to give me chapter and verse on just what a total bounder Magnus was. And that if I hadn't seen through him, I needed to open my eyes. I was quite taken aback, as you can imagine. But of course, I realised he was right.'

'I've never told you, but the week before our wedding, Liam and

I had a wobble.' The words are out before I can stop them. 'He didn't want to have children. We spent a night apart... He came back the next day and begged me to forgive him. He said he did want to marry me. I think it was pre-wedding jitters. Of course, I forgave him...'

As I speak, my mother listens in silence, before getting up. She comes over to me, her eyes glistening as she takes my hands in hers. 'I know relationships are never perfect, but maybe it's as well you didn't marry him,' she says quietly. 'It's hard enough over the years, without being on different pages at the start.'

'I was weak,' I say simply.

'Callie, you have never been weak,' she says sadly. 'You were in love.'

* * *

But over the last year, I've learned who to trust, and who not to. And in spite of the girl I saw at his house, something tells me Nathan's one of the former. Still, it's been a while since I've seen him, And deciding to take matters into my own hands, after work the next day, I drive over to Nathan's.

When he opens the door, he looks pleased to see me. 'I was just thinking about you. Would you like to come in?'

'Thanks.' Going inside, I close the door behind me as the heat from the wood burner reaches me. 'It's nice in here.' I hesitate. 'I'm sorry I haven't been in touch. But as you know, there's been so much going on.'

'I can imagine...' He looks at me. 'I wanted to see you, too. Last time you were here. I'm guessing you saw Emily and jumped to the wrong conclusion. Just so you know, she pitched up here completely uninvited. I want you to know there's nothing going on between us.'

I fold my arms. 'From where I was standing, it looked pretty cosy between you. But... You had asked me on a New Year's Eve date. And honestly, I don't think you would have if you were seeing someone else.' I frown slightly. 'I am right, aren't I?'

He looks relieved. 'You are – completely. It's the kind of thing Emily does. She's impulsive – and pretty determined when she wants something. But I didn't kiss her back – and it definitely was not reciprocated.' He pauses. 'She's an ex. She dumped me when I was ill – there wasn't space in her life for a boyfriend with health problems. She was staying with her parents over Christmas. They had a row and she just turned up here.'

I hold my hands up. 'Honestly, I do believe you – and it's really none of my business.'

'I wanted you to know the facts, that's all.' He looks at me quizzically. 'I still don't know why you came here that day.'

'My dad had just been taken into hospital again.' I pause, remembering. 'I wasn't feeling too good.' I pause again, looking at him. 'I guess it was one of those times I needed a friend.'

'I'm so sorry.' His words sound genuinely heartfelt. 'I wish I'd known.'

I shake my head. 'It doesn't matter.' I walk closer to him. 'I suppose when you believe you're about to lose someone, it does weird stuff to your head – about what's important. I worked out it's my parents and my sisters... But also... you are, too.' I gaze at him. 'Anyway, I just wanted to say that – because so often we don't say these things.' Awkward all of a sudden, I stand there. 'I've said too much, haven't I?'

Shaking his head, he puts his arms around me.

* * *

More and more, I'm aware Nathan and I are growing closer. Meanwhile, I plough my spare time into fine-tuning my plans for the walk in Spain, working out what clothes I need to take and buying some walking boots. Setting off on hikes to wear them in, I walk the coast path.

I express my misgivings to Sasha, that I can't help feeling we should put this off. Since our other sisters live further away, it's feels too soon to leave our parents. But Alice and Rita aren't having any of it. 'We can look after them. We've known for ages that you and Sasha are doing this. You need this.'

And they're right. We do. It's just the timing.

My mother, meanwhile, astonishes me and after clearing out their old clothes, she starts on the house that for thirty-five years has been their home.

'I don't know how I've ended up with so much stuff,' she says time and time again. 'I honestly don't know what to do with it all.'

'We'll get someone in, love.' My father is unperturbed.

'I can't have a stranger going through this house,' my mother says crossly.

'Come and have a cup of tea, Mum.' I pull out a chair at the kitchen table, placing a mug where there's a gap between the boxes, before sitting next to her. 'Have you and Dad decided what's next?'

She looks confused. 'You mean after we leave here?' She glances at my father. 'Good God. I've been so busy, I haven't thought.'

'Well, luckily looking at a laptop is one thing I can do.' My father's eyes twinkle at her. 'I have a short list – when anyone's ready.'

'Perhaps you need to look at them, Mum?' I say gently. 'Once you have an idea of what kind of property you're after, it will be so much easier to work out what you're going to need – and what you won't have room for.'

'Oh dear, I don't know what I've been thinking.' She looks flustered.

'Shall I get your laptop?' I ask.

'I think that's a very good idea.' He glances at my mother. 'What do you say?'

She blinks at him. 'I suppose so.'

After an hour perusing the properties he's picked out, one in particular catches her eye. A cottage with a good-sized garden, it's in a village a few miles away. 'It's a bit small,' she says doubtfully.

'Most houses are compared to this one. But that cottage has four bedrooms, Mum – and two are downstairs. You'll still be able to have us all to stay, but the rooms are smaller and it has a manageable garden. I really like it.'

'I think it looks perfect,' my father says. 'Shall we go and see it?'

I go with them to view it. It has a large kitchen-diner and a cosy sitting room with a fireplace. And while the walls need a lick of paint, it's clearly been someone else's much-loved home. My mother, meanwhile, is smitten with the garden and when she makes up her mind surprisingly quickly, my father takes no persuading.

Already mentally moving in, she looks at my father. 'I really can't be bothered going to see anywhere else. What do we do next?'

'I'll take care of that,' he says quietly.

'I don't think so, Dad. You're supposed to be taking it easy, remember?' I have an idea. 'But if we need some help, as it happens, I know just the person.'

* * *

I stand on Nathan's doorstep, trying to explain. 'They've lived in the house for thirty-five years – and she's extremely capable. But my dad's always taken care of their finances and right now, he's supposed to be taking things easy. Obviously I just wondered if you might be able to help us organise things like surveys and moving – and if there's anything else that needs sorting before they move in.'

Nathan nods. 'I'd be happy to. Shall I go over to see them?' He hesitates. 'Or would you like to bring them here?'

'Oh.' I haven't got that far. 'Could I bring them here? The house is chaotic. I think it would do them good to get out for a bit.'

'Why don't you talk to them and let me know?'

I'm filled with gratitude. 'This is so kind of you. Honestly, I really can't thank you enough.'

* * *

It's late by the time I get home. Going inside, I pick up the post. Sifting through it, I see it's mostly junk mail, with the exception of a letter that's addressed to me. Opening it and reading the first few lines, I take in a second envelope inside, as I stop breathing. I put it down, time seeming to stop as suddenly I'm whisked back to our wedding day, to the moment I was at my lowest just after Liam died.

26

NATHAN

After a call from Callie asking if she can bring her mother over, I tidy the house, plumping cushions, before stoking up the fire and putting on a clean shirt. As I come downstairs, Callie's car pulls up outside.

Standing back from the window, I watch how solicitous she is as she takes her mother's bag, waiting as she gets out, before taking her arm as they walk towards the house.

Halfway there, they pause, standing there for a moment, as Callie gestures towards the garden, talking animatedly as now and then, her mother nods.

Hearing Callie knock, I open the door.

'Hi.' Her eyes seem luminous. 'This is my mum, Diana. Mum, this is Nathan.'

I hold out my hand. 'Pleased to meet you.' Her eyes remind me of Callie's, but the resemblance ends there.

'Hello, Nathan. This is very kind of you. I'm sorry, my husband was supposed to come with us but we've left him resting.' Shaking my hand, she turns towards the garden. 'This is rather lovely.'

'Thanks, but it wasn't always,' I say wryly. 'Not until Callie took it in hand. Would you like to come in?'

'This is charming,' Diana says as she steps inside. 'Have you lived here long?'

'A few months.' I turn to Callie. 'Can I offer you a cup of tea?'

She smiles. 'Thanks – but we don't want to take up too much of your time.'

'I have plenty of time,' I assure them.

'Tea would be nice.' Taking off her jacket, Diana settles herself on the sofa.

After I've made her a cup of tea, Diana talks me through her plans, showing me the details of the house she's thinking of buying. As we discuss the process, from making an offer to organising a survey, now and then I catch Callie's eye, as she sits quietly, listening.

As the conversation comes to an end, she gets up. 'We should go, Mum.'

'There's really no hurry.' I look at Diana. 'More tea?'

'If you're sure.' Diana glances at Callie. 'We don't have to be anywhere, do we?'

'No.' A look I can't read flickers across Callie's face. 'Do you mind if I leave you to it for a bit? I'll be outside.'

Going out the back door, she closes it quietly behind her. Through the window I watch her stand on the terrace, looking around for a moment before going down the steps on to the grass. When I turn back to Diana, her eyes are clouded.

'Her father being ill, after losing Liam... It's been quite hard for her, I think.'

'I'm sure. How is your husband?.'

'He's getting better. Between you and me, though, last time we thought we were going to lose him.' She blinks away a tear. 'It really has been the oddest time. And of course, selling the house makes it even odder. Anyway...' She rallies herself, in the same way I've seen Callie do. 'Given what's happened, we're lucky, really. And a smaller house will suit us so much better.'

I can tell by the way she's talking, she's determined to focus on the positives. 'I know it's not that simple,' I say quietly. 'But I guess for lots of reasons, moving will be a good thing.'

'It's the start of our next chapter – and a very good time to get rid of all the stuff we've collected over the years.' She says it matter-of-factly, before pausing and looking at me. 'So, Nathan, is there anyone special in your life?'

Taken aback, I'm not sure what to say. 'Not for a while. I haven't been well – I'm fine now, but I ended up taking about a year off. Since moving here, though, I think there may be.'

'Callie?' she says quietly.

I'm that transparent? My face feels hot as I nod. 'I know she's working through some stuff. And we're friends... At least, I hope we are.'

Just then, the door opens and Callie comes back in. She looks excited. 'Have you seen the daffodils coming up? You have tiny, wild ones – like yours, Mum. They've probably been there for decades. And you have a clematis in bud.' She pauses. 'I didn't know you'd started a vegetable garden.'

'I've probably done it wrong,' I say hastily. 'I have a book, but I'm learning as I go along.'

'It's cool.' Callie turns to her mother. 'How are you getting on?'

'We've been having a nice chat.' Diana catches my eye. 'But it's probably time we went home and found out what your father's been up to.' There's understanding in Diana's eyes. 'Thank you, Nathan. It's been so very nice to meet you – and you've been so helpful.'

'If you have any questions, feel free to ask.' I'm thinking quickly.

'In fact, if you go back to look at the house again at some point, would it help if I come with you?'

* * *

I walk out to the car with them. As her mother gets in, Callie lingers. 'You don't have to do this.'

'I'd like to help. Property is my thing – as you know.' As I look at her, she seems preoccupied. 'Are you OK?'

'I'm not sure,' she says quietly.

I fold my arms. 'Want to talk about it?'

She hesitates for a moment. 'I suppose it's just a bit weird bringing my mother here.'

But I have a feeling there's something she isn't saying. I wonder if it's the ghost of Liam again – or maybe it's because this is the first time she's brought one of her family into my life. 'It's honestly no problem. I'm happy to help, you know.'

'I know you are. And thank you.'

'You're welcome.'

She gets into her car, then winds the window down. 'You're doing really well with your garden.'

'Believe me, I'm still learning,' I say as she starts her car. But she gives no indication that she's heard me over the sound of the engine. Giving a wave, she drives away.

Back inside, the house feels empty, silent. Thinking about Callie, I have an instinct that whatever's bothering her is something significant. Compared to the last time I saw her, she seemed distracted. I've given her the chance to share whatever it was, and I can't do any more than that. But as I already know, she's trying to find her own way.

27

CALLIE

A constant reminder of Liam, the presence of the letter hangs over me. Though I try to hide it, while my mother was talking to Nathan, once or twice I caught him watching me. It was as though he sensed something was wrong, but I couldn't bring myself to tell him about it.

Not sure I'm ready to face its contents, I put it in a drawer and go outside. Even in winter, the garden is beautiful in less obvious ways. The muted palette of greys and mossy greens; the grasses I've yet to cut back somehow ghostly, ethereal. As I search for the earliest signs that winter is coming to an end, I notice the first buds forming amidst the shoots, while tiny buds of luminous green are appearing on the trees – all signs of spring stealing its way in, bringing with it a tentative sense of hope.

With the walk to Santiago de Compostela coming closer, even with Alice's and Rita's assurance that they'll be spending time with our parents, I'm still not convinced I should be doing it.

Knowing that if I am, I need to start a more organised exercise regime, I call Sasha.

'I'm having second thoughts,' I tell her.

'I thought you might be – because so am I. So I spoke to Rita last night. Honestly, I think we don't need to worry. She's going to stay with Mum and Dad for her Easter break, and Alice is taking leave – and we both know Alice rarely takes leave.'

'But what if Dad has another heart attack?' I say anxiously.

'Then we'll come back,' Sasha says straight away. 'Alice and Rita are going to so much trouble for us,' she adds more gently. 'I really think they want us to do this.'

Relief flows over me. 'OK. Let's do this!' My excitement starts to return. 'I need to start walking more – and so do you,' I say to Sasha. 'I don't want you holding me back, you know. You need to up your training.'

'I am walking,' she says indignantly. 'Pretty much everywhere, as it happens. But it's mostly flattish pavements, as you know.'

'So come and stay this weekend,' I suggest. 'We can walk along the coast path. As a matter of fact, until we go, why don't you do it every weekend?' I'm suspicious all of a sudden. 'You haven't heard from that dreadful man again, have you?'

'I haven't.' Her voice is filled with amusement. 'Finally, he seems to have got the message.'

When she threatened to tell his wife, I'm not surprised. 'That's a really good thing. So, how about this weekend?'

'Why not?' She pauses. 'That way I can see Mum and Dad, too.'

'I have a better idea. They're up to their ears in boxes and packing – they could probably do with some help. Why don't we both spend the weekend there?'

* * *

By the time I arrive at my parents' house on Friday evening, Sasha's already there. When she sees me, she looks slightly shocked.

'I can't believe how much she's done.'

'You know what she's like when she puts her mind to something,' I say wryly. 'She becomes obsessed. And she won't let Dad do anything.'

'I still feel sad that they're leaving here.' Sasha's voice wobbles.

'Sash, she and Dad had already decided to move before he was ill. This will be good for them.'

'She said Nathan's been helping.' Sasha raises one of her eyebrows.

I feel my face grow hot. 'He buys and sells properties all the time. We're trying to take the pressure off Dad. He seemed the obvious person to ask.'

'I think she's taken quite a shine to him,' Sasha says conspiratorially.

'He's a nice guy,' I say quietly.

She looks at me as though I'm mad. 'He obviously likes you. Mum said he barely took his eyes off you.'

I'm silent for a moment. It's hard to explain how I'm feeling, when I haven't mentioned the letter to any of my family. I sigh. 'You're missing the point. Yes, I like him, as it happens. It just isn't the time, OK?'

Sasha takes my hands in hers. 'Will it ever be?' she says quietly.

I blink away the tears that seem to have come out of nowhere. 'I hope so,' I mutter. Wiping my eyes, I pull myself together. 'I think the walk is going to change a lot of things.'

'I'm so pleased to hear that,' she says softly. She smiles at me. 'Now, shall we go and be dutiful daughters? Mum's upstairs mucking out her wardrobe.'

* * *

The following day, the wind is brisk as Sasha and I set off along the coast path. If I'd been worrying that she wouldn't be up to it, it seems pavement walking has done the trick. We walk seven miles seemingly effortlessly.

'We're going to be walking further than this,' I tell her. 'Every day, for weeks – well, apart from the odd day off, that is.'

'Don't worry. I've done my research,' Sasha says calmly. 'I do know what I've signed up for.' She's quiet for a moment. 'I suppose there's no point in me trying to talk you out of taking the ferry?'

'None whatsoever,' I say quickly. 'Aeroplanes are unnatural. I don't trust them.'

'Crossing the Bay of Biscay when you don't have to is just as unnatural.' Before I can speak, she goes on. 'But I'll do it – for you. Just this once, though. As long as you never ask me to do it again.'

'Twice, Sash,' I remind her. 'We need to get back, remember?'

'You know you said you're hoping this walk is going to change things?' She gazes at me. 'Maybe you'll overcome your aversion to flying.'

I open my mouth to argue back. But this, I realise, is part of the problem. If I want things to change, I need to keep an open mind; to be prepared for what right now is the seemingly impossible.

* * *

When my parent's house is put on the market, after a flurry of viewings, it sells almost immediately. With two offers over the asking price, my mother is confused.

'I thought people were supposed to make an offer under the asking price.'

'Not these days, Mum.' I look at her. 'Luckily for you, there aren't enough houses – especially in Cornwall. It's a seller's market.'

'That's what your father said. And I definitely don't want us to sell it as a holiday home,' she says firmly. 'I want a family to live here.'

'Maybe you should talk to the agent about it,' I suggest.

'You know, I think I will.'

True to her word, when she discovers the higher of the two offers comes from a couple who live in London and who only want the house for high days and holidays, after talking to my father, they opt for the lower offer.

'I know to many people it doesn't make sense,' she says matter-of-factly. 'But we're still getting more than we thought we would. And it's important to know it's going to be a home to another family.'

When there's a delay on moving into the house she's found, she's typically impatient. But while my mother's organisational skills are second to none, it doesn't enter her head that other people are not the same. 'They're telling me there's a chain. It could be weeks, apparently. It really isn't very good. I'm ready to move now.'

My father refuses to get drawn in. 'I've told her, it will take as long as it takes.'

Astonishing as it is, everything bar their day-to-day essentials is packed and labelled, ready to go.

'These things happen, Mum.' I frown. 'Why don't you and Dad go away for a few days? Have a change of scene while this gets sorted.'

'We can't leave the dogs,' she says dismissively.

As I drive home, I can't help but wonder if her reluctance to go away is indicative of how she really feels; if moving is going to be more of a wrench than she's letting on.

Letting myself into my cottage, the unopened letter is preying on my mind. Picking it up, I go over to the sofa, a strange feeling coming over me as, slowly, I open it. Unsure if I'm ready for this, I hesitate. But as I force myself to read it, a feeling of disbelief fills me. Then as I read it again, my blood runs cold.

Going over to the dresser, slowly I pick up the card Nathan sent me. Comparing the signatures, I freeze for a moment, as I take in what this means.

Grabbing my keys and running outside, I'm barely thinking straight as I get in my car. On the way over to Nathan's, I'm shaking, crying, angry, all at the same time. I grip the steering wheel tightly, my head exploding with memories that until now I'd blocked out of the afternoon of what should have been our wedding day.

It's a time we should have been joyously celebrating. Instead, I'd been paralysed by shock, overwhelmed by grief; trying to get my head around the fact that Liam had gone, that life as I knew it had changed for ever.

* * *

Lying on my bed, at some point I was aware of Sasha coming in and lying next to me. I remember her stroking my hair, one of her arms over me. A little while later, Alice came in. Crouching on the floor beside me, she took my hand.

'Callie? I have to ask you something,' she said quietly. 'I know it's the worst possible time, but it's really important.' I remember noticing the reluctance in her voice. 'Did you know Liam had registered as an organ donor?'

Unable to speak, I nodded.

'There's a patient in severe need of a heart. If Liam's is a match, it could save their life.' She said it quietly. 'As you're his next of kin, I really need to know you're OK with this.'

My body started to shake. Liam's huge, generous, heart that was the essence of everything he was. The thought of it being removed was too graphic, too incomprehensible, too brutal.

'Callie?' she said gently. 'What would Liam have wanted?'

'He signed up for it,' I sobbed, squeezing my eyes tightly, trying to

staunch my tears. I was unable to give my assent to something that seemed so final. 'It isn't up to me.'

I was aware of Alice leaving my room as Sasha's arm around me tightened. I closed my eyes, trying to shut out the hideousness of it all.

I have only the vaguest memory of the support group getting in touch, even less of what was said. In my grief, I'd been all over the place, struggling to cope with each day, let alone with envisaging the future. And even if I had, I never could have imagined anything like this.

28

NATHAN

Sitting at my laptop, I'm distracted when I hear a car come up the drive, the sound of gravel spraying out as the brakes are slammed on hard. Hearing footsteps come running up the steps, I get to my feet and hurry to the door, opening it to find Callie standing there.

She's distraught, her eyes fill with tears as she waves two pieces of paper at me. 'All this time, Nathan... I can't believe you didn't you tell me. *Why?*'

Seeing the card I sent her, I'm confused. 'I'm not sure I know what you're talking about.' Then I notice the letter in her other hand. It looks remarkably like the one I wrote some weeks back. Shock washes over me. But before I can say anything, Callie goes on.

'I must have known,' she cries. 'Somehow, deep inside me. It's why it never felt right between us. And now...' She stops to wipe her face. 'I don't know what to think, Nathan. I don't know what to feel.' A tormented look crosses her face.

Seeing her in such distress, I feel my heart twist. 'Please come in,' I say as gently as I can. 'I really think we should talk about this.'

She looks poised, as if ready to take flight, and I half-expect her to turn around and run away. But after hesitating, she comes inside.

I close the door behind her. 'Come and sit down.' I lead the way over to the sofa.

'What are the chances?' There's anguish in her voice, but having got it out of her system, Callie seems slightly calmer. 'When I read the letter, I didn't think it could have been from you,' she says tearfully. 'But then I saw your signature... I had this really strange feeling, like I knew it was you. So I compared it to the signature on the card you sent me.'

'Of course they're the same. I'm so sorry—' I start to say, but she interrupts.

'Why didn't you tell me you'd had a heart transplant?'

Under her scrutiny, I feel uncomfortable. 'It isn't something I tend to talk about. I was ill for a long time. This last year, it's felt like I've been given a second chance.' But as I take in that it's Liam's heart that's saved my life, shock washes over me.

'Because Liam's heart is keeping you alive.' As she gazes at my chest, a look I can't read flickers across her face, before tears fill her eyes again, spilling over. 'I don't know what to do with this,' she whispered. 'It's too much.'

It's too much for me, too. But it doesn't stop me wanting to put my arms around her, to hold her close, to comfort her, though I know, right now, it isn't what she wants from me.

A look of incredulity crosses her face. 'It's why you made the sea pictures, isn't it? And why you're suddenly interested in gardening? And in me...' As she stands up, realisation dawns in her eyes. 'This is too weird,' she stares at me. 'You've changed the way you live, haven't you? Since you had a heart transplant? Your choices...' Her voice wavers. '*They're the same choices Liam made...*'

'I don't know,' I say desperately. 'You could equally say having major surgery would make anyone want to find a better way to live.'

I want her to understand how I feel about her, too. But something tells me it isn't the time.

She shakes her head. 'It isn't that.' Her jaw is set. 'I know it isn't. *You have Liam's memories,*' she whispers, a look of pain in her eyes.

'Look, I know how upsetting this is, but this is me, Callie. I think you know how I feel about you – and I think you have feelings for me, too. I've been holding off saying anything, because I know how guilty you feel. But...' I'm lost for words.

Realisation dawns in her eyes, only to be replaced by a haunted look. 'I'm sorry. I can't stay here.'

As she turns and walks towards the door, I hear another car outside. 'Wait,' I call after her. 'Please, Callie. You can't leave like this.'

Turning briefly, she looks distraught again. 'I have to.'

A knock on the door distracts me. When I open it, Robin is standing there.

'Hey, little brother.' She freezes as her eyes settle on Callie. 'Hi.' She looks at me questioningly.

'This is Callie. Callie, this is Robin, my sister.' I don't want her thinking this is a repeat of the Emily debacle. Behind her, I hear footsteps before Max walks in.

As he puts his arm around Robin, a gasp comes from Callie. '*Max*? What are you doing here?'

'Callie?' He looks stumped.

Max and Callie know each other? I stare at them both. This is getting stranger by the minute.

'You know Nathan?'

'We met when Robin and I got together.'

Callie shakes her head. 'This is crazy.' Tears stream down her face as she hurries towards the door. 'Sorry, I don't get any of this. I have to get out of here.'

'Callie,' I call after her. When she doesn't respond, I run after her, catching her up as she slams her car door shut. 'Please. Let's talk about this another time.'

'Max was Liam's best man.' Callie's voice is shaking. 'But I suppose you already know that.'

'I didn't.' As shock washes over me for the second time, my hands close over the top of the window. 'Honestly. It's the first I've heard of it.'

'You're not expecting me to believe you didn't know that Max had been in a major car accident? One that killed his best friend? You must have known. He's going out with your sister, for fuck's sake. You tried to trick me,' she sobs, starting her car.

'I didn't. Look, you're in no fit state to drive,' I say quickly. 'Come back inside. I'll ask them to leave.'

She doesn't reply. Putting her car into gear, she tries to drive away, but it stalls. The second time, she puts her foot down on the accelerator, sending up another spray of gravel. I step back, with no choice but to watch her drive away.

* * *

'Max just told me about Callie.' Robin's face is anxious when I go back inside.

'You don't know the half of it.' I'm still struggling to take in what's just happened. Sitting down, I feel exhausted. 'This is such a mess.' I rest my head in my hands.

Robin comes and sits next to me. 'What's happened exactly?'

Sitting up, I sigh. 'After I had the heart transplant, a woman from a support group came to see me. She left all this info. One of the brochures was about getting in touch with the family of the donor. To start with, I didn't do anything about it. To be honest, I was still getting to grips with the fact that someone else's heart was keeping me alive. But a few weeks ago, I wrote a letter. I had no idea who the donor was – personal details are kept confidential. I gave the letter to the support group to forward on to the family. The family turned out to be Callie...' I still can't believe it. 'She must have had this letter for a while.'

'But how did she know it was you?' Robin frowns. 'I mean, you've just said there's no way she could have linked the letter to you.'

'I signed my first name. But when Callie's father was ill, I wrote her a card. She compared the signatures,' I say miserably.

'Oh, Nathan.' Robin sounds sympathetic. 'She'll work it out. Give her a little time to take it in. It's a lot to process. It isn't surprising she was so upset.' She pauses. 'Are you OK?'

'I'm not sure.' I, too, need time to process this – and I'm worried that this will be the end of any hopes I have of being with Callie. I turn to Max. 'I had no idea your mate died in the crash. I'm so sorry.'

'He was a good guy.' Max's voice wavers. 'I've felt so guilty for surviving when he didn't... I know it doesn't change anything, but it takes some getting your head around. It's why I prefer not to talk about it.'

'While I'm only alive because of his heart.' I feel uncomfortable knowing who the donor was.

'It might just as easily have been someone else.' Robin tries to be matter-of-fact.

But it isn't that simple. 'Heart transplants aren't common. The heart has to be a match... then there's the timing. It isn't like I was local, either. I was in hospital in London. When you add it all together, it's some coincidence.'

* * *

But that isn't all that seems to be coincidental. After Robin and Max leave, I'm deep in thought. Callie was right. Since my heart transplant, my life has changed and so have I – in ways I would never have expected.

Getting my laptop, I sit on the sofa. I start to search for heart transplant patients and personality changes. And stumble across the unimaginable. Needing to talk to someone, I call Robin.

'Have you heard of cellular memory?'

'Can't say I have. Go on, tell me.'

'It's a theory that memories can be stored in the cells of the donated organ. It particularly applies to hearts. There can be changes in your preferences – and personality.' I pause. 'There can be memories, too.' I'm thinking about the sea pictures.

'You think that's happening to you?' She sounds alarmed.

'I don't know.' I'm at a loss. 'But you've said enough times how weird it is that I'd buy a house in the country and get into gardening. I know for a fact Liam did both those things.'

'Yeah. But don't forget also, major surgery's bound to make you have a rethink.'

'I've thought of that, too.' I'm silent, thinking, not sure how I feel about a stranger's unmeasurable influence on the person *I* am.

I think about going to see Callie. But in the end, I decide against it, guessing she'll need time to calm down and think this through. I wonder if maybe Max has gone to check on her – I should have asked Robin.

Sitting back, I sigh. I can't believe I hadn't figured out the connection between Max and Callie. But life can be so frigging complicated – and people so secretive. Half the time, there's no way of knowing who's going through what. It would be so much simpler if we could all be honest.

Callie's the only person I know who says it like it really is – most of the time, at least. OK, so it isn't always what you want to hear. But at least you know where you stand with her. It leaves me with a problem, however, because in spite of all this – or maybe because of all this, I still want to be standing much closer.

I wonder how much of what I feel is because Liam loved her; that in the infrastructure of his heart lay feelings, memories, this incredible sense of connection... The more I think about it, it's uncanny how much I've changed. Whether that's down to coming close to death or the fact that Liam's heart is beating inside me, I can't say.

But deep inside, I know how I feel about Callie. Even without Liam's heart, I would have fallen in love with her. Whatever the reasons for it, I've become this person I like far more than the old Nathan. I like that he has principles, that he likes this way of life, which is just as well, because even if I wanted to, there's no going back to who I used to be.

29

CALLIE

As I drive away from Nathan's, I start to feel calmer. Halfway home, I think about turning around and going back. But after accusing him of lying to me, I'm probably the last person he wants to see.

There's no reason for Nathan to want to deceive me. The fact is, none of this is his fault. He wrote a thoughtful letter of gratitude to the family of an anonymous man who died, thanking them for donating the heart that's keeping him alive. He had no way of knowing it would come to me.

Ignoring the hoot from the car behind me, I slow down. Then reaching a layby, I pull over. Lowering the window, I gaze across the hills and fields towards the sliver of sea that lies beyond, feeling ashamed of how I behaved just now.

But I was upset, I remind myself – and understandably so. I mean, how many people have to figure out something like this? I think about the way Nathan and I met; the way he makes sea pictures on the beach. When apart from Liam, there's no one else I know who does this, it's far too weird to be a coincidence.

Watching the first spots of rain splatter on to the windscreen, I call Tanith.

'I've done something terrible,' I say miserably.

'How terrible?' she says. 'Don't keep me in suspense.'

'I found out something – about Nathan.' I tell her about the letter and how Liam had signed up to be an organ donor; how at the time Liam died, Nathan was in need of a heart. 'On top of that, Liam's best friend turned up at Nathan's. It turns out he's seeing Nathan's sister.'

'Fuck.' She sounds shocked. 'That's some coincidence. In fact, that's a lot of coincidences. How are you feeling about it?'

'So mixed up. It's just the strangest thing to get my head around.'

'It's a massive thing to get your head around.' She's silent for a moment. 'So what have you done that's so terrible?'

I tell her how angry and upset I was; how when I drove away I felt terrible.

'So go and talk to him,' Tanith says calmly.

'What if he doesn't want to see me?' My voice trembles.

'It's a risk you have to take,' she says firmly. 'And from where you are right now, you don't really have anything to lose, do you?'

'I can't.' I still can't work out how I feel.

'Callie... You really can't leave this too long,' she warns. 'Remember, he's one of the good guys – and there aren't many of them, I can tell you.'

'I know. But maybe this is a sign that we're never meant to be more than friends. How could I be with someone who has my ex-fiancé's heart?'

'When you put it like that...' She sighs. 'Only you know the answer to that one.'

* * *

That evening, I hear a car pull up outside. Imagining Nathan coming to see me, I stiffen. Right now, I'm not sure I'd know what to say to him. There's a knock on the door before a voice calls out.

'Callie?'

It's Max's voice. Reluctantly I go to the door and open it.

He looks concerned. 'I thought you might want to talk to someone. Are you OK?'

'I'm upset.' I shrug. 'Why didn't you tell me you were going out with Nathan's sister?'

'Look, it's pissing down out here. Can I come in?'

I stand back to let him in before closing the door. Folding my arms, I look at him.

He holds up his hands. 'I didn't even know you knew Nathan. I knew there was someone who was helping him with his garden, but your name never came up.'

'What about Robin? Surely she must have known who I was?'

He shakes his head. 'I don't think she did.'

I feel the tension start to leave me as I start to believe him – and I know Nathan well enough to know he wouldn't talk about me behind my back. 'You must have known Nathan had a heart transplant.'

Max frowns. 'Yes, but not from him. He keeps to himself about it. It was Robin who told me – in confidence. She worries about him. But the other thing...'

I'm instantly suspicious. 'What other thing?'

His eyes are frank as he looks at me. 'Registering as a heart donor... I had no idea what Liam's view was.'

But I'm not buying it. 'You were his closest friend. You must have talked about it.'

'We didn't.' Max shrugs. 'I've no idea why not. But I guess we all have things we prefer not to talk about.'

I'm astonished. I thought Liam and Max told each other almost everything. 'So you and Robin... is it serious?' I'm still trying to take in these connections I didn't know about.

'Yes.'

I stare at him, seeing how intertwined our lives are. But instead of that being a good thing, all the hopes I had that Nathan and I might one day be something seem to shatter around me. Max will always remind me of Liam. Now that Nathan does too, is it too much?

'We haven't talked about you, Cal,' he says quietly. 'Maybe we should have – but everyone has their own stuff going on. Nathan and Robin... they're really good people – just so you know.'

I shrug. 'I'm sure they are.'

He sighs quietly. 'Look, give yourself some time to think about this. None of this is Nathan's fault.'

'I know that.' But knowing what I do, I'm not sure how to move on from this.

* * *

Deciding that for a while, I'll keep my distance from Nathan, I go to see my parents. As I drive along the familiar lanes it strikes me that this is one of the last times I'll come to my childhood home. No question, everything is changing around me.

But when I go inside, beyond its bare bones, already little remains of the home I love. As I wander through the almost-empty rooms, a strange feeling settles over me. Some of the furniture has already gone, curtains taken down leaving unframed views across the garden. Even the sitting room is spartan, the sofa and armchairs all that remain here, every photo, picture and nick-nack packed away.

In the kitchen, my father is sitting at the table with a mug of tea. 'Can I make you one?' he offers.

'I'd love one.'

I feel a pang of sadness as through the window I see my mother, fork in hand, digging up plants in the rain. 'I'll go and see if Mum would like one.' Pulling on my coat again, I go to join her.

The grass squelches underfoot as I walk towards her. 'Mum! You're getting soaked. Why don't you come inside for some tea?'

'A little rain does no one any harm,' she says firmly. 'I'm just digging up a few plants to take with us.' She pauses. 'Actually, a cup of tea would be a jolly good idea. There's something I want to talk to you about.'

I watch her finish digging up what I know to be a clump of asters. It's winter and they're nothing to look at now, but in autumn they come into their own in a haze of purple.

'Right,' she says. 'That'll do for now.'

'Any news about the house?' I ask as we walk across the garden.

'Not yet.' When she opens the back door, the dogs are waiting, wagging their tails at her. 'You two are fair-weather friends,' she admonishes them, as she takes off her coat. 'They didn't want to go out in the rain,' she tells me.

'I'm with them.' I follow her through to the kitchen where Dad is making cups of tea, as I notice some paint charts on the table.

'You're going to decorate?'

My mother glances at them. 'I'm thinking about colour schemes for the new house. After living with your father's obsession with magnolia, I thought it would be nice to have a change.'

My father raises his eyebrows at her. 'There's nothing wrong with magnolia. It's a perfectly nice, neutral colour.'

'Wow. But Dad, why not? You might even find you like it.' I sit down as he places a mug in front of me.

'That all depends on your mother.' Sitting down again, he starts going through the pile of papers in front of him.

I turn to my mother. 'So what was it you wanted to talk to me about?'

She looks cagey. 'I happened to have a little chat with Nathan yesterday.'

Across the table, my father clears his throat.

'Oh.' I'm not sure I like the idea of my mother and Nathan having a conversation about me. Suddenly I'm on my guard. 'I think I can guess what about.'

'He understands why you were upset,' she says more gently. 'For the record, so do I. Your father does, too.' Glancing at my father briefly, she turns back to me. 'It really is rather extraordinary when you think about it.'

I try to find the words. 'Actually, I'm finding it really weird.'

'It isn't Nathan's fault, you know,' she adds.

'I know that. But I can't help how I feel.' I look at my parents. 'To be honest, I don't want to talk about it.'

When I leave, my father walks out to my car with me. 'Your mother means well, you know.'

I nod. 'I know she does. But she doesn't know how weird this feels. Dad, you should go inside. It's pouring out here.'

He kisses me on the cheek. 'Don't make any rash decisions. Give it some time.'

* * *

After leaving my parents, on impulse I drive to Nathan's. I'm not sure what I'm hoping for, but maybe we do need to talk.

When he opens the door, he looks at me warily. 'Hi.'

'I come in peace,' I say quietly. 'Actually, I was hoping we could talk.'

Standing back, he lets me in, then closes the door behind me.

'I'm sorry about last time.' I gaze at him. 'I was in shock. I didn't know what to think. But then I realised it must have been just as much a shock for you.'

'You could say. I mean, there are so many coincidences in order for it to have happened at all...' He tails off. 'Would you like a cup of tea?'

I hesitate. 'Do you have anything stronger?'

After Nathan pours two glasses of wine, we take them over to the sofa, as I try to explain. 'I suppose, ever since it happened, I haven't wanted to think about Liam's heart being used for a transplant. And when your letter came, I didn't want to open it. I knew it had the potential to take me back to when it happened. It did...' My voice wobbles. 'And then I realised the letter was from you. I couldn't cope. You see...' Looking into his eyes, I take a deep breath. 'You were right, the other day. I do have feelings for you. And I've been coming to the point where I know that's OK. Then when I read the letter, it was like everything was turned upside down again.' I blink at him, slightly tearful. 'Do you understand?'

Sighing, he takes my hand. 'I pretty much worked that out. It's been weird for me, too. I really hope we can overcome this – but I understand if it's too much for you.'

I swallow the lump in my throat. 'Knowing you have Liam's heart... it's quite a lot to take in, isn't it?'

'It is.' He gazes at me. 'I really don't blame you for being upset when you found out, but I genuinely had no way of knowing who the donor was.'

'I realised that,' I say. 'Once I calmed down and thought about it.'

'Thank you.' A look of relief crosses his face, before he frowns. 'It's still odd, though, don't you think? The way we met?'

'Yes.' I gaze at him. 'But sometimes life is, isn't it?'

* * *

Before Sasha and I leave for Spain, I join Tanith for a meeting of the Graveyard Groupies. In a pastel pink sweater, she looks deceptively demure – until she speaks.

'I frigging can't wait for you to go away. If I don't have a break from her, I'm going to murder my mother.'

'Only one week to go, Tanith,' I remind her. 'It isn't long.'

'Honestly, it's going to be heavenly living at your place,' she says.

'Which reminds me. You need to come over so that I can tell you about my plants.'

She rolls her eyes. 'They're just plants. I mean I water them when it's dry... that's about it, surely?'

'We had a deal, remember? And they are not just plants,' I say firmly. 'When you come over, I'll explain.'

When only Joey turns up, I decide to confide in her. I tell her about Nathan's heart transplant, and she looks at me sadly.

'I think it's rather lovely in a way. Even though Liam couldn't have survived, he saved someone else's life.'

As her words sink in, I open my mouth and shut it again. 'I'm finding it weird,' I say at last.

'Of course you are.' Joey looks sympathetic. 'Real life is weird – and it's also messy, painful, confusing, shocking, all at the same time. But when something good comes along, don't you think we should grab hold of it with both hands and celebrate it?'

Not sure what she's getting at, I turn to Tanith.

'Joey's right,' she says quietly. 'Maybe by the time you've done your walk, you'll see why.'

30

NATHAN

There's no question that knowing that my heart was once Liam's has unsettled me. In an increasingly uncertain world, I try to streamline my life; to take each day as it comes; to stop and wonder at the simple things. Taking time out from work, I spend it in the garden, observing it come to life, finding seasonal hidden gems I didn't know about. A clump of scented narcissi, the pale lemon of wild daffodils; the primroses that have colonised under one of the apple trees.

Knowing Callie will soon be going away, I think about going to see her – if only to wish her well.

'Just call round there,' Robin suggests.

But I'm hedging. 'Callie's...' I start to say.

'She's what?'

'I think we both need some time, right now.'

'She probably feels terrible about what happened that day. If it had been me, I know I would.'

'She does. She came round here and apologised,' I tell my sister. 'Not that she needed to.'

'So go and see her.'

'Maybe. I'll think about it.' But with Callie going away soon, my instincts are telling me to leave her alone.

* * *

Work isn't going to plan, either, leaving me no choice but to pull out of the potential deal with the builder. I know immediately it's the right thing to do, but when I meet with him, I'm fully prepared for a backlash.

'You've wasted a hell of a lot of my time,' he says angrily. 'You're not going to find anyone else around here. Word gets about.'

'Don't threaten me,' I warn him. 'You've told me enough about the way you work to land yourself in a whole lot of trouble – if the right person were to find out. Let's see... we're talking about dodgy backhanders, substandard materials, intentionally not fulfilling a brief... and that's just for starters.'

There's a nasty look on his face as he mutters something, and as he walks away, I breathe an inward sigh of relief.

Back at home, though, the idea of the eco-friendly campsite is back on my mind. OK, so the planning application has been refused. But I'm not giving up on it. It has a hell of a lot more to offer than the new builds around here. Maybe if I do my homework, I'll be in a position to appeal.

As I sit there, I feel dizzy all of a sudden, the screen of my laptop blurring in front of me. Telling myself it's stress, I get up to get a glass of water. But as I walk to the kitchen, I feel lightheaded.

I sit down at the table and rest my head in my hands, waiting for it to pass. Half an hour later, when my vision is still cloudy, a feeling of fear fills me. Having been told what to look out for, with my medical history, I know I can't afford to ignore this. There are too many similarities to last time I was ill. Reaching for my phone, I call Robin.

For fifteen minutes I wait, wishing I could call Callie. As my mind fills with different scenarios, none of them appealing ones, and relief floods through me as I hear a car pull up outside, then the sound of Robin's footsteps before the door is quietly opened.

'Nathan?'

'I'm in the kitchen.'

As she comes in, she looks worried. 'Are you OK?'

'I'm not great,' I say. 'It came on out of nowhere.'

'Are you feeling any better?' She sits down next to me.

'Not really.' Her face is blurred as I look at her, my sense of fear growing. 'I'm worried it's just like last time.'

Robin gets up. 'We need to get you to the hospital.'

I nod. 'I've left a message for my consultant.' My legs feel weak as I stand up.

'Here.' Grasping my arm, Robin helps me out to her car.

* * *

Sitting beside the bed I've been given, Robin's face is ashen.

'You gave me such a scare.'

'Sorry about that.' I pat her hand. 'I scared myself. I thought it was happening all over again.'

'At least now you know it's not.'

A feeling of relief fills me. After numerous tests including an echocardiogram, I've been told I'm suffering from high blood pressure and prescribed some pills. I look around for a nurse, raising my hand until one comes over.

'Presumably there's no reason I can't go home?'

'I'll check with the doctors – but they were talking about keeping you in so that we can monitor you.'

I sink back on to the pillow. 'This really is not what I want to be doing.'

'I know.' Robin's voice is quiet.

A couple of minutes later the nurse comes back. 'They're going to check you out in the morning. If everything's OK, you'll be free to go.'

Glancing at Robin, I turn to the nurse. 'Couldn't I stay with my sister?'

Robin squeezes my hand. 'It's only one night. Just do what they say, OK? And get some rest. I want my big brother back healthy and strong. I'll come and pick you up tomorrow.'

As I lie in bed that night, I have a sense of déjà vu as I recall the weeks leading up to my surgery, then the recovery that followed. It was a surreal time, during which I never imagined getting any quality of life back. But as I recovered and grew stronger, not only did I start to feel well again, slowly I became aware of a sense of hope coming back. As more months passed, it was a time that slipped into the background, life returning almost to normal again.

So much has happened since: buying my house, then the land; working on my garden and meeting Callie. And maybe after major surgery, it's been too much. But it's ironic, too, that this setback has happened now, just when I've decided to streamline my life. Maybe more streamlining is required – and less pressure on myself. I'm not in a hurry with anything. I'm just not used to slowing down.

My thoughts are confirmed when a doctor checks me over the following morning.

'Take it easy for a while. Moderate exercise is good, but nothing too strenuous. You should see your GP in a couple of weeks, just to check your blood pressure. It's fine this morning. There really shouldn't be anything for you to worry about.'

'You're sure?' Beside me, Robin's face is anxious.

'He's fit to go.' The doctor's eyes linger on Robin.

'Thanks doc.' Getting up and picking up my overnight bag, I look at Robin. 'Let's get out of here.'

31

CALLIE

The week before Sasha and I leave for Spain, I pack my rucksack and get the house ready for Tanith and her boys. True to her word, she comes over one afternoon so that I can show her everything.

Her dark eyes are shining as she takes in the house. 'This is heaven,' she declares.

'It's quite cosy,' I tell her. 'Though when it's cold, you'll probably need to light the wood burner.'

'The boys are going to love it here.'

'The beach is only about fifteen minutes away. Now,' I open the doors to the garden, 'pay attention, please. This is the important part.' I lead her to the cold frame. 'These pots are sweet peas – or at least, they will be. And these others...' I point to the neat rows of pots sown with various flower and vegetable seeds. 'Please, please can you remember to water them? Everything else...' I glance across the flower beds. 'They'll be fine as long as there's some rain – which let's face it, there's going to be plenty. After all, this is Cornwall... It's all going to start coming to life while I'm away. It'll be very pretty – so just enjoy.'

* * *

When I go to see my parents, I get a strange feeling as I turn into the familiar driveway and park near the house. I stand for a moment, casting my eyes over the large windows, the stone walls and solid timbers, the wooden door through which so many people have passed, knowing this might be the last time I come here.

It would be easy to feel sad. But it's one of those times in life when things are changing – and will go on changing, because nothing stands still. Taking a deep breath, I go around to the back door and let myself in.

'Ah, Callie.' My mother's eyes are bright. 'I'm so glad you're here. I've just got off the phone to the estate agent. He's talking about exchanging contracts as soon as next week.'

'That's good, Mum.' Suddenly I'm regretting going away. 'I wish I was going to be here to help.'

'I knew you were going to say that. But you don't have to worry. Everything is organised – and as long as your father's well, we can cope with anything.' She frowns. 'Is something wrong?'

'I'm realising this is probably the last time I'm going to be here.' My eyes fill with tears.

Coming over, my mother takes my hands. 'I know it seems sad... And in some ways it is. But it's the right time for us to do this.'

'I know it is.' Blinking away my tears, I smile. 'I'm proud of you Mum – for making it happen. And for being so brave – and looking after Dad.'

'I can assure you we've both had our moments, you know.' There's the slightest waver in her voice. 'But there's no point dwelling on things you can't change. In any case, it's the beginning of something new. And really, we have much to be grateful for.'

Before I leave, I take a last walk through the house. Pausing in each room, I recall the happiest of family times we've had here, the life events that have taken place, the conversations that have echoed within these walls; feeling grateful that this house will soon be loved by someone else.

'Good luck with the move, Mum.' I kiss her on the cheek. 'Hopefully when I see you next, you'll be in your lovely new home.'

'Yes.' She nods just as my father comes in.

'I'm glad I've caught you.' He reaches into one of his pockets and takes out a small box. 'I want you to have this. It used to belong to my father. I thought it might be useful.'

Inside the box, I find the compass that was given to him when he was just a teenager. As a child, I remember being fascinated by it. Hugging him, I swallow the lump in my throat. 'Thanks, Dad. I shall really treasure this.'

* * *

With everything else in order, my thoughts turn to Nathan. It doesn't feel right to leave without seeing him. I think about the times he alluded to being ill – including the latest when he said that's why Emily dumped him. He must have been seriously ill if he needed a heart transplant – and she walked out on him.

A terrible realisation comes to me as suddenly my mind is racing. I've been so preoccupied with myself, I haven't properly considered what Nathan's been through – most likely is still going through. Pulling on my jacket, I grab my car keys.

* * *

'I'm so sorry.' Standing on Nathan's doorstep again, my eyes fix on his as I pull my jacket around me against the wind. 'But I really wanted to see you before I leave. Is there any chance I could come in?'

He stands back, and as I go inside, I notice how pale he looks.

Closing the door, for a moment, he doesn't speak.

'Can I make you a cup of tea?'

I breathe an inward sigh of relief. 'I'd really like that.'

After he makes the tea, he brings the mugs over to the sofa and passes me one.

'Thanks.' Sipping my tea, I pause, studying him. 'Are you OK?'

He nods. 'I am now. But I had a bit of a scare a few days ago.'

A feeling of foreboding comes over me. 'What happened?'

'I was working and suddenly my vision blurred. I felt really strange. Robin drove me to the hospital and I had some tests – it turned out to be high blood pressure. So as long as I take my pills, I should be fine.'

Relief fills me. 'Thank goodness.' I pause. 'I wish I'd known.'

'I thought about calling you.'

'I wish you had.' It strikes me that if I'd known, there's no question I'd have wanted to be there. 'Do you mind if I ask you about your illness?'

'I don't. But it's a bit of a long story.' He sighs. 'I was born with a condition called inherited cardiomyopathy. For the first eighteen years of my life, I didn't know anything was wrong. I was a regular guy who used to run and surf and play football. Then one day, at home, I passed out. When I came round, my parents had called an ambulance. They took me into hospital. I was completely convinced I was fine – that I'd just fainted because of low blood sugar or something – and it wasn't that big a deal. I'd been training hard – I thought I'd worn myself out. They did some tests.' A look of bewilderment flickers across his face. 'Lying in that hospital bed, I didn't feel at all bad. But that was when they diagnosed me. Basically, my heart was incapable of pumping my blood around my body. My life changed from that moment. I had to cut out sport altogether.'

'That's why you haven't surfed in a while,' I say quietly.

'Yeah. I lived a much slower life and for a while, it worked. But about six years later, it all got much worse. At one point they installed a defibrillator. I started to feel better. I suppose I went a bit mad – partying and all the rest of it. It was like I was making up for lost time. For about three years, life felt fantastic, but it wasn't long before everything was taking so much effort again. That was when they told me that basically my heart was failing.'

In other words, he'd been dying. A cold feeling comes over me as I try to imagine how that must have felt. 'It must have been so frightening.'

He nods. 'It was terrifying. For a while, life was really tough. I didn't know if I was going to survive or not. They had me on a list for a transplant. Meanwhile, my condition was getting worse. I was giving up hope. I honestly thought I was going to die. But then they found a heart and I had surgery. I spent a while in hospital, but when I came out...' He breaks off, remembering. 'Once I'd recovered, it was incredible, as though I'd been given a new lease of life. I felt completely well – and I could do all these things I hadn't done for years.'

I'm silent, taking it in, as he goes on. 'As far as my heart goes, I could be fine for the next ten, twenty years. The current record is thirty-three years, which would take me into my sixties. But also, it could be much less than that. They might well give me another transplant in the future, if I need one – and if a heart is available.' He looks at me. 'There are no guarantees.'

But as I know, there are no guarantees for any of us. 'Is that part of the reason you moved here?'

'Yes.' He pauses. 'Having come so close to dying, I feel like I've been given a second chance. It's why it's been so important to make meaningful changes in my life. As I got better, I found myself craving peace and space. And in a way, I wanted to challenge myself.'

I'm quiet for a moment, trying to imagine how he feels. 'That makes sense.'

He's silent again. 'I don't know if you've read about it, but there's a thing called cellular memory. The premise is that feelings and personality traits aren't just in the mind – they can be stored in major organs.' Pausing, he looks at me. 'Such as the heart.'

But it fits with what I was thinking last time I came here. 'There are things about you that remind me of Liam.' I hesitate. 'But there's a lot about you that's very different, too.'

'I don't know what to think.' His eyes are troubled. 'I know I'm different to how I used to be. I've always put it down to the fact that after being so ill, it's a miracle to feel well again. But I have wondered if any of it's to do with Liam.'

'We'll never know, will we?' I say softly. 'And maybe the *why* matters less than we think. It's *who* you are that's important.'

'Do you mean that?' His eyes lock on to mine.

I nod. 'I've thought about it so much – and I really don't want this to come between us,' I say quietly.

'Nor do I.' His voice is husky as he gazes at me. 'So how about this.' He clasps one of my hands in one of his. 'When you come back, if I ask you out, what would you say?'

A feeling of warmth comes over me as I smile back at him. 'I think you know the answer to that.'

A smile comes over his face before he changes the subject. 'So, you must be almost ready to go.'

'I am. We leave tomorrow. I'm meeting Sasha at Portsmouth. I'm really looking forward to it. It's funny. It isn't good timing with my parents about to move, but I have this feeling I have to do this.'

He smiles. 'I've told your mother if I can help in any way, she only has to call me.'

'That's so kind,' I say quietly. 'But shouldn't you be taking it easy? Quiet life, no stress?'

'Ha! Yes... supposedly. And I am.' He looks at me. 'I'll be thinking of you on this walk.'

I smile at him. 'When I come back, I'll tell you about it.'

'I'm going to look forward to it.'

Going outside, we take a quick meander through his garden. The hard work of last year is paying off and the garden will soon be glorious. 'I'm sorry I'm going to miss it coming to life, but it's really going to be lovely,' I tell him.

'Thanks to you.' He turns to face me. 'I'm going to miss you.'

'You mean you'll miss my obsessive outspokenness and my weeding skills,' I joke.

'Those, too.' His eyes twinkle. 'But mostly I'm just going to miss seeing you.'

* * *

I feel a quiet sense of peace as I drive away. It lasts only until I park outside my house and my mobile rings.

'Hey, Sash! Are you ready for tomorrow?'

'Callie, something terrible has happened.' She sounds distraught. 'I tripped going up the stairs at work this morning – I've broken my ankle.'

My heart misses a beat. This can't be happening – now of all times. 'Are you sure?'

'Of course I'm sure. I saw the X-rays. I'm in plaster.'

'But the walk,' I say quietly. 'We're supposed to be leaving in the morning.'

She sounds wretched. 'Could we put it off? I'm so sorry, Cal, but I won't be going anywhere.'

'I need to think.' My head is spinning. I don't know what to do – and it will be months before Sasha's up to this much walking. 'Look, just rest up, won't you? I'll call you tomorrow.'

As I end the call, I contemplate calling off the trip. Going outside, I take in the empty flower bed. My roadblock. Suddenly I realise I owe it to myself to do this. Just then, I hear a car pull up outside. It's followed by the sound of doors slamming and children's voices, as I realise Tanith's here.

She's desperate to come here; I can't let her down. I decide here and now that I'm going on my own. that I'm not going to tell her about Sasha.

When I open the door, the boys come scooting in excitedly lugging bags. 'Hi, guys! Make yourselves at home!'

Removing more bags from the back of her car, Tanith looks at me. 'Hey! You all set for tomorrow?'

As I hide my apprehension at making the trip alone, excitement flickers through me. 'As ready as I'll ever be. Want a hand?'

'Thanks.' She passes me a box. 'We have a ridiculous amount of stuff – but that's children for you. We have airbeds, too.' She rolled her eyes. 'The boys insisted – even though they only need them for tonight. I can't thank you enough for this. I had a humdinger of a row with my mother last night. She basically told me I was a terrible role model for my children and they'd probably grow up with all kinds of problems.'

'That's outrageous.' I frown. 'And so wrong.'

'She likes to be the best at everything,' Tanith says bitterly. 'By telling me how rubbish I am, it makes her feel better about herself.

But the worst has been having nowhere else to go, when it's hardly my fault that I can't afford a house around here.'

'Prices are crazy,' I say feelingly, thinking of the market for second homes. 'I'm really glad you have a few weeks away from her.'

'And I'm glad you're going,' Tanith says more gently. 'You need this, don't you?'

'I really do.' It's true. Doing this walk feels like some kind of turning point.'

* * *

We help the boys inflate their airbeds in the guest bedroom and eat giant pizzas together. When I cut the cake I've made them, they shriek delightedly.

'They're great kids,' I say to Tanith when the boys eventually go upstairs to bed.

'Thank you.' She shakes her head. 'They're exhausting at times, but they are these joyous, vibrant little souls and I just love them.' She pauses. 'Thank you for this. The boys and I really appreciate it.'

'Stop thanking me,' I tell her. 'Anyway, you're doing me a favour.'

* * *

Early the next morning, when Tanith takes me to the station, she eyes my rucksack. 'How can you possibly have enough stuff for six weeks?'

'I have to carry it – that's how. I have everything I need in there.' I think of my dad's compass, nestled in one of the pockets. 'Can you give my parents a call? Tell them you saw me on to the train?'

'Of course I can.' She hugs me.

'OK. I'd better go or I'm going to miss it.' I glance into the back of the car. 'See you guys. Look after your mum.' I kiss Tanith's cheek. 'Thanks for the lift. I'll let you know when I get there.'

A few minutes later, I'm on a train. Watching the countryside flash past, I know Sasha won't be expecting me to go without her. On cue, her face flashes up on the screen. I let it go to voicemail. This is taking all my courage; I can't risk anyone talking me out of this.

32

NATHAN

Taking medical advice, I tell myself I need to ease up on work. But the camping project doesn't feel like work. It's fast becoming something I feel passionate about. Lying on the sofa with my laptop perched in front of me, I peruse websites, educating myself about Cornwall's flora and fauna; wishing I was sharing this with Callie. Then looking for a similar model, I start searching for other sites.

It isn't long before I find what I'm looking for. It's almost exactly what I want to create – in a similar location. Hoping to get some tips on how they got planning through, I send them an email.

Now that I'm gathering information, at last I feel I'm on the right track. Newly invigorated about my plan, I drive to St Ives to meet Rick and Gina, who started something similar a couple of years ago. Far enough away that we're not in competition with each other, they're happy to answer my questions.

Gazing around the field, where several bell tents are set in their own area of garden, I start to imagine how mine could look. Rick and Gina suggest suppliers, but the high point comes when they introduce me to Simon, the friend who helped them get their planning application through.

After fixing a date for Simon to come and see me, as I drive home, I'm starting to feel hopeful.

More than once I wonder how Callie and Sasha are getting on, until later on, I take a phone call from her mother.

'I don't suppose you've heard from Callie, have you?' Diana sounds anxious. 'Only she isn't answering her phone. I think she's probably still upset about Sasha.'

My ears prick up. 'What about Sasha?'

'She broke her ankle – the day before they were due to leave. Terrible timing. She's awfully upset. We've both been trying to reach Callie, but she seems to have gone to ground. I just wondered if there's any chance you might have seen her.'

I'm taken aback. 'She came here a couple of days ago, but she didn't mention anything about Sasha.'

'She probably didn't know at that point.' Diana's clearly worried. 'Maybe she's gone on her own.'

I know how much this trip means to Callie, but going alone is a whole different kind of challenge. 'All I know is how much she was looking forward to doing this with Sasha. But I'll pop over to her house later and see if she's there.'

As the call ends, I stand there for a moment, before deciding I'll go over there now. If Callie has cancelled the trip, there's no question she'll be upset. Picking up my keys, I pull on a jacket and go out to my car.

On the way over there, I'm half-hoping to see her, while at the same time, knowing how important it is, I'm hoping she's doing the walk regardless. When I reach her house, my heart lifts involuntarily as I see her car parked outside, in front of another car I don't recognise.

Getting out, I knock on the door. Seconds later, it opens.

'Hi.' A girl with long strawberry-blond hair stands there. 'Can I help you?'

'Is Callie here?'

'No.' She frowns. 'You are?'

'I'm Nathan.'

'Ah.' A look of recognition dawns across her face. 'The guy with the garden.'

'That's me.' I look at her.

'I'm Tanith.' She holds out a hand on which the nails are painted multiple different shades. 'You want to come in?'

'Thanks.' Then the penny drops. 'Tanith as in the Graveyard Groupies?'

'One and the same.' She smiles. 'Like a beer?'

'Please.'

She seems very at home as she goes to the fridge. Passing a bottle to me, as a crash came from upstairs, she rolls her eyes. 'My boys. We're staying while Callie's away. She needed someone to water her plants, and I was desperate to get away from my mother. I live with my parents. It's a long story I won't bore you with.' She chinks her bottle of beer against mine. 'Cheers.'

I was taken by surprise. 'So Callie's gone?'

She nods. 'I took her to the station this morning.' She glances at the clock on the wall. 'She'll probably be waiting for the ferry by now.' She looks stricken. 'She asked me to call her parents to tell them she was on the train. I completely forgot. I'd better call them now.'

'Hold on a moment.' I try to slow her down. 'Did she tell you about Sasha?' When I fill Tanith in, she looks shocked.

'Why on earth didn't she tell me?' she demands.

'I'm guessing she didn't want anyone talking her out of it. I mean, it's a long trip to do on your own.'

'She'll be absolutely fine.' Tanith was matter-of-fact. 'I mean, I'm not saying it isn't a big deal. But she seemed to know what she was doing.'

After another beer and an introduction to Tanith's lively children, she calls Callie's parents, apologising profusely before trying to reassure them.

'I feel terrible.' Coming back into the kitchen, she shakes her head.

'Don't. They know now, and that's what matters.' I pause. 'So how long are you here?'

'Until Callie comes back.' She rolls her eyes. 'To be honest, it's a godsend. I've been living with my parents since my husband died – long boring story. Anyway, I can't afford my own house – and this is the first time in ages we've had some space – just for the three of us.'

'What will you do when Callie's back?'

A shadow crosses her face. 'Move back in with my folks. To be honest, I don't have much choice.'

'It's a real dilemma around here, isn't it? Affordable housing?'

'You could say.' She drinks some more beer. 'And it isn't just housing. It's affordable childcare. What's someone like me supposed to do when the kids are on holiday?'

'I've no idea.' Not having children, it's way off my radar.

She goes on. 'What's needed is somewhere fun – and subsidised. And safe,' she adds. 'But as far as I know, there literally isn't anywhere.'

* * *

Back home, wondering if Diana has spoken to Callie yet, I call her.

'Tanith is staying at Callie's while she's away. It seems Callie's waiting for the ferry – as we speak.'

'I never imagined she'd go on her own.' Diana sounds anxious.

Like Tanith did, I try to reassure her. 'She's waited a long time for this. I think if she'd cancelled it, she'd have felt she was letting herself down.'

'Stubborn, isn't she?' But Diana says it affectionately. 'I suppose we all have to do what we have to. I just hope she's going to be OK.'

'I'm sure she will. And if it doesn't work out, there's nothing to stop her coming back.'

After switching off my phone, I lie back on my sofa and put my feet up, thinking of Callie, hoping she finds what she's looking for. All of a sudden, I feel weary. But it's been a busy few days. I need to remember to pace myself.

As I think about the campsite again, I go over the conversation I had with Tanith, wondering if it would be possible to integrate some kind of community project that addresses her problems. But whatever I do, if the business takes off, it's clearly going be too much for me to do myself. Maybe it's time to think about employing someone.

* * *

On Sunday morning I find myself drawn back to Callie's house. I have an idea on my mind I want to talk to Tanith about.

'It's early days at the moment,' I tell her as we sit down with mugs of coffee. 'And the first time I applied for planning permission, it was turned down. But I have someone who's going to submit the revised application for me. I'm hopeful this time it will be successful.' I sip my coffee. 'You said you live with your parents?'

She rolls her eyes. 'Like I said, it's a long story.'

I'm curious. 'I have time.'

'OK.' She glances out of the window. 'Fuck, they're kicking the ball through Callie's plants. She's going to kill me.'

'Don't worry. Nothing's really started growing yet.' I think quickly. 'You could bring them over to mine, if you like. There's plenty of room to kick a football around.'

She looks startled. 'Are you hitting on me?'

'No way,' I say quickly. 'I promise. I have a large garden and it looks like your boys—'

'They need fucking acres,' she says eloquently. 'Sorry to be so blunt. But I had to ask, you know – firstly, I don't know you, but secondly, because of Callie.'

Itching to ask what Callie had been saying to her, I exercise admirable self-restraint as she tells me about losing her husband. She sips her coffee. 'My dad is great, but my mother... We're chalk and cheese. Basically, she's never had to worry about money and she likes to remind me of my failings.' She frowns at me. 'Remind me why I'm telling you this?'

'I asked. And because...' A victim of circumstances beyond her control, Tanith's exactly the kind of person I'd like to benefit from my project. As I tell her about the idea I've had, I watch her eyes grow round.

'Fuck,' she says at last. 'You're sure about this?'

'Nothing's definite,' I say quickly. 'But if it comes off, then yes, definitely. I'll tell you more as soon as I know, but keep it to yourself for now, OK? And one more thing, too: not a word to Callie.'

33

CALLIE

The ferry pulls out of Portsmouth and as I stand on deck watching England fade into the background, a feeling of freedom comes over me. Breathing in the salty air, I feel the breeze catch my hair as for a moment I think of Liam.

It's strange to be embarking on the trip we were going to do together. More so because so much has happened this last year. But it isn't just about losing Liam and coming to terms with that. There's my father's illness. There's meeting Nathan, too; the realisation that just when you think you know where your life is going, in the blink of an eye it can change.

It's true what they say. Healing takes time. But embarking on this trip is quite possibly the most significant part, as if I'm crossing a line between the past I've lost and an unknown future, one I somehow know is waiting for me.

Not wanting to be charged excessive roaming charges, I switch off my phone. As we head out into the English Channel, the rocking motion of the ferry amplifies. Picking up my bag, I head for my cabin.

I imagined a relaxing afternoon and evening lying on my bunk reading or listening to music, but in reality, it doesn't quite work out that way. Two hours on, the ferry is pitching and rolling as it rumbles towards the Bay of Biscay, as I think about the warnings I didn't heed. Telling myself that even an Atlantic storm can't go on like this, I take some seasickness pills. But it's too little too late, and staggering to the bathroom I'm violently sick.

Huddled on my bunk, I give myself a pep talk, about letting my fears get the better of me. But, if only just, this is still preferable to flying.

A particularly large swell makes the ferry judder. Suddenly I'm terrified. I know ferries do this journey every day of the year, but even those the size of this one must have their limits. Closing my eyes, I try to think about something else, before another wave of nausea has me staggering to the bathroom again.

And so it goes on, through a long, interminable night, until a couple of hours before reaching Santander, the pitching lessens. Relief fills me, followed by a feeling that's almost euphoric. Managing at last to connect to Wi-Fi, I text Sasha.

I have just survived what was quite probably the most horrendous storm in the history of ferry crossings... but I'm nearly there! xxxxx

I make it up on deck as Santander comes into view. It's a pretty town, flanked by green hills, the sea blissfully flat as I stand there taking it in. For so long this has only been a dream; the reality is breath-taking.

While we chug into the port, I make a quick call to my mother. 'Mum? Just letting you know I'm here.'

'I can't believe you've gone alone.' She sounds anxious.

'I was always going alone – until Sasha said she wanted to join me,' I remind her.

'It's just that it is a long time to be away on your own. You will be careful, won't you?' she says.

'Mum, I've been planning this for ages. It's the right time. I need this. Don't worry about me. I'm going to be fine.'

I hear another voice in the background, then Sasha comes on the phone.

'I can't believe you're there,' she says wistfully. 'I was really hoping you'd wait until I could come with you.'

I feel terrible for her. 'I'm sorry, Sash. But it's going to be months before you're going to be up for this. We can do something else? When your ankle's healed?' I pause. 'By the way, you were right about the ferry crossing. You were better off in England. It was horrendous.'

*   *   *

I step off the ferry on to Spanish soil, and feeling a thrill of excitement as I make my way towards the station. Technically speaking, the route I'm walking starts across the border in southwest France. But Sasha and I had decided to start a little further along in San Sebastián in northern Spain.

It's dark by the time my train finally arrives there. A little later, I find the hostel that Sasha and I booked for the first night. I'm not expecting much – we planned this trip on a budget, but up a narrow street, it's quiet and surprisingly comfortable.

Sitting on the bed, without Sasha here, I could let uneasiness take me over. I've never considered myself particularly adventurous. And after Liam died, for a whole year I barely went anywhere. But there's something about the fact that I'm doing this alone that I'm kind of proud of.

After a shower, I go back out, wandering the streets as the

nightlife gets going, stopping at a nearby bar to order tapas and a beer, texting Tanith while I wait.

I'm here!! Just ordered tapas. Ferry journey worst thing ever. Is everything OK at the cottage? xxx

It feels an age since she drove me to the station, but as I contemplate the walk ahead of me, my whole life feels a world away – more so when Tanith replies.

Shit day here, endless rain. Nathan came over to see you. How didn't I know you'd gone on your own???

I picture the view across the Cornish landscape, shrouded in rain, smiling to myself.

Because I didn't want anyone talking me out of going!!

I pause before adding.

Why did Nathan come over?

While I wait for her reply, my tapas arrive, garlicky prawns in a rich tomato sauce and a bowl of croquetas.

He'd found out Sasha wasn't going. He's been over twice, actually. He's really nice Callie. If I were you... Pointless saying it again, you already know what I think. Gotta go and feed the boys. Catch you later xxx

I frown at my phone for a moment. How did Nathan find out? Unless he's spoken to my mother... And how come he's been to see Tanith twice? As I think of them together, a seed of suspicion forms, before I tell myself I'm being ridiculous. There's no way Tanith would do that to me.

*　*　*

The following morning, when I check out of the hostel, there are about half a dozen similarly attired walkers in multi-pocketed trousers and walking boots. Hanging back, I let them pace on ahead, wanting to quietly savour every moment.

After leaving the old town, the route I've chosen hugs the coast. It's a beautiful morning, the fields a soft green, the sea glinting in the sunlight. As I walk, I fall in love with the Spanish countryside. Spring has already arrived here and the grass is speckled with wild flowers.

Away from the familiar, everything's clearer somehow. Thoughts of Liam fill my head, but instead of pain, I feel an aching kind of yearning.

I'm not the same person any more, though, and out here, alone, at last I'm honest with myself. Yes, I've lost the love of my life, the man I built my future around. But as I turn on to the footpath, already it's becoming clearer: even without him, there's still a whole lot of life to live.

That evening I stop at the next hostel Sasha and I booked. Set above a beach, the view is glorious, of green hills sloping down towards pale sand and dark blue sea. Sipping a beer I bought on the way here, I sit on the grass and stretch out my aching legs for a moment.

'Mind if I join you?'

Turning around, I take in the guy standing there. In walking boots and jeans, he's clearly another hiker. 'Hi. Sure.'

Slipping off his rucksack, he sits on the grass beside me. 'I had the same idea.' He opens the bottle of beer he's holding. 'You're doing the Camino?' He has a slight American accent.

I nod. 'The northern route.'

He grins. 'Your first?'

'People do this more than once?' Slightly shocked, I study him.

'It's kind of addictive,' he says. 'This is only my second, though. I'm Ryan, by the way.'

I take the hand he's holding out. 'Nice to meet you. I'm Callie.'

'Beautiful, isn't it?' Leaning back on his elbows, he gazes towards the sea. 'So what brings you here? Or are you just a fellow adventurer?'

'My fiancé and I were going to do this on our honeymoon. He died.' As I explain, my voice remains steady.

'Sorry to hear that.' He sounds sympathetic. 'Must be tough.'

'It was, to start with. Anyway, my sister was going to come with me.' I tell him about Sasha breaking her ankle. 'It seems I'm destined to do this alone, so I'm looking on it as a personal challenge. Kind of closure with the past.' I shrug.

'Tell me about it,' he says feelingly. 'My story's not as sad as yours, but the first time I did this Camino I was with my girlfriend. I thought we were good. I was even going to ask her to marry me – until about a month ago, when she dumped me for my best friend. And I had no idea.'

'That's shit.' I shake my head. 'She clearly wasn't the one.'

He frowns slightly, before a look of amusement crosses his face. 'You know what? You're absolutely right – except everyone at home has been sad for me, or avoided the subject altogether. Not one of them has said it like it is.'

'I'm kind of known for doing that,' I say quietly. 'Sorry.'

'No, it's good. Thank you,' he says. 'So, was it the same for you? When your fiancé died?'

'Not really.' Thinking of my sisters, I feel emotional all of a sudden. 'My family are wonderful. I'm not sure they'll get why I'm doing this alone, but it feels like a defining moment.' I frown. 'I've been thinking for a while I need something more in my life. I'm hoping doing the Camino will help me work that out – amongst other things.'

'Sounds like a plan.' He delves into his rucksack for two more beers. 'On me.' He passes me one.

'Thanks.' I open it. 'So where are you headed tomorrow?'

'I'm thinking Deba.' He glances at my boots. 'You probably don't want to overdo it until your feet get used to it.'

'I'll be OK. These boots have been walking the Cornish coast path,' I tell him. 'Deba's next on my list, too.' After spending the last couple of days alone, I realise company wouldn't be so bad. 'Should we walk together?'

* * *

The next morning, we stop off for breakfast at a café on one of the beaches. After coffee and pastries, we set off.

'So how long were you and your girlfriend together?'

'Too long.' His lips twitch into a smile.

'Obviously.' I roll my eyes. 'You didn't see any warning signs?'

'None. She told me she loved me every day, until the day she told me she didn't and that she loved him...'

'Ouch.' I screw up my face. 'Liam and I had a blip a week before the wedding. It turned out he was having second thoughts. He didn't want kids... But we talked – and we got over it. If anything, it made us stronger.'

'Wow. A week before?'

I nod. 'I was completely in shock. He apologised and I forgave him.' I shrug. 'These things happen, don't they?'

'I guess.' He glances sideways at me. 'So since, has there been anyone else?'

I'm silent for a moment. But because I'll never see Ryan again, I say what's on my mind. 'There is. And I've been fighting it – survivor guilt is a terrible thing.' I pause. 'It makes everything complicated.' But as I think about Nathan's heart, already I'm realising it's only complicated because I've made it so. 'I think I make things more difficult than they need to be.'

34

NATHAN

As spring blossoms across Cornwall, I find myself getting impatient. With the ground drying out, I want to get my camping business under way.

'Can't you chase them?' As a football bounces our way, Tanith picks it up and lobs it back. 'Sorry about that.'

'It's fine.' Since she and her sons have become regular Sunday visitors, I've come to like watching the garden become a playground. 'But in answer to your question, I'm leaving it to Simon. I trust he knows what he's doing – and he knows I'm in a hurry to get on with this.'

Tanith looks at me curiously. 'Have you heard from Callie?'

'Not a word – and I wasn't expecting to.' I pause. 'Have you?'

'I've had a couple of texts,' she says vaguely. 'Sounds like she's really enjoying herself.' She frowns. 'There's one thing I've been meaning to ask you, though. Do you know anything about that empty bit in her flower bed?'

'As it happens, I do.' I tell her what Callie had told me, about the patch of soil she and Liam had intended to plant after their honeymoon that had come to signify the presence of loss in her life.

'We should plant it up,' Tanith says firmly. 'Enough of this frigging symbolic emptiness. It isn't healthy.' She breaks off. 'The problem is I don't know a thing about plants.'

'I'm not much better.' I think for a moment. 'But it just so happens I know someone who is.'

We're interrupted by my mobile buzzing. Seeing Callie's name flash up on the screen, I turn to Tanith. 'Will you excuse me for a moment?'

Going outside, I answer the call. 'Hi.'

'Hello.' The single word somehow conveys her happiness. 'How are you?'

'Good, really good. More to the point, how are you? How's the walk?'

'It's amazing, Nathan. The scenery is stunning, everyone's so friendly...' She sounds bubbly, filled with enthusiasm. 'Honestly, I'm so happy I've come here.'

'I'm so pleased.'

'Thanks.' She hesitates. 'So how are you, really? I have been worried about you.'

Knowing she's been thinking of me warms my heart. 'I'm feeling better, thanks. Trying to take things slowly for once.'

'Progress,' she says teasingly. 'Anyway, it's just a quick call. I'd better get on. I've a few more miles to go before it's dark.'

'Take care,' I say softly.

'I will.' She pauses. 'You too.'

* * *

'This is Tanith,' I say as Diana opens the door.

'Hello.' Tanith holds out her hand.

Diana shakes it. 'How nice to meet you. Come in, both of you.' She closes the door behind us. 'I'll put the kettle on. Sasha's in the kitchen and Stewart's around somewhere – I'm not sure where, though,' she says vaguely.

We follow her along a passageway lined with boxes.

'Do you have a moving date?' I ask.

'Next Friday. Thank goodness. I can't believe what a palaver it's been. Sasha? Nathan's here – and this is Tanith.'

'Not Graveyard Groupies Tanith?' Sasha's face lights up.

Tanith rolls her eyes. 'That's me! How's your ankle?' Going over to Sasha, she sits next to her.

'So annoying.' Sasha shakes her head. 'I've gone from being the fittest I've ever been to a complete couch potato.' She glances at me. 'Mum told me about your plan. I totally approve, by the way. That blinking empty space should have been filled months ago. We even bought her a rose, but she refused to plant it there.'

'She might not be too happy about us doing this,' I warn them.

'You can tell her we're all in on it.' Sasha says firmly. 'And I don't think she'll mind – not if this walk does what she wants it to.'

After cups of tea, Diana and I go outside. 'Now, I have everything ready for you. And I've labelled them all. The tallest ones must go at the back. The rest you can plant in clumps.'

'Sounds straightforward enough.' I pick up the trays of plants. 'I'll put them in my car.'

When I go back in, Sasha and Tanith are deep in conversation. When they see me, both of them look up at the same time.

'What are you talking about?' I say suspiciously.

'You, of course.' Tanith winks at me. 'Well, and Callie, obviously.'

'There really isn't anything to talk about. Callie and I are just friends.'

'So you keep saying. But she called you, didn't she?' Tanith nudges Sasha.

I'm mystified. I intentionally haven't told her about Callie's call. 'How do you know?'

'It's obvious. And we might know something that you don't.' Holding a finger to her lips, Tanith glances at Sasha. 'Not a word.'

* * *

'What was all that about?' I ask Tanith as we drive away.

'Just girl talk,' Tanith says airily. 'I hope you know what to do with those flowers.'

'We dig holes and plant them. Then you have to remember to water them.'

'I can cope with that bit.' She glances at her watch. 'Do you have time to swing by and pick up the boys? It would give my mother such a shock, seeing me with a guy.' She tosses her hair back. 'I'd quite like that.'

'Sure.' But when we reach Tanith's parents' house, my mobile rings.

'You did that intentionally,' she says suspiciously.

I pick up my phone. 'Actually, it's Simon. Why don't you go and get the boys? I need to take this.'

Five minutes later, just as I end the call, Tanith and the boys climb in. 'I have news,' I say quietly.

Tanith's eyes widened. 'And?'

'Well...' I try to spin it out. 'There were a few objections – the usual reasons.'

'Shit,' she mutters under her breath.

'It's OK. Simon sorted everything out.' I smile. 'Looks like we're on.'

'You're kidding.' She gazes at me in disbelief. 'You're not pulling my leg?'

When I shake my head, she flings her arms around me and plants a smacker on my cheek.

'Mummy? Are you and Nathan getting married?' A little voice comes from the back.

'Gross, no.' She glances at me. 'No offence, Nathan, but just the thought of getting married again...' She turns back to the boys. 'When we get home, we're going to plant some flowers. Then after, if you're really good, I'm going to tell you something so exciting you won't believe it. Even I can't believe it.' Her eyes are shining as she looks at me, adding more quietly, 'I can never thank you enough for this.'

* * *

Now that planning has been approved, I can't get started quickly enough. Contacting suppliers, I start placing orders for materials and find a local hard landscaper. As work gets underway, it isn't long before the project is drawing interest from the local press. There's a fair amount of opposition, too, but I'm more than ready for that.

'We don't need any more second homes around here.' The voice belongs to a woman who's marched across my land simply to make her opinion heard. 'Places like this should be preserved.'

'I completely agree.' I take the wind out of her sails. 'You're welcome to come back when we've finished and see for yourself. But meanwhile, I'd like to point out that you're trespassing.'

With the help of a local garden designer, I divide up the land into sections, leaving them to source fruit trees and plant them exactly where Callie suggested.

'This is frigging awesome.' Tanith already loves it. 'When do you hope to open?'

'With any luck, by early summer.' Or not long after. I need to start clawing some money back.

'Around the time Callie gets back.' She arches one of her eyebrows.

'I guess so. You haven't mentioned this to her, have you?' I remind her.

She shakes her head. 'But I can't wait to see her face when she comes here.'

* * *

It seems the universe is on my side as almost all the deliveries arrive on time, while the greatest joy of this project is the relative simplicity of its installation. But the high point is when the house starts going up, swiftly followed by the café.

Tanith is beside herself. 'I can't wait to quit my job. Honestly Nathan... Being part of this is a dream come true.'

'It's working for both of us, remember,' I say. 'But if this takes off, you do realise how busy you're going to be?' And there's another element to this I need to talk to her about.

'I don't mind that... And I know the boys are going to be so happy here.' She pauses. 'You asking me to manage all this, I can't tell you what it means.' She's uncharacteristically sober as she turns to me. 'I don't know why you've chosen me... But you've changed our lives.'

I'm touched. 'You were dealt a bad hand, that's all. I always wanted a local family to benefit from all of this. I couldn't be happier that it's you.' I pause. 'What you said about there being a shortage of the right kind of childcare around here, I've been thinking about it. We're going to have a huge great tepee, the ground is going to be securely fenced... I'm wondering if out of season, we couldn't use it for kids. I'd love you to manage that side of it, too, and employ a couple of people qualified in childcare, but I was thinking of it being a place where they would have freedom – to roam and explore nature, all within the safety of the campsite... I'm exploring funding options. What do you think?'

'I think it's inspired.' Tanith's eyes are bright. 'It's the kind of idea I'd love for my boys.'

'OK. I'll keep looking into it.' This is turning into much more than I'd planned, but in a way that feels good, while I can't help feeling Callie will love it.

Later that afternoon, after taking the boys to the beach for an hour, I drop them back to Tanith. It's playing on my mind that everything is going a little too smoothly. But when I get home there's an unfamiliar car parked in the drive. As I go over to it, I take in the figure with long brown hair hunched over the steering wheel, the bags and cases piled in the back. As she looks up, my heart sinks. It's Emily.

35

CALLIE

As my Camino continues, I settle into a pace of life I've never known before. One of simplicity, breath-taking landscapes, of regional Spanish food. After a week walking with Ryan, when he branches off on another more challenging route, I'm more than happy to be alone for a while.

But I'm not, I'm learning. There are always other hikers, people to breakfast with, times for company and days I'm happy to be alone in this wilderness.

Most of the time, I'm content in my own company, but in the evenings, listening to other people's stories only serves to remind me that challenging things happen to all of us.

'If they didn't, we'd always stay the same people.' Josefine is a Danish girl I meet almost halfway into the walk. Having nursed her girlfriend through a terminal illness, she'd decided to travel. 'All the shit stuff makes you strong.'

'Actually, it broke my heart,' I tell her.

'Mine was broken, too.' She shrugs. 'It's strong now – and yours is, too. Otherwise, you wouldn't have come here. These experiences change us. They give us freedom, too. My girl was adventurous, but she wouldn't have wanted to walk a Camino with me. And I don't think I would have come here alone if she was still alive – which seems crazy when you think about it.'

But I know exactly what she means. 'I'd never have done this alone if I was still with Liam.' It's true. I would have happily stayed in my comfort zone.

. 'Then this is good,' she says approvingly. 'It is a waste of a life never to have an adventure.'

'Not everyone wants them,' I point out. 'For some people, doing a Camino, sleeping in dormitories, not having creature comforts, would be their idea of hell.'

'Perhaps. So tell me, what made you do it?'

Already it seems strange to think about how I came to do this. 'Well, to start with, it was because Liam and I were going to do it. I felt like I was doing it for both of us. But while I've been walking, I've realised something. I'm not doing it for him – or anyone else. There's only one person I'm doing it for. Myself.'

'Good for you.' Josefine high-fives me. 'I'm doing it because I can't bear to stay in Denmark. After this Camino, I'm going to Canada. I will work for a while – I have a friend who owns a bar. I can stay there until I've saved for the next trip.'

I'm intrigued. 'Don't you miss having a home?'

She shrugs. 'Occasionally. But not enough to stay in one place – for now, anyway. It's a big world. I want to see more of it.'

And I get what she's saying. Ever since starting this walk, not only have I met all kinds of people. I've been given a window on to an unencumbered, nomadic way of life; one which encapsulates a rare kind of freedom.

That evening, we stop in Llanes. On the beach, Josefine strips down to her underwear.

'I have to swim, Callie. You should, too.'

I laugh at her. 'No way. It's too cold.'

'It is cold, but that is good,' she says sternly. 'You will feel incredible afterwards. Come on...'

The sea is beautiful, sparkling where the low sun catches it; small waves uncurling on to pale sand, as a sudden recklessness takes me over. Stripping off my clothes, I follow her.

Josefine's right. The same cold that takes my breath away makes me feel vibrantly, ecstatically alive. Josefine duck-dives under the water, her eyes sparkling as she surfaces. 'Under,' she orders.

Holding my breath, I do as she says. Feeling the water close over me, for a moment I'm lost from the world, revelling in the sensation, before coming up for air.

* * *

Deciding it's to be the first of many cold-water swims, I can't believe I haven't done this in Cornwall.

The following day, I get up early and watch the sunrise. It's the best time of day, the streets quietly stirring into life, the beach almost empty when I reach it. Walking along the high-water mark, I peruse the tiny pebbles and fragments of shells, collecting a handful. When Josefine joins me, I show them to her. 'In Cornwall, I used to make sea pictures,' I tell her.

Her brow crinkles. 'Sea pictures?'

'I'll show you. But they can be anything.' Crouching down on the sand, I carefully mark out the outline of a heart shape.

'Don't tell me. You're going to write a guy's name in there.' Josefine doesn't sound impressed.

'Actually, I'm not.' Laying the last of my shell-pieces, I trace a single word inside it with one finger. *Life.*

We catch the café on the beach just as it opens. After a café con leche, we collect our backpacks and continue walking. When we stop for a break and I glance at my phone, I gaze at the date.

'What is it?' Josefine frowns at me.

'It's my dad's birthday,' I say at last.

She looks at me oddly.

'He's been really ill. He almost died.' My vision blurs. 'I can't believe I've forgotten his birthday.' Rummaging in my rucksack, I unzip the pocket and take out the compass. 'Before I left, he gave me this. It used to be his.'

She takes it carefully. 'This is beautiful. And it's perfect, don't you see? With this, wherever you are, you'll find your way.'

As I look at her, a strange feeling comes over me. 'It hasn't felt like that, but I think you're right.'

'Ah, Callie.' Her arms go around me. 'Go. Call him. I'll wait here.'

Walking away, I find my parents' number and call them. My mother answers almost immediately.

'Callie! Where are you? Are you all right? I hope you're eating enough. And I hope you're being careful.'

'Mum! Stop! I'm fine. And I'm eating enough. It's wonderful here. Do you have a date for moving yet?'

'Next week,' she says hurriedly. 'I'm so sorry, but I'm just about to go out. I have to take Sasha to the hospital. Her foot has swollen up.'

Thinking of Sasha and my mother together, I feel a pang of homesickness. 'I hope she's OK. Give her my love.'

'I will. Let me pass you over to your father.'

'Hello, darling.' My father sounds bright. 'How's it going over there?'

'Happy birthday, Dad.' For no reason, there's a lump in my throat. 'It's wonderful here – really beautiful and peaceful. I'm loving it.'

'I'm so pleased.' He sounds like he's smiling.

'So are you up to anything today?' I want to keep him there, savour the feeling of comfort his voice brings.

'Apart from having a lie-in,' he chuckles. 'Your mother says we're having a few people over tonight. As if we haven't enough to do, what with moving next week.'

Suddenly I remember Spanish time is an hour ahead of England. 'Sorry. I hadn't realised how early it was.' But here, days have come to revolve around daylight hours. I don't even measure time the way I used to.

'Not at all. I'm just enjoying the peace and quiet before I go and face a little more packing. This move can't happen soon enough. It's like we're camping – no offence. But I want to unpack and have a home again.'

'You will have before long.' I pause. 'So how are you – really?'

'Don't you worry yourself about me. All in all, I'm not bad. I've had another check-up and my consultant is very happy with me.'

'That's really great.' Relief fills me. 'Look, I should probably go. Have the best day, Dad. I love you.'

'I love you, too.' He sounds emotional. 'I hope that compass is coming in useful.'

'More than you know,' I say softly.

Going back to Josefine, I sit on the grass and tell her about my dad, then about my childhood; then about his heart attacks when we all thought we were going to lose him; how my parents are moving from our family home. She listens until I finish speaking.

Her eyes are kind. 'You are lucky to have known all that love.'

'I am lucky.' I blow my nose. 'I haven't said it to my parents, but them moving now feels like the end of a huge chapter of my life.'

'I get that. Chapters end, but new ones begin... That happens in life.' She pauses. 'You may think I'm mad, but I don't think we ever really lose the people we love. My girl still talks to me.'

I think of that day in Cornwall, when I could have sworn I heard

Liam's voice. 'I don't think you're mad. There was one time, on the beach... I just knew Liam was with me.' I frown. 'It took a while, though.'

Josefine shrugs. 'Maybe he knew you had to find your own way.'

Her words stick with me as we carry on walking, as more things fall into place. Loss and grief, as well as leading me to find my strength, have shifted me on to a path I wouldn't otherwise have taken.

'We are about halfway,' Josefine tells me as we climb another headland. 'Another three weeks or so and we'll be in Santiago de Compostela. We will have completed our Caminos, my friend.'

Stopping for a moment, I take in the view of the rugged coast and green hills of Asturias. 'Are you flying out straight away?'

'As soon as I book a flight. How about you?'

'I'm going to look into trains.' I tell her about the horrendous ferry crossing.

'I don't get why anyone would put themselves through that. Why didn't you fly?'

'I have a deep-seated and pathological fear of being airborne,' I tell her. 'It simply isn't natural. And if something goes wrong, I can't get off.'

'The ferry is better?' She cocks an eyebrow at me.

'I don't like ferries either,' I say quickly.

Josefine looks confused. 'You're brave enough to do this walk on your own, but too scared to get a short flight back to the UK. I don't understand.'

'That alone tells you how terrified of flying I am,' I say firmly.

'It doesn't make sense, but I'm not going to try to change your mind. What will you do after your long and expensive train journey?'

I hesitate. I haven't thought much beyond completing this walk. 'I'm going to get a job.'

'Doing what?'

'I used to work in a bookshop. They've said they'll keep my job for me, but I'm thinking it might be time for me to find something else – something new.' I think of the pleasure Nathan's garden has given me. 'I've been helping a friend – he doesn't know a thing about gardening. I might try to do something like that again.'

'A friend?' Josefine sounds curious. 'A man?'

'A friend,' I say firmly. Then I sigh. 'Actually, it's frigging complicated. I met him too soon after losing Liam.' I go on, telling her how we met and about Nathan's heart transplant.

She looks thunderstruck. 'I see what you mean about complicated. I mean, what are the chances?'

'I was quite upset when I found out. I'm not now. It's just a strange reality that I'm gradually learning to live with. Sometimes I'm OK with it. Other times,' I shake my head. 'It's just too weird.'

'Do you like this guy?'

I turn to her. 'Honestly?'

'What other way is there?' She sounds frustrated.

'OK. Yes. I've tried not to, but I really like him.' But then I think about his heart again. 'I was hoping this walk would help me work things out in my head.'

Josefine's silent for a moment. 'I think you should forget about Nathan's heart. You've been through some shit – and so has he. It's rather cool that you've found each other.'

'I suppose when you put it like that...' As her words sink in, I find myself looking at it differently. 'Anyway, I've probably put him off me.'

'Do not be so negative,' she says crossly. 'Seriously, Callie. Most people end up kissing a lot of frogs before they find their prince.' She breaks off. 'Your Liam... he wasn't a frog, was he?'

'Definitely not,' I say softly. 'He was a prince.'

'And this Nathan?' She arches her eyebrows.

'Not a frog, either.'

'Two princes?' Josefine sounds incredulous. 'I think you don't know how lucky you are.'

I frown at her. 'You know what? You're right.'

'Of course I'm right. Anyway, you know what I think about love.' Josefine makes it sound distasteful. 'It is overrated and fucks your life up.'

'That is so much rubbish and you know it,' I tell her. 'You loved your girl.'

'I did. It seriously screwed me up, too.' Going on, Josefine tells me about the ups and downs before they finally got it together. 'Then one year later, she was diagnosed with cancer and almost five months after that...' Josefine shrugs. 'Sometimes I think we are better off without love.'

I slip my arm through hers. 'My cynical friend, one day you will fall in love again – and you will think back to this conversation and you'll say to yourself, I was wrong and Callie was right...'

She stifles a giggle, but then she bursts out laughing. 'My little English friend, I very much hope so.'

* * *

That evening, when we stop for the night, after another cold-water swim, while Josefine catches up with one of her Danish friends, I call Tanith.

'Callie! How's it going?' She sounds elated to hear from me.

'It's great,' I tell her. 'Stunning countryside and beaches, interesting people... I'm about halfway. How's everything?'

'It must be amazing. I'm great! Something incredible has happened. Don't ask me what – I can't tell you about it until you're home.'

'Wow. You sound happy.'

'I'm over the moon!' She pauses. 'I should go, Cal. Nathan's just come back with the boys.'

What's Nathan doing with Tanith's sons? Or am I missing something? 'Say hi to him – to all of them,' I correct myself.

'Will do. Catch you later.'

Ending the call, I stand there for a moment as suddenly it strikes me: when I think of Nathan with Tanith and her boys, I really, really miss him.

I go to find Josefine. 'I've just realised something.'

She looks at me quizzically. 'You have spoken to Nathan?'

I shake my head. 'I spoke to Tanith. She's great – she said something amazing's happened. She wouldn't tell me what. But she sounded so happy. She couldn't talk for long, though, because Nathan had just got back with her sons.'

'Your friend is seeing this man you like?' Josefine frowns.

'Not like that. He's a nice man. He's probably helping her out with her boys. They are quite... energetic, is the best way to describe them. Anyway, Tanith's my friend.' I gaze at Josefine. 'But there was definitely something she wasn't telling me.' Suddenly I'm thinking about Nathan, getting on with his life while I'm away. 'What if I've blown it?' I stare at Josefine. 'I mean, here I am miles away, thinking Nathan's going to wait for me. What if he doesn't?'

'If he doesn't, it wasn't meant to be.' She passes me a piece of tortilla. 'Here. Eat this. Then we'll go and get a beer. We are not meant to bring our worries on a Camino,' she adds more sternly. 'We are meant to breathe clean air, enjoy the beauty of this place and embrace the freedom it offers...'

The tortilla is delicious and as I eat it, I take in the glorious view, the peacefulness that surrounds us. Josefine's right. There are times to park your worries, to savour the moment. Feeling the softness of the breeze, I listen to the chorus of birdsong as the sky changes colour. No question in my mind, this is one of those times.

36

NATHAN

Opening the passenger door of Emily's car, I lean down. 'What are you doing here?'

'I have nowhere else to go.' Emily's face is tearstained. 'And I've lost my job. Please Nathan. Can I stay? While I sort something out? Even if it's only for a week?'

I sigh. 'Sorry, Em. This really isn't a good time. I've a lot going on right now.'

Sitting there, she starts to sob. 'It isn't a good time for me, either. I've lost my flat, Nathan. I haven't been able to afford my mortgage repayments. I have nothing.'

I hesitate. It makes no sense that instead of going to her parents, she's come here. 'Can't your parents help you out?'

Her jaw is clenched as she shakes her head. 'I can't ask them. They're so angry with me.'

'Angry?' I frown. 'Isn't this what family's about? Helping each other out when times are tough?'

'My parents aren't like that,' she mutters through her tears.

I sigh heavily. 'One week.' I watched her wipe her face. 'But there will be several conditions.'

'Anything.' She looks at me bleakly.

'Firstly, you tidy up after yourself. Secondly, while you're here, there's a list of jobs I need help with. And thirdly...' I give her a stern look. 'Absolutely no funny stuff.'

* * *

Inside, I make her a cup of tea and sit her down at the table. 'I know you don't want to, but if things are this bad, you really should talk to your parents.'

'After what they said, I can't.' She shakes her head. 'Anyway, they wouldn't want to see me. I've made such a mess of things.' Tears spill down her cheeks.

As I look at her, something doesn't add up. 'Is there something you haven't told me?'

She's silent for a moment. 'Last time I was in trouble, they bailed me out – on the understanding that from there on, I had to manage my finances more carefully. But the trouble is, it's been so difficult. Money goes nowhere, does it?'

I take in the designer clothes she's wearing, her perfectly manicured nails. 'What you're saying is you didn't stick to your part of the deal.' I gaze at her in disbelief. 'New clothes, expensive manicures, they're not essentials, Em. Not when you have a mortgage to pay.'

Her cheeks flush pink. 'I have to look the part for work.'

'You just told me you've lost your job.' I shake my head. 'As for your parents, sometimes the simplest solution is a good old-fashioned apology. It's you who's fucked up. You've had it far too easy. It's time you woke up to some harsh realities.'

'Say it like it is, won't you?' she says bitterly.

'There is no point in anything else,' I say more gently. 'Sleep on it. Think about going over there – tomorrow.'

* * *

The following morning, it's a very sober Emily who makes me a cup of coffee and tidies the kitchen.

'I've been thinking about what you said.' She looks preoccupied. 'And you're right. I have fucked up. I suppose I've been so used to unlimited money coming in, I've found it really difficult...'

'You know, in a way your parents are doing you a favour,' I say gently. 'It might feel harsh, but having to stand on your own two feet can only be a good thing.'

'Yeah.' She rolls her eyes. 'I just wish they could have done it a long time ago.'

'Maybe they hoped you'd use the money sensibly,' I point out. 'It was entirely down to you what you did with it.'

She's silent for a moment. 'So what do I do now?'

'Apologise. Tell them what you've told me and that you're not asking for another handout. Ask them if there's any way they can give you a loan. Then make sure you pay them back.'

Gripping her coffee mug, she grimaces. 'I know what my father's going to say.'

'You don't, actually. And in any case, you're going to have to take it on the chin. If you drop the stroppy act and you're straight with him, he might surprise you.'

I leave her with a set of gardening tools and point her in the direction of a bit of garden that needs digging. It won't do her any harm. A bit of time surrounded by the elements might even help her sort her head out.

It's still early as I drive away, reaching the campsite before anyone else. Stopping on the newly gravelled car park, I get out. As I stand there for a moment, a feeling of pride comes over me. Each day it seems the countryside is growing greener and as I look around, it's gratifying to see how little impact the work I'm doing is having on it.

I walk through the line of fruit trees. The palatial chicken run is finished to my right, the beginnings of a large veg patch underway to my left, while further on, the ground is almost ready for the setting-up of the tepee and half a dozen tents.

Just as I've planned, the land beyond has retained its unruly wildness and already wild flowers are starting to appear. By summer, I'm hoping it will look as it did when I first came here.

Turning around, I head for the log cabin that's going to be Tanith's home. In time it will weather and blend into the site. It was cheap to build and easily assembled from sustainably sourced wood; it's proved the perfect solution. With two good-sized bedrooms and a large open-plan kitchen-diner, all that remains to be done is the plumbing and electrics.

I haven't told Tanith, but right now, the house is my top priority. The fact is, I need someone on site and with Callie home soon, I know Tanith would rather move here than back to her parents' house.

It's looking good for opening by early summer, though. Today, however, is a special day. Going into the chicken run, I lift the hatch for the first time, watching proudly as a dozen hens hop out.

* * *

'Do you know when Callie's back?' I ask Tanith when she and the boys come over to my house. 'And you are watering her garden, aren't you?'

'Yes and yes.' Coming over, she sits opposite me. 'She's into the last week. But she was talking a load of nonsense about coming back by train, so goodness knows how long that's going to take.'

'So ferries are out of the picture too?'

Tanith shrugs. 'Seems that way.' Gazing out of the window, she frowns. 'Who is that?'

'Ah. I'm afraid that's Emily.'

'Emily?' Tanith's eyes bore into mine.

'Ex-girlfriend who, to use her own words, doesn't have anywhere else to go. I've told her to sort it – and that she has to earn her keep. Emily's more into manicures than gardening – I don't think she'll want to hang around for too long.'

'That really is rather devious of you.' Tanith seems impressed.

'Not intentionally. I'm doing her a favour.' I break off as Emily comes over to us.

'I need a rest. My back is bloody hurting.' Looking curious, she turns to Tanith. 'Hi. I'm Emily.'

'This is Tanith. I was just telling her you're here for a few days.'

'He's come to my rescue,' she says to Tanith. 'He's probably told you I've fucked rather a lot of things up.'

'He hasn't, actually.' Tanith looks surprised. 'Nothing you can't put right, surely.'

'Hopefully not.' Emily glances at me. 'I've decided I'm going to see my parents this afternoon.'

'Good.' Relief washes over me. Hopefully if she eats humble pie, they'd bail her out one last time. She still needs to change her ways and make sure it doesn't happen again, but I'll talk to her about that later.

'Posh, isn't she?' Tanith whispers as Emily goes inside.

'And spoiled, I'm afraid. But I'm hoping this is a turning point.' I'm silent for a moment. 'You know, I still don't have a name for the campsite.'

'Meadow Farm,' Tanith says instantly. 'Actually, that's far too boring. Let me think.' She's silent for a moment. 'If I were you, I'd call it Wild – or maybe Wyld, with a y. After all, it's what it's about, isn't it?' She paused. 'You need a beautiful sign – and a website. And we need to plan a grand opening.' A look of excitement crosses her face. 'Why not have a party? Invite friends and family, and all your suppliers and local people... We could get the press to feature us! It would be a brilliant opportunity.'

I like that she says *we*. I love her enthusiasm, too. 'I've been thinking about that. We also need a menu.'

'Leave that with me. I have a name for the café, too – how about Homegrown Kitchen? I know it isn't going to be this year, but that's the plan, isn't it? I've made a list of local suppliers – I'll base it on that, and we can rejig it seasonally...'

I smile. 'In that case, I'll check out having a sign made.'

* * *

After Tanith and the boys leave, Emily comes outside. Wearing less make-up than usual, and in trainers instead of heels, she seems slightly less sure of herself.

'Are you and her...?' She looks at me quizzically.

'She and I are not,' I say firmly. 'And even if we were...'

Emily interrupts. 'I know, it's none of my business.'

I look at her. 'Are you going to see your parents?'

'Trying to get rid of me?' She sounds more like the old Emily again.

But I've been thinking. 'Actually, before you go, maybe there's something you can do for me... Your uncle works for Cornwall Council, doesn't he?'

'He's a councillor, yes.' She frowns. 'Why?'

As I tell her about my idea for using the campsite for childcare, she surprises me. 'It's a really good idea. When I've seen my parents, I'll go and talk to him.'

'That would be great.' I'm taken aback. It's unlike Emily to put herself out for other people. 'And good luck. Remember what I said.'

'Got it.' Rolling her eyes, she walks to her car.

As she drives away, a feeling of relief settles over me. When life is suddenly so busy, I'm glad to have the house to myself for a while. Sitting back, I gaze across the garden, thinking about Callie for a moment. I wonder whether the walk is helping her order her thoughts; if she's met anyone else along the way. If not, when she comes back... I imagine asking her out to dinner. But I have no idea what's going through her mind, though knowing Callie's capacity for outspokenness, I guess I'll find out soon enough.

37

CALLIE

I've loved every part of this walk, but I fall headlong in love with Galicia's windswept beauty, its verdant hills, quiet lakes and fairy-tale waterfalls. I've never seen so many shades of blue and green, or felt such magic in a place.

'I have to come back here,' I say to Josefine.

'Come with the guy,' she says promptly. 'If he loves it as much as you, it will be a sign.'

It's also the slowest part of the walk as I savour every footstep, stopping to photograph flowers or butterflies, collecting more pebbles to take home with me.

'You are mad,' Josefine says more than once. 'All that extra weight.'

'I don't mind.' I tell her about my garden and the last empty section of flower bed. 'Planting it after this walk is my way of finding closure.'

'Then what?' she asks. 'I've been asking myself the same thing. For me, I think wallowing in grief has been easier than moving on...' Her voice wavers as she stops to wipe away a tear.

I'm astonished – yet at the same time, I'm not, because she's lost the woman she loved. But it's the first visible sign of emotion she's shown. 'Hey,' I say gently. 'You are doing so great, you know.'

Looking up, she blinks away tears as she tries to smile. 'Thank you, but I'm not so sure. Sometimes, I think I am this ridiculous mess of a human being who is running away from her pain, hiding her sorrow in walking hundreds of kilometres... Pretending I'm Josefine the brave adventurer, when underneath, I'm like everyone else. Muddling through this life, searching for happiness.' She blows her nose noisily. 'Fuck. What self-indulgent nonsense. What is wrong with me?' she demands.

'Nothing at all,' I smile, linking my arm through hers.

She looks outraged. 'Why are you smiling when I am telling you how shit I am?'

'You are so not.' I pause. 'You're just so wonderfully human sometimes.'

The last night we stop in a small village just ten kilometres from Santiago de Compostela. Set amongst mostly derelict houses, the hostel is basic and functional, the mattresses thin, but it will for ever have a place in my heart as our final stop along this journey we've made.

Inland from the coast, our final cold-water swim is in one of the waterfalls Galicia is known for.

'It's freezing!' After jumping in and coming up for air, my teeth are chattering.

'You feel alive, no?' Beside me, Josefine's cheeks are pink as she treads water.

'So alive!' Getting out, I climb one of the rocks, shrieking loudly, the sound echoing as I jump in again. The water is crystal clear, the sound of its flow the sweetest of music. It's an experience I wouldn't have missed for anything.

It seems impossible to imagine that by this time tomorrow, our walk will be over. Josefine and I have a last simple meal. Then as we watch the sunset, we clink our beer bottles together.

'I wish this wasn't coming to an end.' My body feels stronger, while my mind is clear, more focussed than it's ever been.

'Me neither.' Josefine pauses. 'It has been so good, walking with you.'

'You, too.' I clink my bottle against hers again. 'Cheers, my friend.'

'Santé. A toast to life,' Josefine says.

'And to adventures.' We clink them again.

'One more toast.' Josefine looks at me. 'To the future. May yours be everything you deserve, my friend.'

There are tears in my eyes. 'Yours too,' I whisper.

Finishing our beers, as darkness falls, we lie on our backs, stargazing.

'This doesn't feel real,' I say to Josefine.

'I agree. But has it given you what you were looking for?'

I watch a shooting star arc overhead. 'You know, it has – but it's given me so much more than that.'

'Ah,' Josefine says knowingly. 'Adventures have a way of doing that. So tell me, what have been the best parts?'

'The landscape,' I say immediately. 'And the people. Meeting you. The beauty and the peacefulness... After that, it's like I've reminded myself that life is filled with the most surprising, amazing moments – and I should never lose sight of that.'

'Agreed.' Josefine's silent for a moment. 'I think that's something you feel much more when you've lost someone close.'

'Once you get over the survivor guilt,' I add.

'Hmm. True. But we have, haven't we?'

'I think so.' But she's right. In the part of me where guilt used to reside, I've rediscovered the joyfulness in being alive. 'I think I've even come to terms with Nathan's heart.' It's how I think of it now, because it's his body it's beating inside. That Liam gave him the gift of life is something I'll always be grateful for.

Her voice is quiet. 'I am so pleased. I know how difficult it has been for you.'

There's a lump in my throat. 'I'm going to miss you so much.'

'I will miss you too.' She reaches for my hand. 'But we will keep in touch. Are you really getting a train home?'

'I don't have much choice.' The thought of a ferry crossing like last time fills me with dread.

'Oh, but you do...' Her hand tightens around mine. 'You are brave, Callie. So brave.' She pauses. 'You could fly.'

* * *

The next morning, we do as many have done before us and take our final steps along the Camino towards the city of Santiago de Compostela. As it looms up ahead of us, it's magnificent, the ornate spires of the cathedral standing out above the other buildings.

After the emptiness of the countryside, the streets feel crowded and as we make our way towards the cathedral, up close it's even more spectacular.

Taking in the intricacy of the architecture, I gaze at it in awe. 'I've never seen anything like this.'

'Me neither.' Beside me, Josefine doesn't move. Then she nudges my elbow. 'Come on. This is what we've come for. Let's go inside.'

* * *

Just like that, this adventure I've dreamed about is over. After a night celebrating with tapas and beer, in the morning I see my friend off.

'Thank you, Callie.' Josefine hugs me tightly. 'You have been the best ever walking buddy.'

Holding her at arm's length, I gaze at her one last time. 'So have you. It's going to be so strange without you. Enjoy Canada, won't you?'

'I will. I have to go. This is my bus.' She picks up her backpack. 'Good luck with everything – and with the guy. Don't forget to tell me what happens!'

The bus doors open, then after everyone gets on, they close. Standing there, I wave to her as the bus pulls away, watching until it disappears into the traffic, feeling very alone.

As I make my way back to the hotel, I think about all the things I could do here today. Maybe wander the streets, check out one or two clothes shops – most of what's in my rucksack needs throwing away. But nothing really appeals, and suddenly I know why. I want to go home.

* * *

After six weeks in Spain, England seems crowded and noisy. As I sit on the train to Bodmin, I text Tanith.

I'm back!!! Getting into Bodmin at 6.30pm, can you pick me up? xxx

She gets back to me straight away.

Yay!!!! We can't wait to see you xxx

Closing my eyes, I think back over the hundreds of kilometres I've walked as nostalgia comes over me for the Spanish coast I've come to love. It's an experience that will stay with me always, one that's changed me and opened my mind; that's given me a deeper sense of connection in this world.

It's a lovely afternoon to be arriving back in Cornwall. It's cooler and less luxuriant than Galicia, but achingly familiar and no less beautiful. As the train pulls into Bodmin station, Tanith's waiting on the platform for me. Picking up my backpack, I wince slightly. Josefine was right about the extra weight, but I know when I plant my garden, it will have been worth it.

I step off the train and Tanith hurries towards me, flinging her arms around me and hugging me.

'You look amazing.' As she pulls away, her eyes are lit up in a way I haven't seen before.

I smile at her. 'So do you. You'll have to fill me in on what's been happening while I've been away!'

'There's so much to tell you, I don't know where to start.' Reaching her car, she lifts my bag in. 'I've loved being at your place. The boys have, too. I can't thank you enough.'

'I'm just sorry it means you have to go back to your parents' house.' When she doesn't reply, I'm curious. 'Is there something you're not saying?'

'There's something I have to tell you,' she sounds mysterious. 'But you're going to have to wait.'

* * *

Back home, the cottage is oddly quiet. 'Where are the boys?'

'At a friend's,' Tanith says vaguely. 'Can I get you anything?'

'I'd love a beer.' Opening my backpack, I start delving amongst my clothes until I find what I've been looking for. One by one, getting out the pebbles I've gathered, I put them on the table. 'I found these mostly in Galicia. It's amazing there. The sea is every shade of blue and the beaches are stunning.'

'I hope you have loads of photos.' She passes me a beer.

'Thousands.' I glance around the house properly, noticing for the first time how tidy it is. 'Thanks so much for looking after everything.'

'It's me who needs to thank you.' Her eyes are solemn for a moment. 'You have no idea how since coming here...'

'What?' I frown at her.

'Nothing,' she says hastily. 'It's just made all the difference in the world – that's all.' She glances at my pebbles. 'Hey, these are cool.'

'I brought them back for my garden. In fact...' Picking up my treasured stones, I take them outside.

The garden is coming into its summer finest. The grass is neatly mown, the first sprigs of lavender flowering, many of the roses already in bloom. Making my way over to what's to become my memory of Santiago de Compostela, I'm aware of Tanith following me. But as my eyes find what used to be an empty patch of soil, it isn't at all as I left it. I take in the patch of earth that's been carefully planted with daisies and bright orange marigolds, the tall yellow rudbeckia that's just starting to come into flower. A funny feeling comes over me as I turn to look at Tanith.

'We wanted to fill it with sunshine colours,' she says quietly.

'We?' I shake my head. 'But this was supposed to be Santiago de Compostela. I have all these ideas. I've even brought back a piece of driftwood.'

'These came from your parents' garden,' Tanith says gently.

'All of them?' Turning back, I study the plants, memories come flashing back – of my childhood, of playing with my sisters, of the many family occasions for which these and many other flowers were the well-tended backdrop. As my objections fade, there's a lump in my throat. I've been so hellbent on doing it my way, or the way Liam and I had planned. But it doesn't matter any more. Life moves on; these plants represent family, friendship, love. It's impossible to be anything other than grateful for them.

'It's perfect.' My voice wavers as I turn to hug Tanith.

'I'm so glad you think so.' Sounding relieved, she hugs me back. 'It wasn't my idea – though I have to say I did totally agree.'

I look at her quizzically as she goes on.

'It was Nathan's. He spoke to your mum about it and she dug up the plants. He and I planted them – according to her strict instructions, obviously.' Tanith rolls her eyes. 'By the way, Sasha thought it was a good idea, too.'

Wondering what else I've missed, I open my mouth to speak, before closing it again as I take in how all these people in my life have been planning this together. 'You've met Sasha?' I say at last.

'She's great, isn't she?' Tanith smiles mischievously.

'You're saying this was Nathan's idea?' I'm puzzled as to why he'd go to all this trouble. 'How is he?'

'He's really good. By the way, if you still want to plant Santiago de Compostela, there are a couple of other ideas you might like to consider. But we can talk about those later. Why don't you have a shower and get changed? There's something I need your opinion on.'

I've no idea what she's talking about, but I do as I'm told and after a blissfully hot shower, I put on the first dress I've worn in weeks, a little make-up, too. Gazing at my reflection, I try to discern if I look different. But as I already know, the change I'm feeling is more on the inside.

'You're being very cryptic,' I say as we get into Tanith's car. 'I've walked hundreds of miles, I've spent all day travelling – and all you want to do is drag me out?'

'Don't expect me to be sympathetic.' She starts the car. 'You could have flown back. You didn't have to take the train.'

'Actually...' I glance sideways at her. 'Believe it or not, that's what

I did. All the way from Spain to Bristol. I only got the train for the last bit.' All through the airport, I had to stop myself chickening out and as I boarded the plane, my legs were shaking. But however scared I was, I was mesmerised by the view of the coast as we flew over it. Gazing out, I wished it a silent farewell, promising I'd soon be back. Then I'd ordered a gin and tonic and simply told myself that now I was up there, there was nothing I could do about it.

The car judders to a halt. 'Fuck me.' Tanith's jaw drops. 'After everything you said about flying... What changed your mind?'

I shrug nonchalantly. 'Just a friend, who told me I was brave.'

38

NATHAN

It's a perfect Cornish early evening, the air still warm with the softest of breezes and after a hectic afternoon, I can't believe how easily things are coming together. Standing there, I survey the almost finished café, the awning we've put up in case of rain; upcycled chairs and tables are arranged underneath it, the long table shortly to be filled with food.

Thanks to Tanith, there's bunting strung across the car park and jars of flowers on all the tables, with cutlery rolled inside brightly patterned napkins. While I've had my eye on the large scale, as I'm finding out, it's details like these that make all the difference.

Noticing people start to arrive, I feel nervous all of a sudden. This isn't just an opening party. It's a chance to showcase what this project is about and impress people; it's a major milestone in the life of Wyld, too. And by chance, the timing has worked perfectly to welcome Callie home.

Coming over, Emily mops her brow. 'My uncle's just arrived. He's going to be really impressed. What else do you want me to do? Those kids, by the way...' She nods towards Tanith's boys. 'They've been helping me.'

'They're great, aren't they? Maybe you can you finish setting up the bar. And see if the band wants a drink?' I've noticed she has her eye on one of the musicians. 'Tanith texted me. They should be here in five minutes or so.'

'Cool.' There's been a noticeable change in Emily since she talked to her parents, and at long last she's starting to sort her life out, to the extent that it was her idea rather than mine to help out today. 'I'll just come over and see my uncle with you.'

We go to find Emily's uncle. When she arranged for us to meet, he had already flagged up a lack of local childcare. After agreeing to subsidise places, he gave the idea the green light. And there's more to do but at least we're over the biggest hurdle.

After talking to him briefly, Robin and Max wander towards us. 'This is fantastic.' Robin kisses me on the cheek. 'Emily...' She glances at me quizzically. 'I didn't know you were going to be here.'

'Hi. Well, I thought I'd make myself useful. Contrary to popular belief, I'm not a bad waitress.' She disappears for a few seconds.

'Looks great.' Max shakes my hand.

'Thanks,' I say just as Emily reappears with a tray. 'Would you like a drink?'

Taking a couple of glasses, after she's gone, Robin looks at me again. 'So, are you going to give us a tour?'

I watch another car pull up before Callie's parents get out, followed by Sasha and another girl who's presumably another of Callie's sisters. 'I'm kind of tied up just now. Why don't you help yourselves?'

'No worries.' As Robin and Max wander off, Sasha waves at me. Coming over, she kisses me on the cheek.

I glance at her leg. 'You're out of plaster!'

'At last. I still have to be careful though.' She sounds relieved. 'I can't believe how incredible this looks. Does Callie have any idea?'

I shake my head. 'Not so far as I know.'

'She'll be blown away.' Sasha's eyes are bright as her sister joins us. 'This is Rita. Alice sends her apologies. She would have been here if she could, but she has a shift tonight.'

'Hi.' Rita looks slightly stunned. 'You've done all this for Callie?'

I feel slightly awkward. 'To be honest, it started out as an opening party. I didn't know exactly when she was coming back. But as it turns out, the timing has worked perfectly.'

'I'm rather impressed, Nathan.' Joining us, Diana looks at the board outside the cafe. 'Not sure how vegan will go down, but the rest...'

I let it go. 'Thank you.' A plant-based menu is a calculated risk. But it's an important one.

'Very good.' Stewart shakes my hand. 'Thank you for inviting us.'

'Thanks for coming.' I look past them just as Tanith's car pauses in the entrance before pulling in and parking. As Emily comes over with a tray of drinks for Callie's family, I make my excuses. 'I'll be right back.'

As I walk towards the cars, through the small crowd, I register Callie's look of astonishment as she gets out of the car. Then as our eyes meet, I'm rocked by a surge of emotion.

I stand there as she comes towards me. She's wearing a flowery dress, her hair lighter, her skin more tanned than when I last saw her. Then there she is, standing in front of me.

'I can't believe this.' Her eyes are wide. 'It's everything we talked about. But I don't understand. When I left, you didn't even have planning permission...'

'Quite a lot has happened since you went away. How are you?' I gaze into her eyes. 'How was your trip?'

'It was amazing,' she says quietly, her eyes darting around. 'This is too much to take in.'

'I've had a lot of help.' I watch her eyes glance around again before latching on to mine. 'With planning... and I found some brilliant suppliers. Once we got started, everything seemed to fall into place.'

She looks at me incredulously. 'You've planted fruit trees and built a café – in just a few weeks. You even have a sign – and the letters are made of tiny seashells. Something like this doesn't just fall into place...' Her voice tails off.

'Ah. That depends on who's helping you,' I say wryly. 'When there's a powerhouse behind the scenes...'

Joining us, Tanith is beaming as she kisses my cheek. 'You have to admit it looks pretty fucking awesome, doesn't it?'

A look of confusion crosses Callie's face. 'You've been helping?'

Tanith flashes a smile. 'I have. There's so much to catch up on, Cal. I don't know where to start, except to say if it wasn't for Nathan—'

Before she can finish, Sasha comes over and flings her arms around Callie. 'I've missed you! I can't wait to hear about it all. Sorry,' She glances at Nathan and Tanith. 'Do you mind if I steal her?'

Callie turns to me. 'I'll see you in a bit?'

'Is she pleased?' Tanith looks excited.

'I think so. But it must be quite an adjustment after being away.' This isn't turning out to be the romantic reunion I've been hoping for. I've been hoping she'd come back ready to move on. Plus I thought when she saw what we'd done here, she would be thrilled; excited, even. But the evening is still young. There's time.

I turn my attention back to the party. Many more people have turned up than I've dared to dream. Not just local contacts and friends, but the press and most of my suppliers. I catch Emily as she passes.

'We're not going to run out of anything are we?'

'Not a chance.' She winks at me. 'Quit worrying. Go and enjoy yourself.'

After talking to the journalist, in between chatting to guests, now and then I catch a glimpse of Callie, surrounded by her family, her face animated as she speaks, no doubt regaling them with tales of her trip. When I hoped she'd be more than a little pleased to see me; I can't help feeling disappointed. But with everything else going on here tonight, maybe it isn't the time.

At one point I'm aware of Max talking to Diana, as Robin comes to find me.

'You OK?' She sounds slightly anxious. 'Not overdoing it, are you?'

I shake my head. 'I have a lot of help.'

'So what's eating you?' She follows my gaze. 'Callie?' Patting my arm, she confirms what I'm already thinking. 'She's been away a while. If I were you, I'd give her time.'

An hour into the evening, before the band starts playing, there are one or two things I want to say. Going to the makeshift stage, I pick up a microphone, tapping it. As it crackles, the hum of voices dulls to a hush.

'Good evening to all of you. And welcome to Wyld.' As applause breaks out, I wait for it to fade. 'Thank you. And thank you so much for joining us tonight. We're very proud of what we're building here – not just in terms of providing wonderful holidays, but we're trying to be an example of how a business can succeed without damaging the environment. Everything here is sourced from sustainable materials. We've upcycled. We also aim to be zero plastic. We've brought in the most skilled craftspeople this part of Cornwall has to offer. Our café is another example of our philosophy. We're not even going to try to give you the same food every week of the year. Instead, our menu will vary according to what we're growing in our vegetable garden. Oh – and our chickens are already in residence! In time you'll be able to buy our eggs.' I pause as a murmur of laughter goes around. 'The inspiration behind this isn't mine, though. It came from a friend. I'll be honest with you. Before I heard her idea, I was planning to put up a handful of eco-homes, which presumably would have sold at inflated prices to second home owners. But... that isn't what Cornwall needs.' I clear my throat. 'It needs us to be more mindful of the lives of people around here, and of this beautiful environment we're blessed to call home. And that's what this is all about. A way of life that respects this landscape. I'd like you to join me in raising your glasses.' I pause again. 'To Wyld.'

As I raise my glass, I register the shocked look on Callie's face. Catching her eyes, I think I see her lips form the words, *thank you*.

* * *

Having said what I want to say, I feel a weight lift from me. Grabbing a beer, I notice Callie walking towards me.

'Great speech.' Emily's voice comes from behind me.

I turn around. 'Thanks. And thanks for your help tonight.'

'No worries.' She grins at me. 'It isn't entirely unselfish on my part. I needed to feel a little less like I owe you.'

'Hi.' Stopping in front of me, Callie looks at Emily. 'You're Emily, aren't you?'

'That's me.' Emily gives her a breezy smile. 'Anyway, I have work to get on with. I'll leave you to it.'

As Callie turns to look at me, there's confusion in her eyes.

I try to explain. 'Emily offered to help. That's all.'

Distracted, suddenly her eyes grow wide as she sees the house. 'I can't believe I haven't noticed that before.'

'I'm pleased you said that! Right now, it looks a bit new, but it'll blend in better as the wood weathers.' I pause. 'Tanith and the boys are moving in in the next few days. She's going to be helping to run this place. Actually, I'm hoping she'll be doing most of it, if I'm honest! I could do with a break.'

'It's great.' Callie looks puzzled. 'I feel like there's something I'm missing.' A frown furrows her brow. 'Anyway, I came over to say I loved what you said just now.'

'Thanks. You know the friend I mentioned...' I pause. 'It's you.'

Her cheeks tinge with pink. 'I wondered if it was. I really like what you've done here.'

'Thank you. But I meant it. It wouldn't have happened without your vision.'

'Maybe it would have.'

'There's so much more to tell you about.' My eyes search hers. 'The tepee is going to host community events – and when the campsite is closed, we're going to offer affordable childcare that gives children the experience of being in nature. It's another reason for keeping the chickens. We have the support of the council now and it's going ahead.'

Her face lights up. 'You've found your way to give something back.'

I hesitate. 'I hope so.'

A small smile flickers on her lips as she changes the subject. 'You wouldn't believe how tired I am. At this time of night, I'd usually be horizontal on the grass stargazing. My feet...' Looking more like the Callie I remember, she shakes her head. 'They've walked hundreds of miles these last few weeks. You have no idea how much they ache.' She smiles, slightly wistfully. 'This has been really lovely, but would you think me rude if I left soon?'

'Not at all.' Taking one of her hands, I raise it to my lips and kiss it. 'Maybe we can catch up when you feel more rested. I'd love to hear about your trip.'

A look of uncertainty crosses her face, before she nods. 'I'd really like that.'

39

CALLIE

After Rita drops me home, I go outside to my garden. It's been a long day and the peace is welcome. Sitting on the grass, I think about what Nathan's achieved while I've been away, slightly regretting I couldn't have been a part of it.

Gazing up at the sky, I think of Josefine and the Camino. It seems surreal that only a couple of nights ago in Galicia, we were lying on the grass together looking at the stars. I sigh. Though it's lovely being home, it doesn't feel the way it used to. Getting up, I wander among the familiar plants, recalling their significance to me and Liam. But only now do I realise I've found the closure I was seeking; that at some point during the walk, I crossed the line I wanted to find, between the past and what lies ahead as I move forward.

Already I'm craving the sea and early the following morning, I make my way to the beach. Instead of walking or looking for sea glass or sitting on the sand, I strip off my clothes and wade in. Savouring the coolness of the water, I close my eyes for a moment. Feeling myself whisked back to that last swim in Galicia, with Josefine, as I hear the echo of her laughter, the last piece of the puzzle falls into place.

Memories are precious – and some will stay with you always. They're a gift to be treasured. But we shouldn't let them hold us back. Instead, we carry them with us. Always.

Our lives can be so short – and I lost a year of mine when Liam died. Suddenly aware that I don't have time to waste, I wade towards the shore. As I dry myself and pull on my clothes, the first drops of rain fall.

Since arriving at the beach, I haven't even looked at the sky. When for the last six weeks I've gloried in it, *how haven't I looked at the sky?*

The heavens open as I grab my things and run for my car. By the time I reach it I'm soaked again. As I start driving towards Nathan's house, I don't care that my clothes are wet, that my hair is straggly. I feel alive in every cell of my being, my heart racing, my stomach filled with nervous energy. Filled with an overwhelming desire to see him, I rehearse what I want to say to him, butterflies flutter deliciously inside me. *I know what I said before, and I don't know if you have anything going on with anyone else – but I have to say this: all the time I've been away, I haven't stopped thinking about you.*

If I'm too late, I'll live with it. I'll go and walk another Camino, or go on another, different adventure. But in my heart, the next adventure I want is with Nathan.

When I reach his house, I sit in the car for a moment, smoothing my hair as best I can. It's still raining as I get out, and barely registering the garden I take the steps to the front door, pausing there, inhaling deeply before I knock.

Almost immediately he opens it. 'Hi.' He looks surprised to see me.

'Hi.' Suddenly I'm not so sure. 'Is this a good time?' I half expect him to say he's busy.

Standing back, he opens the door wider. 'You're soaked. You'd better come in.'

'I'm fine. I just want to say something.' Standing there in the rain, the words pour out of me. 'I know I haven't been making sense. I've been confused – and I know I've confused you, too. But since going away, I've realised that I want to be happy again – and that it isn't wrong to want to be with someone again. The timing...' Shaking my head, I have to ask. 'I know before I left, you said you'd ask me out, but that was six weeks ago and I don't know what's been going on in your life. Is there someone?'

He looks confused. 'No – except I'd like there to be.' As he pauses, his eyes meet mine. 'But it's a little tricky when she's been hundreds of miles away.'

I breathe a shaky sigh of relief. 'It's just I've figured out life's too short to look for obstacles all the time. There's a risk of one of us getting hurt, but it would be riskier, wouldn't it, if we didn't try?'

I watch his face. First uncertainty flickers across it, but as he realises what I'm saying, he looks astonished.

'What happened to just being friends?' he says quietly.

I hesitate. 'To be honest, I was hoping for a little more than that. You see...' I hesitate. 'While I was away, I couldn't stop thinking about you. I've finally worked it out.' I pause, because this is the risky part. But as I've learned, life is nothing without risk. 'I love you. And I love your heart.' When he doesn't react, I go on. 'I'm sorry if that's too much... But you know me. I like to say what's on my mind.' I pin on a smile, trying to hide how anxious I feel.

'Are you sure?' He frowns. 'I mean, if you're not and this is just a reaction to being away, I'd rather know now.'

'I am so sure.' My voice wobbles.

He stands there for a moment, before a smile spreads slowly across his face. 'Then you'd better come in – as long as you're not planning on running away again, that is.'

Stepping towards him, I pause in front of him. 'I'm not running anywhere.' Reaching up and closing my eyes, I kiss him.

* * *

It's a kiss I will never forget. There is no guilt, no backlash, just the sweetest sense that I've come home. After closing the door, Nathan shows me where the bathroom is and finds me an oversized sweatshirt to change into while he dries my clothes. Smoothing my hair back, I gaze at my reflection. My eyes are bright; there's colour in my cheeks. But it's how I feel inside, like the part of me I lost for a while is glowing brightly.

After what feels like a momentous revelation, on my part at least, I come downstairs to find Nathan in the kitchen making tea. Going over to him, I wrap my arms around him. 'Thanks. I'm warmer now.'

But when he turns around, as I take in the troubled look on his face, my heart misses a beat.

'Callie, I think we should talk.'

The blood drains from my face. 'What is it?'

'Come and sit down.' Taking my hand, he leads me over to the sofa.

'When I've just put my heart on the line, you're really scaring me,' I try to joke.

Holding my hand, he looks at me intently. 'I've thought a lot while you've been away. Up until last night, I was hoping you'd come back and want us to be together. But last night I couldn't sleep.' He hesitates. 'I know I'm well at the moment, but it hasn't been without its glitches. I had a funny spell a little while back. I spent the night in hospital. But next time, it might not be so simple.'

'So next time, we deal with it together,' I say gently. 'I'm not going to run out on you because you're ill.'

'It isn't that.' There's pain in his eyes. 'Like I told you before, I may have twenty, thirty years ahead of me. But also, I may have far less.'

'I know. But that's how life goes, isn't it?' Gazing into his eyes, I've thought about it, too. 'I know we all think the future is almost unlimited, but it isn't, for any of us. Look at Liam.'

'That's exactly it.' He swallows. 'You've been through so much. I've watched what it's done to you. I can't be that person who does it to you again.'

My heart starts to race. 'Isn't it possible, too, that it might never happen?' I say quickly. 'You can't live the rest of your life as though it's going to end tomorrow.' I pause. 'You know the way I've always noticed small things, like tiny shells and shards of sea glass? I learned while I was walking, that it's the same with love.' Taking his hands in mine, I try to explain. 'It's about treasuring those sweetest, precious moments, however short they are, however few of them. You know there will be sadness too,' I say gently, 'but that's OK, because it means you loved.'

When Nathan's silent, I go on. 'If you had one day left, or one week, or a year, it would make no difference. I'd still want to spend every moment with you.'

When he looks at me, his eyes are filled with tears.

'Say something,' I whisper, my eyes searching his. 'Anything.'

He says it quietly, stroking my still-damp hair off my face, as at last my heart calms.

'I love you, too, Callie.' He hesitates. 'By the way, there's something else I wanted to mention.'

I feel myself tense. 'Yes?'

He shrugs. 'Just a thought, but if you're looking for somewhere to plant Santiago de Compostela, I have an empty flower bed or two...'

A smile spreads across my face as my arms go around him. It's the perfect conclusion. It strikes me that walking to Santiago de Compostela turned out not to be the end of a chapter. It was a beginning.

40

NATHAN

Outside, I show her the flower bed where she can plant her memory of Santiago de Compostela, watching as she arranges the pebbles she's collected, setting the piece of driftwood before scattering seeds.

'Don't tell, will you? You're not really supposed to bring seeds back.' She looks at me slightly anxiously.

'Your secret's safe with me.' I frown at the flower bed. 'Is that it?'

'Haven't you learned about patience yet?' She wags a finger at me. 'The seeds will grow if we give them time – and they'll do their own thing. They'll be a little bit of Spanish wildness...' A wistful look crossed her face. 'I saw a lot of wildness on that walk.'

* * *

When we go back inside, Callie's quiet. Pulling off her boots, she comes over to me, her eyes not leaving mine. 'I want you to know I meant what I said earlier. I want to be here for you, Nathan.' She carefully slides up my T-shirt. As she exposes the scar on my chest, I've never felt more naked. Very gently, she traces it with one of her fingers, before laying her hand over my heart. When she turned to me, tears glisten in her eyes. 'I can only imagine what you've been through,' she whispers to me. 'I want to be here for you, no matter what lies ahead. Always.'

While she's speaking, I feel something click into place and it becomes crystal clear to me. Life is short; this rare kind of love so precious. If you're one of those who find it, you're lucky. Slowly, I put my arms around her. 'I want you to be here,' I whisper into her hair. There's a momentary hesitation as her whole body seems to sigh, before her arms go around me. I feel a weight lift, leaving in its place a sense of quiet peace I've never felt before.

Just like that, the next chapter of my life finds me. Actually, it's a chapter that tentatively started the day I made my first sea picture. It just needed time.

41

CALLIE

Since Liam died, I've plunged the depths of human existence; learned how it feels to almost give up. Yet at the point I came close, a tiny ember deep inside me fought to stay alight. It's felt like a battle – with the past, with guilt, and not least with myself. But the darkest times teach us something about ourselves. And as they pass, they illuminate the beauty of this world.

I'll never know if Liam and I would have stood the course of time. But that isn't the point. What happens, happens. There isn't always a reason – and however hard it is, sometimes all we can do is to go with it. For a long time, I didn't. I fought, clung to grief, to the past, to my dreams, when what I should have done was let them go.

That's another thing I've learned. Letting go doesn't mean forgetting. It means holding on to those tiny precious moments somewhere deep inside your heart, knowing whatever happens, they will never be lost; that they will always be there; that life is about collecting more of them.

'Callie?' Tanith calls up the stairs. 'Your sisters are here!'

I leap up. 'I'll be right down.'

In Tanith's bedroom, I take a last look in the mirror. My dress is sage green, my hair loose and lightly curled, my make-up minimal, my perfume the same one I've always worn. As I think about the day that lies ahead, I know that in spite of the heartbreak I've known, I'm one of the lucky ones.

I slip on the ornate gold flip-flops I've bought specially for today before applying a coat of pink lipstick. And as I look at my reflection again, I know I'm ready – for absolutely anything.

Downstairs, my mum and my sisters are in Tanith's kitchen. I pause in the doorway for a moment, watching them, my heart filling with love for them before they turn and see me.

'Callie!' they cry in unison, coming over to hug me.

'You look stunning,' Sasha says.

'I'm so proud of you.' There's a tear in my mum's eye.

As I catch my father's eye, there's a lump in my throat. We came so close to losing him; I know how lucky we are to have him here.

'Here.' Tanith passes me a glass of champagne.

'I probably shouldn't.' My hand rests protectively on the beginnings of a small bump.

'A sip won't hurt. Go on,' she coaxes, before turning to my wonderful family and raising her glass. 'A toast – to Callie.'

Looking at each of them in turn, I lift up my glass. 'To all of you. I honestly don't think I'd be here without you.'

'Stop it,' Rita mutters, wiping away a tear.

'Look at the time.' Glancing at the clock, Tanith sounds horrified. 'Come on. We should be out there.'

'It's fine.' I smile at them. 'It's only us. We can go out together.'

'We cannot,' Tanith says firmly. 'Give us five minutes, Callie. OK?'

I watch them go outside, then through the window, as they pass the café before disappearing through the trees into the garden beyond. I'm not sure quite what awaits me out there. For the last twenty-four hours, I've been under house arrest.

I watch the clock as the minutes tick past. In the year since I walked the Camino, so much has fallen into place. I've found my next step, too, one in which I've joined the ranks of my sisters, educating myself in the ways of the broken-hearted. After training as a bereavement counsellor, I've started a group which meets weekly in Wyld's tepee, christened appropriately the Lonely Hearts.

Briefly I think of Liam. *I still love you,* I whisper, before another thought takes its place. *But this is my future.* Then taking a deep breath, I let him go. My heart swells with love as I think of Nathan, as, taking my most precious of memories in my heart, I join the others.

It's quiet as I walk and I'm reminded of the day I first came here. But since then, so much has changed. Through the trees, ahead of me, I take in my friends and family as they turn to look at me. It's a simple ceremony, a million miles from the elaborate country wedding I'd planned with Liam, but that's exactly what Nathan and I wanted. Either side of the path, rows of chairs have been arranged in which are seated the most important people in the world to us.

In front of the tepee, an arch has been decorated with wild flowers. Standing in front of it is the man I love. As my eyes meet Nathan's, my heart is overflowing, and as I go to join him, the most incredible feeling comes over me.

Life has taught me there are no certainties, but as moments go, this one is perfect, because when our lives are about so many things, there's only one that truly matters.

And that's love.

ACKNOWLEDGMENTS

This is my third book to be published by the super-talented team at Boldwood Books. A huge thank you to all of you, especially Claire and Nia. And to Tara Loder, my brilliant editor. It's so wonderful to be working with you. I'm thrilled my books have a home with you.

Huge thanks also to my lovely, superstar agent, Juliet Mushens. And to the whole fabulous team at Mushens Entertainment for everything you do.

Much love to my friends. To Dad and my sisters. To my amazing children, Georgie and Tom. And to Martin. Thank you so much to all of you for being such loyal and tireless supporters of my books.

And thank you to you, my readers. I've loved writing Callie's journey through her grief and the way she found her way forward. It's been inspired by so many things: not least the loves and losses we all experience, as well as the enduring strength of family and true friends.

It's also about the way we find something surprising in ourselves when we push ourselves out of our comfort zone. There's something, too, about spending time in another country. We are such habitual creatures! It can take breaking away from the familiar to open our eyes to not only a different way of life, but of thinking, too – and I really love where Callie's adventure took her.

I also owe this story in part to the last few years of travelling. A nomadic way of life isn't for everyone, but it's enabled us to meet wonderful people and live in many gorgeous places, while experiencing different cultures has set my writer's mind off in several new directions... And as Callie's outspoken friend Josefine says: *It is a waste of a life never to have an adventure...*

Thank you so much for reading and sharing my books, and to book clubs for choosing them. To everyone who's been moved by them, thank you from the bottom of my heart. Without you, I wouldn't be doing this. x

MORE FROM DEBBIE HOWELLS

We hope you enjoyed reading *The Shape of Your Heart*. If you did, please leave a review.

If you'd like to gift a copy, this book is also available as an ebook, large print, hardback, digital audio download and audiobook CD.

Sign up to Debbie Howells' mailing list for news, competitions and updates on future books.

https://bit.ly/DebbieHowellsnews

Explore more heart-warming, page-turning women's fiction from Debbie Howells...

ABOUT THE AUTHOR

Debbie Howells' first novel, a psychological thriller, *The Bones of You*, was a Sunday Times bestseller for Macmillan. Four more bestsellers followed, including most recently *The Vow*, published by Avon. Fulfilling her dream of writing women's fiction she has found a home with Boldwood.

Visit Debbie's Website:

https://www.debbiehowells.co.uk

Follow Debbie on social media:

Boldw**oo**d

Boldwood Books is an award-winning fiction publishing company seeking out the best stories from around the world.

Find out more at www.boldwoodbooks.com

Join our reader community for brilliant books, competitions and offers!

Follow us
@BoldwoodBooks
@BookandTonic

Sign up to our weekly deals newsletter

https://bit.ly/BoldwoodBNewsletter

Lightning Source UK Ltd.
Milton Keynes UK
UKHW040828260223
417684UK00005B/165